D1742387

E.R. PUNSHON
DARK IS THE CLUE

ERNEST ROBERTSON PUNSHON was born in London in 1872.

At the age of fourteen he started life in an office. His employers soon informed him that he would never make a really satisfactory clerk, and he, agreeing, spent the next few years wandering about Canada and the United States, endeavouring without great success to earn a living in any occupation that offered. Returning home by way of working a passage on a cattle boat, he began to write. He contributed to many magazines and periodicals, wrote plays, and published nearly fifty novels, among which his detective stories proved the most popular and enduring.

He died in 1956.

The Bobby Owen Mysteries

E.R. PUNSHON

DARK IS THE CLUE

With an introduction
by Curtis Evans

DEAN STREET PRESS

Published by Dean Street Press 2017

Published by licence, issued under the
UK Orphan Works Licensing Scheme.

First published in 1955 by Victor Gollancz

Cover by DSP

ISBN 978 1 911579 09 0

www.deanstreetpress.co.uk

Detective Stories, the Detection Club and Death: The Final Years of E. R. Punshon

> . . . but, they dead,
> Death has so many doors to let out life,
> I will not long survive them.
>
> *The Custom of the Country* (c. 1619-23; 1647)
> JOHN FLETCHER AND PHILLIP MASSINGER

WHEN IN 1949 E.R. Punshon published *So Many Doors*, his twenty-sixth Bobby Owen detective novel, the Englishman was seventy-seven years old, with nearly a half-century of published novels behind him and a comparatively scant seven years of life and letters remaining before him. 1901, the year of the appearance of Punshon's first novel, *Earth's Great Lord*, saw the death of Queen Victoria, the long reigning granddaughter of King George III for whom a regal age of European global dominion has been named; while 1949, a year during which a convalescent Europe was still bleakly recovering from a world war that had reduced much of its civilization to ashes and rubble, saw the testing by the USSR of its first atomic bomb and the proclamation of the formation of the People's Republic of China. The world was changing with a fearsome fleetness that not merely old men who had first glimpsed light in the Victorian era were finding hard to follow.

Rapidly changing too was the craft of crime and mystery fiction that E.R. Punshon had long practiced (this admittedly a minor thing compared to unsettling phenomena like armed revolution and atom splitting). Like the once seemingly imperishable British Empire, the hegemony of the between-the-wars "Golden Age" clue-puzzle detective novel was breaking asunder, under pressure from increasingly popular rival forms of mystery fiction, such as hard-boiled, noir, psychological suspense and espionage. Already stalked by Raymond Chandler's famous gumshoe, Philip Marlowe, as well as ill-humored and hard-drinking would-be Marlowe doppelgangers like Mickey Spillane's brutish Mike Hammer, Punshon's well-born English policeman Bobby Owen, along with other of his surviving gentlemanly detective colleagues from the era of classic crime fiction, soon found himself in the sights of no less deadly a professional killer than James Bond. Agent 007's creator, Ian Fleming, who cited as his literary influences Raymond Chandler, Dashiell Hammett, Eric Ambler and Graham Greene, published his first Bond spy novel, *Casino Royale*, in the United Kingdom in 1953, where it enjoyed immediate popular and critical success. In the United States, where the novel appeared in 1954, the same year as Raymond Chandler's much-lauded *The Long Goodbye*, *Time* magazine wryly declared that "Bond . . . might well be [Philip] Marlowe's younger brother, except that he never takes coffee for a bracer, just one large martini laced with vodka."

Upon the publication of *So Many Doors* in the UK and the US (in the latter country it would prove the last Punshon mystery published during the author's lifetime), crime fiction reviewers deemed the novel and its author representatives of a vanished era. "The twenties were the plotter's heyday (consider Freeman Wills Crofts, J.J. Connington, Dorothy L. Sayers)," observed the Democratic-Socialist *London Tribune* in its review of the "well-plotted" and "studiously told" *So Many Doors*, "and to the twenties, in spirit at least, belongs Mr. Punshon." In the United States, Anthony Boucher, dean of American mystery critics, allowed in the *New York Times Book Review* that the narration of *So Many Doors* was "leisurely"; yet, after noting the seventeenth-century English stage derivation of the novel's title, he approvingly added that there "is something Elizabethan, even Jacobean, about the obscure destinies that drive [Punshon's] obsessed and tormented characters, and about the frightful violence that concludes the story." Punshon, it seemed, still had something to say in the harried and hectic atomic age, when crime fiction reviewers and readers alike seemed increasingly to believe that brevity was the soul of death.

To his death in 1956 E.R. Punshon maintained a loyal following in the United Kingdom among readers who staunchly adhered to the strict standard of fair play puzzle plotting associated with Golden Age detective fiction. During the Fifties the aging but seemingly indefatigable author, who still lived quietly with his wife Sarah at their house at 23 Nimrod Road, Streatham, produced, through the medium of his prestigious longtime publisher Victor Gollancz, nine new mystery titles--*Everybody Always Tells* (1950), *The Secret Search* (1951), The Golden Dagger (1951), *The Attending Truth* (1952), *Strange Ending* (1953), *Brought to Light* (1954), *Dark Is the Clue* (1955), *Triple Quest* (1955) and *Six Were Present* (1956)—that detailed the final criminal investigations of his longtime series police detective, Bobby Owen, now risen to the august rank of Commander (unattached), Metropolitan Police. Additionally Punshon continued to remain active in his cherished Detection Club, a London-based social organization of distinguished detective novelists, in which the author had been inducted, along with Anthony Gilbert and Gladys Mitchell, in 1933, three years after the Club's founding, joining such luminaries from the crime writing world as G.K. Chesterton, Dorothy L. Sayers, Agatha Christie, E.C. Bentley, Anthony Berkeley, R. Austin Freeman and Freeman Wills Crofts.

Like other British institutions the Detection Club from 1939 to 1945 bore the bitter burdens of war, including the devastating Nazi air raids known collectively as "the Blitz." When the Club revived its meetings and annual dinners in 1946, it became immediately apparent that time had wrought cruel changes with its membership. On seeing his brother and sister detective novelists again at the Club premises after the long interval of war years, John Dickson Carr, a comparative stripling at the age of forty, recalled that he had been "shocked" by their appearance, which he had found decidedly "greyer and more worn."

By 1946 eight of the original twenty-eight Detection Club members, including G.K. Chesterton, R. Austin Freeman and Helen Simpson, had passed away and many other members were now elderly and inactive. Several more members would expire over the next few years. Even the formerly quite engaged Freeman Wills Crofts and John Rhode (Cecil John Charles Street), now in their sixties and living in the country, became markedly less involved with Club affairs, as did an increasingly infirm Henry Wade (the landed baronet Henry Lancelot Aubrey-Fletcher). For his part, John Dickson Carr, deeming British life under postwar conditions and the governance of the Labour party intolerable, would in 1948 depart for his native United States. Besides Punshon, only Christie, John Rhode and Henry Wade, among original members, and Anthony Gilbert, Gladys Mitchell, Margery Allingham, John Dickson Carr, Nicholas Blake, Christopher Bush and E.C.R. Lorac, among the smaller number of Thirties inductees, remained substantially active as crime writers into the 1950s. Of these Lorac and Wade, like Punshon, would not survive the decade, and another, John Rhode, would barely outlast it.

Clearly some new blood was badly needed. During Punshon's remaining span of life the aged and ailing Detection Club received transfusions, so to speak, from seventeen new members. Although with the deaths of Baroness Emma Orczy and A.E.W. Mason (in 1947 and 1948 respectively), Punshon became the oldest surviving member of the Detection Club, the author, who served as Club treasurer between 1946 and 1949, during the postwar years remained extensively involved in Club affairs, actively participating in hearty debates concerning prospective new members, like Christianna Brand, Michael Innes, Michael Gilbert, Elizabeth Ferrars and Julian Symons, as to whether or not they practiced fair play and sufficiently respected the King's (later Queen's) English, the Club's chief requirements for induction. (These debates are chronicled in detail in my CADS booklet *Was Corinne's Murder Clued? The Detection Club and Fair Play, 1930-1953*.)

In 1949 Punshon found himself at odds over the matter of new enrollments with the man who unquestionably was the Club's crankiest and most cantankerous member: Anthony Berkeley, famed author of *The Poisoned Chocolates Case* (1928) and, under the pseudonym Francis Iles, of *Malice Aforethought* (1931) and *Before the Fact* (1932), three of the best regarded British crime novels from the Golden Age. In April Berkeley wrote a provocative letter to Punshon in which he claimed that as the Club's "First Freeman" he possessed blanket veto power over prospective members, despite the fact that he no longer served on the membership committee. During the early days of the Detection Club, Berkeley had observed at a meeting that the Club had two "Freemans" as members (R. Austin Freeman and Freeman Wills Crofts), and he pronounced that as the person who had originally suggested forming the Club he would be its "First Freeman." To this suggestion everyone else had laughingly assented, taking the office as a joke; yet now, nearly two decades later, it seemed that Berkeley had not been joking.

Incensed by Berkeley's gambit and the rude language in which he had couched it, Punshon wrote Sayers, enclosing his antagonist's "offensive" letter (which evidently has not survived) and warning that "[Berkeley] intends to make some sort of fuss." Punshon speculated that "possibly it is better to take no notice [of the letter], except perhaps as regards the absurd claim of his to hold some special position as what he calls 'First Freeman.' I have a vague idea that once before he put forward a claim to be a permanent member of the [membership] committee on the same ground." He noted dryly that while he had forborne responding to the specifics of Berkeley's letter, he had sent the notoriously tightfisted "First Freeman" a reminder that his annual membership fee was due, to which he had received no reply.

"Bother AB!" responded Sayers in a letter to Punshon that she composed the day after receiving his missive. "I do wish he was not so rude and silly." She entirely concurred with Punshon's recollection of the once comical but now rather annoying office of First Freeman and added resignedly: "If he tries to make a fuss at the meeting, the committee will have to cope; but I hope he will have more sense. I am sorry he should have written to you so impertinently."

By the summer of 1949 the First Freeman's irksome machinations had been checked--but only, Punshon feared, for the moment. With considerable skepticism Punshon wrote Sayers, "I gather the reconciliation with Anthony Berkeley is now complete and the hatchet well and truly buried. Until dug up again." Sayers, who soon would succeed E.C. Bentley as President of the Detection Club, advised members to tread carefully around Berkeley's tender sensibilities. "Let a (more or less) sleeping Berkeley lie," she urged. Nevertheless Sayers agreed with Punshon that the Club members would have to keep Berkeley off the membership committee, because were he to be on it the Club would "never get any new member . . . he turns them all down on sight." She lamented that "Berkeley is a difficult man to work with."

Sayers found working with Punshon, whose detective fiction she had enthusiastically promoted as a book reviewer for the *Sunday Times* between 1933 and 1935, to be an altogether more pleasant experience. Surviving correspondence between the two authors suggests that Punshon was, along with Anthony Gilbert (Lucy Beatrice Malleson), the Detection Club member with whom Sayers got along most amicably at this time. The two communicated fairly frequently during the postwar years, chatting not only about Detection Club matters, but more personal affairs as well.

As treasurer of the Detection Club, Punshon gave his attention to matters large--such as any taxes the Club might have to pay to a revenue-hungry British government ("we have to remember that we may be dropped on by the Income tax people")—and matters small. As an example of the latter, Punshon advised Sayers in December 1948 that the Club should give a "small Christmas present" to Mrs. Buchanan, caretaker of the Club premises at 12 Kingly Street, Soho. ("A room and loo in a clergy house," Christianna Brand bluntly recalled of the locale.) Although payment for services was included with the rent, Punshon pointed out that "services included are very often badly neglected and so far as I have noticed in this case they have been quite well carried out and the room always seemed neat and tidy." "[E]ven in this sordid age," he reflected with characteristic gentle irony, "a few thanks and expressions of satisfaction . . . often please as much as gifts—at any rate if accompanied by a gift." A few days later Sayers gave Mrs. Buchanan a £1 Christmas tip (about £32 today).

Sadly, Punshon suffered a serious setback to his health in August 1949, not long after a busy summer that saw the English publication of *So Many Doors*, his nettlesome skirmish with Anthony Berkeley and the annual Detection Club dinner at the Hotel Café Royal, Piccadilly. (Recorded treasurer Punshon of the latter event: "L87/9/9—Miss Gilbert paid L6/9/4 for after dinner drinks. I gave the head waiter L1. Total 95/9/1. Great success.") After writing Freeman Wills Crofts and John Rhode to inform them about the Berkeley brouhaha, Punshon went into hospital for an operation. In September Sayers wrote Punshon that she was pleased to hear from his wife that he was "making a really good convalescence," adding: "We will miss you greatly at the October meeting, but of course you must have a good long holiday and get quite fit."

By early November Punshon, recuperating at Christopher Bush's house, Little Horsepen, near Rye in East Sussex, was able to report that he was "very much better," though the same month he resigned as Detection Club treasurer. (Christopher Bush succeeded him to the office.) Later that month Punshon wrote Sayers from Bournemouth, where he was taking a "long rest." He wished her good fortune with the recently published Penguin paperback edition of her translation of Dante's *Inferno*, remarking, "I don't know any translation of Dante except the old one [1805] by [Henry Francis] Cary, and that was a fairly pedestrian performance." He also heaped praise on Penguin's ambitious paperback publishing scheme, deeming it a "very praiseworthy attempt to turn us into a nation of book buyers instead of borrowers. A Real

Revolution—if they can bring it off." Punshon had particular reason to applaud Penguin's effort, as the previous year the company had issued a pair of 1930s Bobby Owen mystery titles as paperbacks. (Three more titles would follow in the next half-dozen years.)

Punshon remained active in Detection Club affairs in 1950, though he urged that Michael Gilbert be tapped to replace him on the membership committee. "Would [Anthony Berkeley] take the suggestion as an insult," he sarcastically queried Sayers, obviously still smarting over the events of the previous year. Punshon also participated in evaluations of the work of proposed new member Julian Symons (1912-1994), one of Britain's new wave of consciously self-styled "crime writers." Of Symons's recent *Bland Beginning* (1949), a novel based, as was Punshon's own *Comes a Stranger* (1938), on the Thomas J. Wise literary forgery scandal, Punshon wrote Sayers, "On the whole I should be inclined to say 'yes,' even though I think the character drawing deplorable and the construction and final explanation a bit shaky. But he does manage to produce a readable story and it is certainly an intelligent and clever book."

By 1952, Punshon's health had declined to the point where he felt unable to attend the Detection Club's annual dinner. "[A]s they used to say in the war, the situation on the (health) front has deteriorated," he mordantly wrote Sayers, adding ominously that he had scheduled an "appointment with a specialist." The next year, however, both he and his wife, now octogenarians, managed to make it to the dinner, much to the pleasure of Sayers, who promised, "you shan't be bothered with the [initiation] ceremony at all—there will be plenty of people to carry candles." Sayers promised the Punshons good seats at the High Table to hear philosopher Bertrand Russell speak, and in a contemporary letter Christianna Brand somewhat cattily reported observing Mrs. Punshon sitting "terribly close to the speakers so as not to miss a word, and sound asleep."

Sometime in the 1950s an increasingly fragile Punshon took a dreadful tumble down the landing steps at the Detection

Club premises at Kingly Street, an event Christianna Brand vividly recollected many years later in 1979, with what seems rather callous amusement on her part:

> My last memory, or the most abiding one, of the club room in the clergy house, was of an evening when two members were initiated there instead of at the annual dinner [possibly Glyn Carr and Roy Vickers, 1955 initiates]. As they left, they stepped over the body of an elderly gentleman lying with his head in a pool of blood, just outside the door. . . . dear old Mr. Punshon, E.R. Punshon, tottering up the stone stair steps upon his private business, had fallen all the way down again and severely lacerated his scalp. My [physician] husband, groaning, dealt with all but the gore, which remained in a slowly congealing pool upon the clergy house floor. . . . However, Miss Sayers had, predictably, just the right guest for such an event, a small, brisk lady, delighted to cope. She came out on the landing and stood for a moment peering down at the unlovely mess. Not myself one to delight in hospital matters, I hovered ineffectively as much as possible in the rear. She made up her mind. "Well, I think we can manage *that* all right. Can you find me a tablespoon?"
>
> The club room was unaccountably lacking in tablespoons. I went out and diffidently offered a large fork. "A fork? Oh, well . . ." She bent again and studied the pool of gore. "I think we can manage," she said again, cheerfully. "It's splendidly clotted."
>
> I returned once more to the club room and closed the door; and I can only report that when it opened again, not a sign remained of any blood, anywhere. "I thought," said my husband as we took our departure before even worse might befall, "that in your oath you foreswore vampires." "She was only a *guest*," I said apologetically.

"Dear old Mr. Punshon," no vampire he, passed through a door to death in his 84th year on 23 October 1956, four years

E.R. PUNSHON

after his elder brother, Robert Halket Punshon. On 25 January 1957 the widowed Sarah Punshon presented Dorothy L. Sayers with a copy of her husband's thirty-fifth and final Bobby Owen mystery, the charmingly retrospective *Six Were Present*. "He would like to think that you had one," wrote Sarah, warmly thanking Sayers "for your appreciation of my husband's work during his writing life" and wistfully adding that she would miss her "occasional visits to the club evenings." Sayers obligingly invited Sarah to the next Detection Club dinner as her guest, but Sarah died in May, having survived her longtime spouse by merely seven months. Sayers herself would not outlast the year. As Christianna Brand rather flippantly reports, Sayers was discovered, just a week before Christmas, collapsed dead "at the foot of the stairs in her house surrounded by bereaved cats." Having ascended and descended the stairs after a busy day of shopping, Sayers had discovered her own door to death.

* * * * *

Dorothy L. Sayers's literary reputation has risen ever higher in the years since her demise, with modern authorities like the esteemed late crime writer P.D. James particularly lauding Sayers's ambitious penultimate Peter Wimsey mystery, *Gaudy Night*--a novel E.R. Punshon himself had lavishly praised in his review column in the *Manchester Guardian*--as not only a great detective novel but a great novel, with no delimiting qualification. Although he was one of Sayers's favorite crime writers, Punshon was not so fortunate with his own reputation, with his work falling into unmerited neglect for more than a half-century after his death. With the reprinting by Dean Street Press of Punshon's complete set of Bobby Owen mystery investigations—chronicled in 35 novels, five short stories and a radio play—this long period of neglect now happily has ended, however, allowing a major writer from the Golden Age of detective fiction a golden opportunity to receive, six decades after his death, his full and lasting due.

Short Stories by E.R. Punshon

FIVE BOBBY OWEN detective short stories complement E.R. Punshon's 35 Bobby Owen detective novels, and these short stories are reprinted, one to a volume, with the new Dean Street Press editions of Punshon's *The Attending Truth*, *Strange Ending*, *Brought to Light*, *Dark Is the Clue* and *Triple Quest*. Although Punshon's Bobby Owen detective novels appeared over nearly a quarter-century, between 1933 and 1956, the publication of the Bobby Owen short stories was much more concentrated, with the first one, "A Study in the Obvious," appearing in the London *Evening Standard* on 23 August 1936 and the remaining four, "Making Sure," "Good Beginning," "Three Sovereigns" and "Find the Lady," in the *Evening Standard* in 1950, on, respectively, 15 February, 1 August, 17 October and 21 December.

"A Study in the Obvious" appeared as part of an *Evening Standard* series devoted to "famous detectives of fiction," edited by Dorothy L. Sayers. Besides Bobby Owen, fictional detectives included in "Detective Cavalcade" were Sherlock Holmes, Sexton Blake, Raffles, Eugene Valmont, Father Brown, the "Man in the Corner," Max Carrados, Dr. Thorndyke, Dr. Priestley, Dr. Hailey, Hercule Poirot, Reggie Fortune, Philip Trent, Albert Campion, Lord Peter Wimsey, Roger Sheringham, Ludovic Travers, Mrs. Bradley, Mr. Pepper, Mr. Reeder, Mr. Pinkerton, Chief Constable Sir Clinton Driffield, Inspector French, Superintendent Wilson, Inspector Head, Uncle Abner, Trevis Tarrant, Charlie Chan and Ellery Queen.

As editor of the series Dorothy L. Sayers warned Gladys Mitchell, who was contributing an original Mrs. Bradley short story, that the *Evening Standard* "will probably say they want it as short as possible and as cheap a possible! Don't let them screw you down to 4000 words, because I know they are prepared to go to 6000 words or thereabouts. . . . I have almost broken their hearts by pointing out to them that all the older people, like Conan Doyle and Austin Freeman, run out to something like 10,000 [words] and their columns will be frightfully congested."

In her *Evening Standard* introduction to "A Study in the Obvious," (2814 words) Sayers wrote:

> E.R. Punshon's detective novels are distinguished by two things: a delicate, sub-acid humour and a fine vein of romantic feeling. They fall into two groups—the stories about Inspector Carter and Detective-Sergeant Bell, and the more recent series about Superintendent Mitchell and Detective-Sergeant Bobby Owen.
>
> In this short story . . . Owen—that nobly-born and Oxford-bred young policeman—appears alone, exploiting his characteristic vein of inspired common sense.
>
> The crime here is a trivial one; those who like to see serious crimes handled with delicate emotional perception should make a point of reading some of the novels, such as "Mystery Villa" and "Death of a Beauty Queen."

"A Study in the Obvious," which appeared the same year as *The Bath Mysteries*, a Punshon detective novel that delved into Sergeant Bobby Owen's aristocratic family background, is Bobby Owen's origin story, showing how he came to be a policeman. Though light, the tale is one of considerable charm that should delight Bobby Owen fans.

The later *Evening Standard* stories are shorter affairs, though they are all murder investigations. "Good Beginning" and "Find the Lady" take us back to earlier years in Bobby Owen's police career, when he held the ranks of, respectively, constable and sergeant. "Making Sure" and "Three Sovereigns" capture something of that quality of what American mystery critic Anthony Boucher called "the obscure destinies that drive [Punshon's] obsessed and tormented characters," which so impressed Dorothy L. Sayers about Punshon's novels.

Curtis Evans

CHAPTER I
THE ATROPOS

COMMANDER BOBBY OWEN, of the Metropolitan C.I.D., was driving rather carefully down the narrow, twisting main street of the small but quickly growing village of Twice Over, past the old village church, from which the village itself was rapidly receding, preferring perhaps proximity to the railway station to proximity to the church, and so on towards Over Abbey, erected in Victorian Gothic early in the last century on the site of the very ancient, venerable, and once-famous Benedictine Abbey of Over Once, and now the seat of Sir Charles Stuart, well known and prominent in all local affairs.

A little outside the village, but nearer to it than was the Abbey, stood the Old Dower House, dating from at least a century earlier, and if of no architectural pretension, at any rate showing that sense of proportion which seems to have been innate in the master builders and craftsmen of the period.

It was here that Bobby halted his new Du Guesclin Twelve he had preferred to use on this trip rather than one of the Yard cars. He alighted to open the gate admitting to the long, straight, rhododendron-lined avenue leading to the house. A well-kept garden, he noticed—no trace there of the difficulty often experienced in these days of keeping lawns and flowerbeds in good order. Possibly, though, Mr Willoughby Wynne, the occupier of this attractive little place, looked after it himself.

Before the front door Bobby halted his car again, and then, as he was in the act of alighting, a young girl came flying out of the house in a flutter of skirts and little cries of delight.

"Oh, Marty, how lovely!" she called; and then gasped and stood still as Bobby turned to face her and she saw it was a stranger. "Oh, I am sorry," she said, changing all at once from a whirlwind in petticoats to a dignified and sedate young lady. "I thought it was a friend I was expecting. He's buying a new car and he said it would be either a Du Guesclin Twelve or a Tiger Ten and he would bring it for me to see, so when I saw it was a Du Guesclin I made sure it was him, and I got so excited; wouldn't you?"

"I'm sure I would," Bobby agreed; "and I'm so sorry to disappoint you. I hope your friend will like his new car as much as I do mine—I've only had it a week. I believe Mr Willoughby Wynne lives here. Do you think I could see him for a few minutes? It's a small matter of business."

"I expect he's in his study or somewhere," the girl answered. "Stamps, isn't it? It almost always is. Or chess? I do think they are both so utterly boring, but Daddy loves them. If you'll come in, I'll see if I can find him."

Bobby did not attempt to correct her assumption that it was either stamps or chess with which his errand was concerned. They were two subjects of which he knew little, except that you could spend a fortune on the one and a lifetime on the other. He produced his card—private, not official. He said:

"You are very knowledgeable about cars. Not every young lady would be able to tell at a glance a Du Guesclin Twelve from a Tiger Ten."

"Oh, but you've simply got to know about cars, haven't you?" she protested. "You couldn't live without one, could you? Vital."

She was an attractive-looking young woman, though not because of any exceptional claim to beauty, or indeed to beauty at all. Her best point was her complexion, which was very much as God made it, owing little to that excessive use of cosmetics by which some girls manage to give themselves so striking a resemblance to a new-laid egg. Her eyes were good, too—of an unusually clear light brown. But her hair could have been fairly described as 'mousey', and her features were irregular: her mouth too large and her nose too small. None the less—though this she hardly knew—she often drew an admiring attention prettier girls sometimes missed, and would occasionally find herself sought out in apparent preference to these others. It was a result, one supposes, of a sense of joy in life that she seemed, though so unconsciously, to spread about her, as though every passing moment were a fresh delight. As a baby in its cradle may be seen at times to chortle to itself as with the sheer pleasure of being here at last, so now an incarnate joy this girl appeared, as she almost literally danced up the few steps leading to the front door, and then turned, with a smile Bobby knew was not meant for him but for all existence, to see if he were following. And the thought came suddenly into his mind that this was how life was meant to be for all created things.

The lofty hall they now entered was paved in alternating squares of black and white marble, the coldness of this effect much relieved, however, by the rich colours of several oriental rugs lying here and there, and by a soft amber light where the late September sunshine penetrated through the glass cupola in the roof. Opposite the door a graceful semi-circular stair, in gilt and iron, rose to a kind of balcony above. On one side a columned alcove sheltered a striking marble statue—of Atropos, Bobby guessed, to judge by the 'abhorred' shears she carried and by the darkly grave expression the sculptor had managed to give her. His guide saw how Bobby paused involuntarily to look, for it was indeed a magnificent piece of work. She said:

"Doesn't she look a sulky, solemn old thing? I always make a face at her when I remember," and this, having remembered, she now proceeded to do. "Daddy's awfully proud of her, though. He found her in an old back-yard somewhere. Genuine Grecian antique by Phidias or someone, and worth pots of money. People write to Daddy to ask if they can come and look at her. Sort of film star in stone. When I was a tiny years ago I used to be scared she might come walking into my room one night."

So, chattering happily, she led the way down a corridor into a room commanding a gay prospect over lawn and flowers and shrubs, with in the distance a background of tall tree-tops, now golden with autumn foliage. On this french windows opened, and these were swung widely apart, as though through them the occupant of the room had only that moment left.

4 | E.R. PUNSHON

"Daddy can't be far off," the girl said. "I'll see if I can find him. Sit down, won't you?"

With that she ran out into the garden, and Bobby watched her as she crossed the lawn so swiftly and so lightly it might well have been she went on wings and not on mortal feet. A corner of the house hid her from sight, and Bobby turned his attention to the room itself, hoping to gather from it, as he always tried to do, some impression of the character of its occupant.

In this he failed. It seemed to him entirely impersonal, withdrawn, as if inhabited only by some disembodied spirit, a ghost from past times, or even as if it guarded jealously secrets it did not mean any should ever know. A fanciful impression for which he could not account. The room was of fine proportions, the walls panelled in gold and white, with blue-and-white medallions at the corners, the plaster ceiling showing in the centre a gilded floral device. The general effect was charming, though, again, a little withdrawn. It was furnished so impeccably in the style of the period that instinctively the name of a famous firm in Tottenham Court Road came to mind. Even the books on the shelves of a magnificent Gothic library bookcase seemed chosen to be typical of the time, and, closely packed as they were, gave but little the idea of ever being read. Bobby told himself that whoever used the room lived a life entirely apart from it. He found himself beginning to wonder if the complete impersonality of these surroundings did not in itself constitute a clue to the personality of their owner.

From such rather dreamy thoughts he was abruptly recalled—his back had been to the open french windows as he stood admiring the bookcase—by a sudden conviction that he was no longer alone. He turned quickly. A man was standing just inside the room. The windows he had closed noiselessly behind him as he entered. He appeared to be of middle age, of medium height and build, dark eyes and dark complexion, clean shaven, as are most men to-day. In one hand he was holding both a pair of horn-rimmed spectacles and Bobby's card. His voice when he spoke was low and soft, and he had a trick of running his words into each other, so that it was not always easy to catch what he was saying. He came forward. He hardly seemed to move, and yet he was suddenly in the middle of the room. He said:

"Mr Owen, isn't it? I am Mr Willoughby Wynne. Sylvia tells me you have called on business. Not, I hope, about my Atropos? But won't you sit down?"

He waved Bobby to a chair which was either genuine Chippendale or else a remarkably good reproduction, seated himself and waited—waited as if he were prepared to wait for ever, indefinitely and indifferently, with the same unvarying grey patience. Bobby himself knew well how to wait, but he with a controlled force and passion that often brought forth the response that it demanded. The manner of tired attention, as if to what could not possibly be of concern to him, shown by this apparently withdrawn and secret man was new to Bobby, and he did not think that he much liked it. He produced his official card and handed it to Mr Wynne, who took it, looked at it, laid it down.

"Yes?" he said, as though well used to visits from highly placed Scotland Yard officials.

"My information," Bobby said, beginning to talk more formally, "is that there is a private entrance from these premises to the copse at the back. The copse, I am informed, is the property of Sir Charles Stuart, of Over Abbey, your neighbour, but you have a right of way across it to the public footpath running between it and the fields beyond."

"Perfectly correct," said Mr Wynne. "Yes?"

"We have reason to believe," Bobby continued, "that an attempt may be made to-night to recover stolen property of considerable value buried there by the thieves. We are asking your permission to have access to the copse by your right of way. We wish to avoid any risk of attracting attention in the village. It is vital no suspicion should be roused of our presence here, or the attempt may be put off for weeks or even for months."

CHAPTER II
TALE FOR A MORALIST

MR WYNNE'S gaze had wandered away to one of those blue-and-white medallions at the corners of the ceiling. He might not have heard a word of what had been said, and yet that was certainly not the impression Bobby received. In the same low, toneless voice as before, his aloof gaze still upon that blue-and-white medallion in the furthest corner of the room, he said:

"I have the greatest respect for the police and the very high level of efficiency they invariably display. You may naturally rest assured that I shall be most happy to co-operate in every way in my power," and as he spoke there came and went a smile, so small, so swift, so fleeting, it had vanished almost before it could be seen. It was as though in his quiet, hidden way it amused him to think of taking part in police operations. He laid down the outsize horn spectacles he had been holding, and thus allowed Bobby to notice that the forefinger of his right hand was missing. A war wound, perhaps, or some accident. Possibly the 'blitz'. On a finger of his other hand he wore a large signet ring. Opening a drawer of the writing-table at which he was seated, he took out a box of cigarettes, offered one to Bobby, gave him a light, lighted his own cigarette, and went on: "I am wondering if the Mr Dowie who has been staying at the Over All Arms for the last day or two is one of your men. If he is, I fear it is a little too late to hope to avoid attention. I should imagine he is about the only topic of conversation all through the village."

"He has nothing to do with us, whoever he is," Bobby said quickly. "What makes you think he might have?"

"Well," Wynne answered, "it seems he has some sort of contraption he claims will show the whereabouts of any hidden treasure. Do you know of the old story about the monks of Over Abbey burying the church plate and so on at the time of the Reformation to save it from Cromwell's Commissioners? When you spoke of stolen property buried in the copse,

I began to wonder if there was any connection. Very likely it is only a coincidence, but I thought I had better mention it."

"I am very glad you did," Bobby told him, and he was beginning to look a little worried. "If it is a coincidence it is a most unlucky one. It is the first I have heard of it. Has he said anything about where it is supposed to be hidden or what it is?"

"Not that I know of," Mr Wynne answered, "but really I didn't pay much attention." Again that same small fleeting smile came and went almost in the same fraction of a second. "I'm afraid I've no great belief in hidden-treasure stories," he added apologetically.

"Can you give me any description of him?" Bobby asked.

"I'm afraid not," Mr Wynne answered. "I've never even seen him, that I know of. I heard him spoken of as a tough-looking customer who might give our Sir Charles Stuart as good as he got if it came to that. Evidently Stuart has heard about it and is very much on the alert as a result. He's saying he's not going to have anyone trespassing on his property looking for treasure or anything else. If there is anything there, then that's his business and no one else's."

"I see," Bobby said, and looked even more worried than before. It was clearly going to be all much more complicated than he had expected. But, then, village life so often is. And who was this Mr Dowie so suddenly making so abrupt an entrance on the scene? Mr Wynne, however, for all his manner of reserve, seemed inclined to be communicative, and Bobby's habit was always to encourage people to talk. The more they talked, the more information came out—some of it entirely irrelevant, of course, but also some of it sometimes very much to the point. Occasionally, too, it was information they themselves had not known they possessed. 'You understand all this is highly confidential', was a favourite gambit of his, and one that seldom failed to loosen the tongues of even the shyest, the most taciturn, the most distrustful. He made up his mind suddenly and went on: "As a matter of fact I came to ask your help because I heard it was so much more secluded here than at Over Abbey. As well as easier to get to the copse unobserved. If the attempt we think from our information may be made tonight to recover the stuff if it's still there, then a sharp look-out will be kept beforehand to make sure all's clear. The least hint of a suggestion we are on the look-out, and that will be the end of it for goodness knows how long, and we can't continue watching indefinitely. The initiative is always with the criminal."

"You don't mean Dowie may be one of the gang, do you?" Mr Wynne asked. "On the look-out? If gang is what you call it," he added doubtfully. "Gang sounds so melodramatic, doesn't it? Unreal."

"Oh, gangs are real enough," Bobby told him. "Much too real for my liking or the safety of the public. Criminals do tend to work in gangs. They have cut themselves off from society, and so they feel the need to create a fresh society to belong to. Solitary criminals are rare, but when they exist they are formidable. Like rogue elephants."

"I can understand that," Mr Wynne said. "But I should have expected, too, a tendency, after a really big haul, to slip back into society and shelter in the shadow of an accepted respectability. Even to make oneself as prominent as possible, so as to get accepted, so to say. Rather on the principle of Edgar Allan Poe's lost letter. The easier to see, the more conspicuous, the less likely to be noticed. But that might be too dull a life for gangsters, and no doubt you speak from experience, not theory. You have evidently given much thought to the subject— gone into it very deeply, if I may say so. No doubt a great help to you in your work, though I am afraid all that would rather puzzle our good Sergeant Jenkins in charge in the village here. I was going to suggest your getting Dowie to try out his machine and see if it was any help. Water-divining works, so perhaps that might, too. But hardly advisable if Dowie is one of the gang himself. Though it would be rather amusing," and now again came and went that faint, fleeting smile so nearly imperceptible it was more communicated than seen. A secret and hidden sense of humour, at any rate. "Amusing, I mean," he explained, "to enlist the help of one of the gang responsible for the theft to recover what he himself had helped to hide."

"I think, perhaps," Bobby remarked, "that we will wait and see what happens to-night. We hope, of course, that whoever appears will go straight to the hiding-place. If we can arrest them with the stolen property in their possession it will be much easier to get a conviction. Clever counsel won't be able to persuade the jury it was only blackberrying or taking an innocent midnight stroll before bed, or something like that, took them there."

"You'll have to keep a sharp look-out for Stuart as well as for your other visitors," Wynne warned him. "He is very much in evidence just now. Sylvia—my daughter, you know: you've seen her, her room overlooks the copse—says she's seen a light there two or three times lately. It may have been Dowie and his machine. More likely Stuart on the prowl for trespassers. Very possessive person, Sir Charles. Likes to keep his own to himself."

Bobby had made up his mind now. He said:

"You understand all this is highly confidential? Anyhow, even if Dowie and his machine are both genuine, they wouldn't be much help. What we believe may be hidden in the copse isn't jewellery or anything like that. Do you remember the robbery shortly before the war ended of a Post Office van? A number of mail-bags were taken. They contained used pound-notes from branch banks in the provinces sent up to be cancelled. There was another such robbery later on, but they don't seem to have been connected in any way. In this first one notes to the value of about £200,000 were secured. The driver of the van tried very pluckily to resist. He was shot and wounded by the gang leader. Fortunately he recovered."

"Well, that was a good thing," declared Mr Wynne. "I don't expect killing was ever intended. They shouldn't have had guns at all. Most likely told not to, but thought they knew best. But what a tremendous haul! I'm afraid I don't remember much about it. Seven or eight years ago, wouldn't it be? A long time, and I daresay I wasn't very much interested even then. All that sort of thing seems so remote from this quiet little backwater of ours. A dull life you may think it, but at least a safe one. Isn't it all rather ancient history by this time? Are you taking it up again? There was no arrest at the time, was there?"

"No," Bobby answered. "But we knew very well who had carried out the robbery. Names were being mentioned in pubs and cafés in Soho, and we were getting together a fair amount of evidence. But what we didn't know, and very much wanted to know, was who did the very highly efficient planning and staff work—the 'backroom boy', as they say, or the 'master mind', as the papers like to put it."

"Are you still hoping to find him?" Mr Wynne asked; and once again Bobby had the impression, though this time no least shadow of a smile had shown, that any such hope was regarded as distinctly amusing—which annoyed Bobby. "A 'master mind'," Wynne was repeating. "I confess I always thought the 'master mind' idea was just newspaper talk—journalistic colouring. I should expect any 'master mind' to do a lot better in the city—and very likely a peerage thrown in as well."

"Well, there's always that," agreed Bobby; "but this time there was definite information to go on. There was certainly someone of the sort in the background—very carefully in the background. But all the same, though the other members of the gang never saw him, they all seem to have gone in deadly fear of him. He kept very strict discipline. Even among themselves when they met to receive his instructions they always wore gloves. There was one member of the gang we thought we had identified, but he turned out to be only a hanger-on, a runner or scout. We got a glimpse of him once or twice—generally running away—and even he always wore gloves."

"Finger-prints," said Mr Wynne, nodding understandingly. "I've heard of them."

"Well, finger-prints—'dabs', we call them—aren't much use unless there are others to check up with," Bobby explained. "Of course, if 'dabs' are on record at Central, we know at once who to look for. So we should if everybody had to have them registered on a kind of identity card. But the public wouldn't have that at any price."

"Well, you know, I rather feel like that myself," Mr Wynne remarked.

"Most people do," Bobby agreed. "So do I, for that matter, as a private citizen, that is. As a policeman I should find it a great help."

"You don't expect this unknown leader to be one of your visitors to-night, do you?" Wynne went on. "The men who carried out the actual raid, perhaps, but surely not the master-mind gentleman?"

"Not the actual men," Bobby said. "Their heirs and successors, perhaps. The actual thieves are all dead."

"Dead? All of them?" Wynne exclaimed. He was showing more animation now—to have grown, so to say, less grey, less secret and withdrawn. "Surely not all of them? All?" he repeated.

"Two of the gang," Bobby said—"the two against whom the strongest case had been worked up—were killed the very night their arrest was to have been made. A direct hit scored on the house where they were hiding by one of the last V2's to fall on London. Nothing much left either of them or of the house. We believe their share of the stolen notes went up with them—probably £20,000 each."

"Ironical," pronounced Mr Wynne. "The notes had been sent up to London to be destroyed, and destroyed they were—very efficiently. A tale for a moralist. And the remaining two men? What about them? Were they killed the same way?"

"No," Bobby answered "One was a man named Frank Farmer. He was apparently what might be called 'Operation Chief'. He was always in charge of actual raids, and we were able to get good evidence that he was the man who shot the driver. But before he could be brought in he was discovered in a ditch outside London with half his head shot away."

"A quarrel over sharing out the stolen money, probably," Mr Wynne suggested. "I imagine these sort of people often fall out among themselves. One of them made drunk, put in a car, taken out into the country, shot, and dumped where you found him. The American technique I've read about. It must have been a great disappointment to you."

"Oh, it was," Bobby agreed. "There had even been hopes he might turn King's evidence, as it was then, and tell who it was did the planning—the 'Boss', as the others called him."

"What about him?" Mr Wynne asked. "But perhaps he had the sense to leave the country?"

"His difficulty would be in getting the money abroad," Bobby remarked. "A hundred thousand pounds or more in paper money would make a sizeable package to smuggle out of the country. Several suit-cases, I should think. And then there's the changing into foreign currency. We worked on the idea, but it came to nothing."

"What about the other man?" Mr Wynne inquired. "Did he get away with it? Or was he unlucky, too?"

"He was a man named Charley Cream," Bobby answered. "Charley Cream. Naturally he got called 'The Milkman'. He was brought in for questioning, and enough came out for him to be charged with an entirely different offence. A burglary. Violence had been used and he was given rather a stiff sentence. Twelve years. We tried to get him to talk, but he wouldn't. We knew though that he was boasting to other convicts that there was money waiting for him, safe put away, enough to live on like a gentleman for the rest of his life. Only he died first."

"Their success doesn't seem to have brought any of them much luck," Mr Wynne observed thoughtfully.

"No," Bobby agreed. "Now another convict has been released. A man named Rogers—Jolly Rogers they call him. I don't know why. He was the Milkman's special pal in gaol, and we have information that he's boasting he got a tip from the Milkman before he died about where the money is hidden, and it's somewhere in Twice Over, so he's going to give Twice Over the once over."

"How very extraordinary!" said Mr Wynne. "A treasure hunt in our quiet little village! Sylvia will be excited. Oh, I won't say a word till it's all finished and done with. I know how to hold my tongue. So does she, for that matter," and he smiled affectionately in a way that seemed to change his whole personality, to open it out as it were and show beneath that cold outward reserve of his unexpected depths of warmth and goodwill, as at the magic touch of his daughter's name. "I wonder," he went on, "if you've ever thought of the possibility that this unknown 'Boss' in the background was merely camouflage for the Frank Farmer you mentioned. A useful screen for him to operate from if he really was the hidden 'master mind'. It would give him a claim, too, for a double share—one for himself, one he would collect for the non-existent 'Boss', both of them big ones—and he could dodge responsibility for unpopular orders and for failures and mishaps—if there were any."

"Not many," Bobby said, surprised Wynne had so soon suggested a plausible idea it had taken the investigating officers at the time much longer to arrive at. "An objection is that Farmer doesn't seem to have had the necessary brains, from what we heard of him. A good subordinate, but had to be told what to do. First-class sergeant, but no staff officer. Anyhow, we're still hoping that if the attempt we expect is made to-night, and the buried money is recovered, we may also recover with it, or from the men concerned, information as to the identity of the man behind it all. Personally I feel sure there was one—and not Farmer. It may be Farmer discovered who he was, and that's why he was shot. That information, if Farmer had it, may have been buried with the money. At any rate there seem to be hints like that in the talk that we've heard is going on."

"Well, if you brought that off," exclaimed Mr Wynne with sudden unexpected enthusiasm, "that would be splendid, wouldn't it? A big feather in your cap," he said, positively beaming.

CHAPTER III
LOGANBERRY BUSHES

THE VEHEMENCE, the emphasis, with which this was said surprised Bobby. But natural enough, he supposed, that the sudden prospect of the arrest of a violent criminal almost at his own back door should prove rather exciting to any normal citizen, especially one who, like Mr Willoughby Wynne, seemed to live so quiet and cloistered a life. Wynne had risen from his chair now and had gone to stand at the french windows overlooking garden and copse. Perhaps, Bobby thought, he wished to reassure himself that the old familiar scene remained the same, even though strange events might soon be enacted there. He turned round and said:

"I am wondering if you would care to take a stroll through the copse to get an idea of the lie of the land. There's rather a tangle of undergrowth, and it's not too easy always to follow the right-of-way path. Especially at night, of course."

"Thank you very much," Bobby said warmly. "It would be a great help, if it's not troubling you too much."

"Not at all," declared Mr Wynne. "For that matter, a plain duty to help the police. We are all indebted to them. We'll go out the front way, shall we? I had better tell Sylvia, or she won't know what's happened."

Bobby followed him into the hall. Mr Wynne, murmuring something about a cap and scarf, disappeared into a cloakroom. Bobby, waiting, turned to look again at the Atropos statue which had previously caught his attention. A magnificent thing. He was still looking at it with increasing admiration when he found the soft-footed Mr Wynne back at his side.

"You've noticed my Atropos," he remarked. "A fine bit of work, isn't it? The experts seem to think it does really date from very early Greek times. At the moment an art dealer's trying to buy it for an American client—very persistent. I expect he scents a big profit. I thought at first that's what you had come about. Sylvia wants me to get rid of it," he added reflectively.

"Miss Wynne told me you had come across it somewhere near here," Bobby said. "A wonderful find. If it were mine, I should hate to part with it, and yet—something rather ominous and strange about it. But that may be what the sculptor intended. I can quite imagine Miss Wynne wouldn't be altogether sorry to see it go."

"She makes faces at it sometimes," Mr Wynne observed. "I've seen her put her tongue out at it as she passes," and now, as he was speaking, his voice was no longer low and toneless, but charged with a sudden great tenderness.

"I wouldn't do that," Bobby said, half seriously. "I think I would offer propitiatory sacrifices instead—a cup of wine and a garland of flowers."

"It might be wiser," Mr Wynne agreed, and he, too, spoke half seriously. "I wonder where the girl's got to," he added. "Sylvia," he called, "where are you? Sylvia." When no answer came he went over to a Chinese gong near by and struck it one reverberating blow. "Our private signal," he explained, "when we want each other."

Almost at once the front door burst open and with her light, dancing step, Sylvia came running in.

"Hullo, Daddy dear," she called. "Want me?" and then she saw Bobby, flashed one of her smiles at him, and then another, a different smile, not general to all the world, but particular to her father and to him alone.

Strange it was to see how under the radiance of that lovely smile he seemed to grow, to change, how that grey, withdrawn personality of his dropped from him. It was as though she brought with her a brightness from another world, so that the light within her illumined all around—all but the Atropos still shadowy in her sheltered alcove.

"I'm taking Mr Owen to have a look at the right of way," her father said, that new warmth and tenderness still making his voice so different Bobby could hardly believe it was the same man speaking. "We shan't be long. Could you have some tea ready for us when we get back?"

"Right-oh," said Sylvia. "Only mind you aren't long, because I'm ravenous," and then she looked to see if either of them were shocked by this announcement.

"That's very kind of you," Bobby said; "but really, I ought not to trouble you."

"Sylvia likes trouble," Mr Wynne said. "Unlike her father, who doesn't."

"Marty's here," Sylvia said. "It's a Tiger Ten he's bought." She looked at Bobby. "I like it just as much as the Du Guesclin, even if it isn't so big. But I don't think I like things for being big. Besides, it's miles cheaper. He's paid every penny, too, because I told him you"—the 'you' was to her father—"said it was always a mistake to owe anything to anyone."

"I'm glad to hear it," Mr Wynne said. "I thought he said he hadn't enough to pay cash?"

"Oh, he hadn't, poor boy," Sylvia agreed; "but his publisher made it up. Wasn't it nice of him?"

"Well, then, he owes it to his publisher, doesn't he?" Mr Wynne asked.

"Oh, no," Sylvia protested; "it's only what Marty's going to get for his book when he's got it done." It was an explanation, Bobby thought, more satisfactory to the daughter than to the father. But Mr Wynne only smiled at her—not a secret, swift, elusive smile this time, but warm and open. "Do come and look at it," Sylvia added. "It's awfully swell."

She danced away then, and her father and Bobby followed, Mr Wynne explaining as they went that 'Marty' was a Mr Martin Maxton, a young neighbour of theirs, a writer living alone in a small cottage but often away for long periods at a time. It was information given quite casually and naturally, and yet Bobby got the impression that Mr Wynne was not altogether happy about the friendly relationship that evidently existed between the two young people. Natural enough that any father, especially such an adoring father as Wynne appeared to be, should eye somewhat critically any young man coming near his daughter. Natural, too, that Mr Wynne, with his preference for a life of calm routine, placid and unadventurous, should regard with especial doubt young men who were 'writers', lived alone in small cottages, and were often absent for long periods. Probably a bank clerk or a civil servant would have found greater favour in his sight.

Outside were the two cars, the Du Guesclin and the Tiger Ten, ranged behind each other on the gravel drive with Sylvia, in a bustle of admiration, fluttering between them. Watching her adoringly was a tall young man, presumably the Martin Maxton Mr Wynne had spoken of.

Hearing the two older men approaching, he turned towards them as if in greeting, and then stood very still. He was a tall, dark youth, good looking, with strong, well-marked features and dark, deep-sunken eyes. Nothing did he show of that happy, gay acceptance of life in which Sylvia moved as in a bright cloud of joy. It was almost as though, young as he was, he had known the depths, and it was with something of a shock that Bobby realized that Martin knew him and that that was why he had so suddenly stiffened and stood still, and why now there was distrust and even fear showing so clearly in those deep, sunken, troubled eyes of his—the eyes of one who did not sleep well. It came to Bobby that he himself had either seen the young man before or else someone strangely like him.

There were, of course, Bobby was well aware, many who knew him but whom he himself had either never seen at all or else had had of them only a mere passing glimpse. Few officers of police, indeed, remain for long unknown to criminals and undesirables generally, and Bobby was probably as well known as any. A drawback, of course, but inevitable; and inevitable, too, that many of those who thus knew him should have reason to regard him with distrust and fear.

All this passed through Bobby's mind in a flash, and only later on was recalled to be given more careful and prolonged consideration. At the moment the customary ritual of introduction was being gone through, and Bobby and Martin were trying to express a pleasure at making each other's acquaintance that neither of them felt. Sylvia was busily inspecting and admiring the two cars and occasionally calling attention to this or that point about one or other of them. Mr Wynne was apparently fully engaged listening and answering her very knowledgeable comments, but also, at the same time, as Bobby suddenly realized, watching both him and Martin Maxton with a silent, close attention. Evidently he had not failed to notice the sudden moment of strain and tension when the casual glance which Bobby and Martin had at first bestowed upon each other had become so abruptly charged with a deeper significance. But now again Sylvia's clear young voice intervened, for she at least was plainly quite unaware of anything unusual or unexpected.

"I like the Tiger Ten ever so much better," she announced. "I think it's just perfect." Then she added, as if afraid she might have hurt Bobby's feelings by so pronounced a judgment in favour of another car: "Of course, the Du Guesclin's lovely, too."

"So long as a car takes me where I want to go, that's all I ask," Mr Wynne remarked, "but Sylvia's an expert—nothing she likes better than taking bits of a car to pieces and then putting them together again. It looks as if there will have to be a visit to the Motor Show next month if the bank balance seems like running to a new car."

"Oh, Daddy, you are scrumptious," Sylvia cried.

"Sounds as if I were a toasted tea-cake," Mr Wynne chuckled, and to Bobby he said: "Shall we push on?"

"Has Sir Charles been worrying about that old right of way again?" Sylvia asked. "You know, Daddy, I don't think he's really been awfully nice about it," and it seemed as if, to her, not 'being awfully nice' was something that almost passed human comprehension.

"He would be even less awfully nice if he got half a chance," retorted Mr Wynne, and then, as he and Bobby walked away, and as soon as they were safely out of earshot, he remarked half to himself apparently and half to Bobby: "I'm a little worried about that young man. He always gives me a feeling that there's something in his past—something he doesn't want known. It's his eyes, I think. I've seen men with eyes like that before. Fanciful, no doubt. Do publishers generally provide authors with cars?"

"It seems very generous of them if they do," Bobby answered cautiously. "Does Mr Maxton write under his own name?"

"I don't really know," Wynne answered. "Last week Sylvia showed me something in the Open Air Weekly, I think it was. She said it was his and he did it every week. It was signed 'Max o' the Fields'. And I rather think she said he had to do with guide-books, but that's hardly being an author, is it?"

Bobby did not attempt to answer this searching question. Mr Wynne lapsed into silence; and it was very noticeable how, as they moved further away from that circle of light and joy Sylvia's own innate happiness seemed to spread around her like an aura, so her father seemed to grow less, to contract as before he had expanded, to sink again into that grey withdrawal which had been so apparent when Bobby first saw him.

The path they were following led directly to a door in the garden wall, topped by barbed wire with specially long, ugly-looking spikes. The wall itself was about six or eight feet in height, and along its foot ran a hedge of loganberry bushes. Wild, untrimmed, even overgrown they looked: a contrast to the trim tidiness of the rest of the garden. Wynne saw Bobby looking at them, and laughed softly—the first time Bobby had heard him laugh. He said:

"My first line of defence against the village boys, who seemed to think I grow fruit for their special benefit. Very effective, too. They climbed the wall with no trouble at all, but I've not been bothered so much since one of them tumbled over it right into a specially deep tangle of those bushes. Scratched himself more than badly getting himself free," and he laughed again, the same soft laugh, as if he found this tale very amusing. Then, as he took some keys from his pocket and began to look for the right one, he repeated: "No, I'm not altogether happy about him. Very pleasant to talk to, but I do have that feeling that he has a past, and not an altogether agreeable one. Not that I take any notice of the gossip about him. I've no doubt there's gossip about every one in the village as well. Including me, very likely. I know there is about Stuart. But when it comes to talk of blackmail, it seems a bit more serious. Actionable."

"A criminal matter," Bobby corrected him, a little startled by the use of a word of such ominous content. "Is it thought that Maxton is blackmailing someone?"

"No, no," Wynne answered quickly. "The idea seems to be that he is the victim—at least that's what I gather. There's nothing said in so many words, of course—it's all nods and winks and so forth." He had found the right key now and was opening the door. Bobby noticed that it was a mortice lock and that it had recently been oiled. "It's not much used," Wynne went on to explain, "but I always keep it locked. I've had an electric bell fixed. It rings in the kitchen. So far as I can make out the whole of the blackmail story depends on the fact that once a month or so a woman calls on him and apparently he gives her fairly large sums of money. At any rate on one occasion she lost her handbag after a bicycle accident. She was knocked down, and afterwards her handbag was found in a ditch. There was a hundred pounds in pound notes in it. Rather a large sum for an impecunious young man to hand over. Very likely there's some quite simple explanation."

"Can you give me any description of her?"

"Well, I've seen her once or twice near Maxton's cottage—if it's the same woman, that is. Tall and stout, middle-aged, I should say, but trying hard to look younger. Rather a furtive look about her, as if she didn't much want to be seen. Hair dyed, I thought. I remember especially her nose: it was very prominent."

"That's a very good description," Bobby said. "Much better than those we generally get."

"I suppose it was the stories about her made me notice her," Wynne said carelessly.

CHAPTER IV
TRESPASSING

ON THEIR WAY through the garden they had been walking in bright, warm sunshine—exceptionally bright and warm for the time of year, and very welcome after recent persistent rain. But now as they passed on into the copse the change was immediate. Here the rays of the already declining sun were entirely cut off by the high wall, and much of the remaining daylight was lost in the thickly growing trees from which the leaves had not yet begun to fall. A dark, chill silence reigned, like that of a neglected cemetery. Even their footsteps on the sodden ground sounded dull and muffled, and here indeed no bird sang—or ever would, Bobby thought. It was an all-pervading damp, one to penetrate even to the bones; and as Wynne carefully locked the door behind them, he said with some appearance of uneasiness:

"I hope we shan't run across Stuart on the prowl for trespassers. He often is. My landlord, and unfortunately we are not on good terms—don't speak to each other, like a couple of school-girls. Awkward, of course, and if he hears you came to me rather than to him, he'll be definitely hostile. Put a spanner in the works if he can."

"I hope it won't come to that," Bobby said. "It will have to be dealt with if it does. As I said before, it is necessary to avoid attracting attention, and I did hear there was a lot of coming and going at Sir Charles's place—Over Abbey, isn't it?"

"Coming and going is a nice tactful way of putting it," Mr Wynne observed. "Not that any one worries—except the Vicar. Nothing to lay hold of, except that Stuart seems to have almost as many nieces—most attractive young ladies, all of them—as a mediaeval pope had nephews. And why shouldn't he? Some elderly but still skittish visitors as well. Aunts, probably. All Vicar can do is to look worried, and meanwhile Stuart subscribes most liberally to all good causes in the village. Puts me quite in the shade. Not that I mind. Have you any idea why these people should choose this particular spot to hide their loot? I shouldn't have thought it very suitable. How did they know about it?"

"Frank Farmer," Bobby explained, "the gangster I told you we found shot—probably by one of his pals—was born here. His father was a farm worker in the district. He is sure to have known this copse—blackberrying, for one thing—and then it's easy of access and yet private. As soon as we heard of the rumours going about we got out an Ordnance map, and this struck us all as the obvious place."

"Probably Dowie thinks that was the old monk's idea, too," remarked Wynne. "Looks as if the copse is going to be busy, and if Stuart doesn't upset it all I shall be surprised. I don't want to say anything about people behind their backs, but he really is unreasonable. He threatened me with proceedings over my right of way."

"But surely there can be no question of that," Bobby said, "if the lease says so?"

"It's a yearly lease," Mr Wynne explained, "but renewable at the option of either party. Stuart's lawyers wrote me that that applied only to the duration of the war. They said their client held letters from old Lady Stuart—his great-aunt, I think, he was her heir, to prove that was her intention, and that as he had to dispose of the property on account of death duties, he would be unable to consent to its renewal. I told them liability for death duties was hardly my concern and I stood by my lease. They wrote again, I took no notice and next thing Sir Charles came to see me. Thought we might come to some friendly arrangement, he said. What he meant was that he thought he might bully me into going. I remember very well now that he started by chatting about the Post Office van robbery you mentioned. The papers were full of it. The oblique approach technique. He soon worked round to asking me to go. I gave him a pretty blunt refusal, and he went off in a huff. And I must say I've heard no more about forced sales to meet death duties. He seems to splash his money about—death duties or none—the legendary uncle from America, perhaps. After all, if there really are master minds in the underworld, why not rich forgotten uncles in America? Anyhow, I know that was the village gossip at the time. But what I'm rather afraid of is that if Stuart sees you, especially in my company, he would try to do what he is saying he'll do to Dowie if he catches him trespassing, looking for hidden treasures or anything else."

"Oh, what is it he intends to do? Nothing too drastic, I hope," Bobby asked, not because he was very greatly interested in Sir Charles Stuart's possible reactions to trespassing, but because he wanted to keep the conversation going as long as Mr Wynne remained in his present communicative mood.

"Take him by the scruff of the neck and run him out in double quick time," answered Mr Wynne; and once more that faint, almost unseen smile of his flickered and was gone, and once more Bobby was slightly annoyed, for it was as though in his secret thoughts Mr Wynne was enjoying a mental picture of a high Scotland Yard official getting embroiled in a scuffle with this apparently bellicose neighbour. Working off a grudge against that neighbour, perhaps, or even possibly against the police. As Bobby knew, some motorists have rather biased views about police activity on the roads.

"Well," he said mildly, "let's hope it won't come to that."

"Not when you tell him who you are, it won't," Wynne agreed. "But the trouble is that he would at once rush off to Sergeant Jenkins to check up, and on the way tell everybody he saw all about it. Any accomplice of this man you mentioned, watching to see if the coast were clear, would soon know it wasn't."

They had come now to the end of the right of way where it joined up with the public footpath running between the copse and the fields beyond. Mr Wynne began to explain how the spot where they now were stood in relation to the village, the church, the more distant railway station, and to Over Abbey, the residence of Sir Charles Stuart. Bobby listened carefully. Topography was always important. Turning one way instead of another might easily ruin a whole careful plan. But all the same with a part of his mind he was considering the problem presented by this apparently truculent, talkative Sir Charles. None knew better than Bobby the mischief a clacking tongue can work. He said with a gesture down the public path, as if directing his companion's attention there, but really to prevent his turning round too abruptly:

"Do you think it might be Sir Charles watching us? I had the impression once or twice that we were being followed. I might be wrong."

"I don't think so," Wynne answered. "I rather had the same idea myself. It would be just like Stuart, ready to jump out on us if we moved an inch from the right of way."

"If it is him, it won't matter so much," Bobby said. "I can deal with that. I could make him understand there would be unpleasant consequences if he really interfered. But it may be Rogers or some pal of his on the look-out. If it is, we may as well call the whole business off."

"Easy to make sure," Wynne told him. "There's one spot where the right of way is nearly overgrown, so that it is quite easy to leave it and trespass unless you know. If it is really Stuart watching, he would be sure to jump on us the moment he thought we had wandered far enough away from where we had a right to be."

Bobby, feeling it was necessary to know who was there, agreed to the suggestion. He added that they had better go on chatting so that any watcher, if there were one, might not guess his presence was suspected. Wynne said that was a good idea and continued:

"There was one thing I was wondering if I might ask, even though you may think it's no business of mine. Are these buried notes likely to be any really considerable amount of the stolen money? Of course, if it's confidential, all right."

"Well, we don't really know," Bobby explained. "The total amount stolen was about £200,000. Our information—it may be reliable or it may not—is that each of the three subordinates got £20,000 each. Farmer got £50,000, and the odd £90,000 or thereabouts, the lion's share, to the unknown in the background. Possibly Farmer himself, as you suggested might be. It's all rather vague. We were hoping that to-night might help to make things clearer."

"Yes, there's a good chance of that, no doubt," Wynne agreed, and then continued, almost apologetically: "You know, Mr Owen, in spite of what you said, I should be willing to lay odds that your unknown 'boss' got out of the country as fast as he could. For a master mind—not too difficult, I should have thought. Anyhow, you are hoping, if you can arrest these men you are waiting for to-night, to get some sort of proof of his identity? A great score if you did, especially if he is really living quietly somewhere in England, thinking himself quite safe. But when notes have been buried in damp earth all these years, aren't they likely to have rotted away?"

"Oh, I don't think so," answered Bobby. "We expect them to be all right. Tight wads of pound notes are nearly indestructible and then very likely they are in waterproof wrappings of some sort."

"Yes; I hadn't thought of that," Mr Wynne agreed, and went on, lowering his voice a little, "This is where we ought to go straight on, but instead we'll go through this gap in the bushes as if we had mistaken the path. Then we'll be trespassing, and then we'll see what happens—if anything."

To Bobby, the right-of-way path seemed clear enough, but Wynne had already pushed through the indicated gap, and Bobby followed. Now he was sure someone was close behind, hidden by the thick undergrowth of bush and bramble. He could hear footsteps, the sound of a stumble once. Wynne was pushing ahead rather quickly. He said something over his shoulder that Bobby did not catch, though he thought it was a warning to be on the look-out for trouble. Bobby reflected grimly that he generally had to be. But he was not prepared for the wild panic scream that now came so suddenly, shrill through the trees—such a cry as even he had not often heard. Both he and Wynne stood still, immobile under the shock of that great cry. Crashing through the thickly growing undergrowth that hitherto had sheltered him came a tall, burly man, waving his arms, his naturally red face as white as that of a woman's recently powdered, shouting incoherently. Bobby turned:

"What on earth . . . ?" he began and paused.

"A woman . . . she's dead . . . dead . . . murdered. . . . It's round her neck. . . . I saw it. God in Heaven! I saw it plain. Who are you? what are you doing here? Trespassing," and there was now something in his voice that suggested he held trespassing to be only a little, if any, less a crime than murder.

"Where? where do you mean? Show me," Bobby said sharply. "I'm a police officer."

Wynne, who had pushed on a little ahead, came hurrying back.

"It's Stuart, Sir Charles Stuart," he called. "What's he mean? Dead woman? Nonsense! Rubbish! How can there be a dead woman here?"

"I nearly tumbled over—over—" Sir Charles was saying. "My God!" He was still trembling violently and he leaned against a nearby tree for support. "You, Wynne, what are you up to here?" he asked suspiciously. "Both of you? I'll get the police."

"I am a police officer," Bobby repeated. "Show me the place."

"Oh, you're a police officer, are you?" Stuart said, still more suspiciously. "Then you had better come with me. Sergeant Jenkins must be told at once. Wynne can stop here. He can't run away."

"Don't stand talking there," Bobby said sharply, by no means convinced, since the man was so obviously near to hysteria, of the literal truth of his tale. "Where is this body you say you've seen? Show me. Is it far?"

Sir Charles shook his head and pointed. Bobby hurried in the direction shown. He had to force his way through undergrowth, he had to dodge as best he could the sprawling blackberry bushes that made an obstacle as impenetrable as any coil of barbed wire—more so, indeed. He came to a spot, clearer than most of all such bush and undergrowth. Here more light penetrated, Wynne had followed, but with hesitation, as though reluctant to see what was waiting to be seen, and yet drawn by a dreadful fascination. Sir Charles hung back, but still he followed, drawn apparently by the same dreadful fascination he would have resisted had he known how. Partly hidden by a wild-growing loganberry bush, Bobby saw where lay the body of a woman, prone, plainly visible the knot at the back of her neck where one of her own stockings had been tied round her throat and then twisted tight by the aid of a small piece of broken branch from a tree near. Nor did it need more than that one glance to show that death had ensued, for swiftly indeed is it to be seen when the living spirit has left its earthly habitation.

Turning, Bobby said:

"Mr Wynne, will you hurry back at once and ring up Jenkins? Tell him to report here immediately to Commander Owen. If he is not on hand, say he must be found at once. My orders. And to bring a doctor. Then please ring up Scotland Yard. Inform them of what has happened, and ask them to get in touch with the local people. I'm carrying on till they arrive." Wynne nodded and hurried away, slipping through the hampering undergrowth with a clean, swift dexterity, breaking into a run as soon as that became practicable. Sir Charles seemed inclined to follow. Bobby put up a hand to stop him. "Stay here, please," he said. "I don't expect Jenkins will be long."

Sir Charles seemed a little more composed now, but if anything even more suspicious, and he was dabbing with his handkerchief at his face, his hands trembling.

"If you're police, what are you doing here?" he demanded. "You and Wynne—trespassing both of you. How do I know Jenkins is going to get that message? How do I know what you are up to?—Wynne and you, and all this talk of buried treasure going on. Did you know what was there—waiting for me to find?"

"Oh, for goodness sake," Bobby said angrily. He was trying to concentrate on that dead body, on every detail of the scene around, for who could tell what might or might not prove to be significant? "You can see my credentials if you like. You found the body, though, and it might not look too well if you hurried away."

"You sent Wynne off," Stuart said, suspicion unallayed in every word. "I'll stay all right, if only to watch you."

"Good," Bobby approved, more mildly. "Your present evidence is important. Mr Wynne's isn't."

CHAPTER V
DISCOVERY

IT WAS NOT long before Sergeant Jenkins arrived, flushed, excited, breathless, nervous, for never before had he had any such serious crime to deal with, inclined, too, to be thankful that a senior officer was there to take some of the responsibility off his shoulders.

"Inspector George will be here immediately, I rang him at once," was the first thing he said. "Is that—her?" he asked as he saw where that still form lay, half hidden under the spreading, sprawling, one might have thought protecting, loganberry bush. "Is she dead?" Without waiting for the unnecessary reply, he went on: "Dr Harrison is coming at once; I rang him, too. Is it—is it murder?"

"I'm afraid so," Bobby answered, looking up from his notebook in which he was already jotting down details. "There's no handbag," he said, for he had noticed immediately the absence of this that now every woman carries.

He had noticed, too, how closely this dead woman answered to the description of the woman Mr Wynne said he had seen going to or coming from the cottage of young Martin Maxton. For she, too, had been stout, heavily built, middle-aged. Her hair looked as if it might have been dyed and her nose was large, well shaped and prominent. But now there was no furtive look about that still, contorted face, rather did it seem, swollen and discoloured as it was, as if from it there issued some great cry. But this information Wynne had given him, Bobby decided he would keep to himself till Inspector George arrived. He or a senior officer would be in charge of the investigation, and it would be for them to decide what use should be made of it.

"Must have had a handbag—every woman has," Jenkins was saying. "Stolen most like. There's your motive. Robbery." He turned to Bobby. "Or will it be what—what you've come about, sir," he asked, afraid to be more explicit since it had been so strongly impressed upon him that the strictest secrecy was to be observed concerning Bobby's presence in Twice Over and his errand there.

"All this buried-treasure talk," Sir Charles intervened. "All over the whole place. That's what's done it."

"Was it you found the body, sir?" Jenkins asked; and then, without waiting for an answer, for Mr Wynne had already told him as much over the 'phone, he went on, speaking to Bobby: "There's a Mr Dowie been staying at the Over All Arms, and now he's left without warning like, but reported as seen last night near where the copse footpath starts. Hurrying he was and almost running like."

"There you are," said Sir Charles. "What had he been up to? Trespassing and dug up something and had to"—he stopped, looking quickly at the body and then as quickly away again— "had to do that to keep it all for himself."

"Yes, sir, I shouldn't wonder if that isn't how it was," agreed Jenkins, much relieved at being presented with so plausible a theory so quickly; one, too, that assumed the guilt not only of a stranger in the village but of a stranger already under suspicion, what with that contraption of his warranted, according to him, to disclose the presence of objects hidden underground. "Done a quick-time bunk, so he has," Jenkins added. "Good enough, if you ask me."

Ignoring equally both the suggestion made by Stuart and Jenkins's acceptance of it, Bobby said:

"Sergeant, do you know if any other stranger has been noticed here the last day or two?"

"Instructions to keep a sharp look-out for same, but none reported or seen as far as I know," Jenkins answered. "Except a chap in the Over All Arms last night as no one liked the looks of. Came in just before closing time, knocked back two quick whiskies. Spoke surly like; and barman had his foot all ready on the alarm behind the counter, just in case."

"What was he like?" Bobby asked. "Got any description?"

"Well, no, sir," replied Jenkins. "You know what it is, getting descriptions. Only as being the sort of ugly customer nobody wouldn't want to meet on a dark night. But drank up, paid up, and was off immediate, so nothing to complain of."

Bobby thought all this sounded so much like Jolly Rogers as to make it fairly certain he was the Over All Arms visitor. But also it might equally well have been some associate of Rogers come on ahead to reconnoitre. Before he could say more, however, Dr Harrison arrived, followed almost immediately by Inspector George who, from his headquarters in Magna Minor, a town more than ten miles away, had come full speed on that modern magic carpet, the motor cycle. Bobby, having no wish to share in the usual routine now beginning that the local police would take full charge of, said he thought he had better go back to the Old Dower House, where he had left his car and where he would ask Mr Wynne to allow him to wait till Inspector George was ready to hear what the two of them had to say. Not much, Bobby added deprecatingly, but he would be very interested to know what Mr George thought of it all, and Mr George replied politely, and also truthfully, that he would be more than equally glad to hear any observations or comments Mr Owen might feel able to make. He added that Mr Wynne was a very nice gentleman, always ready to co-operate in every possible way and very well thought of. From which remark Bobby gained the impression that Sir Charles Stuart had not always been found equally ready to cooperate and was now receiving an invitation to be more so and thus earn also the tribute of being very well thought of.

So Bobby, walking slowly back along the right-of-way path, much troubled in thought, for here, he could see, were threatened developments that might affect many lives, was not much surprised when presently he was overtaken by Sir Charles.

"Nice sort of thing on one's own property," he said in a very injured tone. "In my humble opinion, there's a lot more to it than you would think at first."

"I expect so," Bobby agreed. "Only what? There often is behind murder. Long, complicated histories of hate and rivalry. One never knows. Difficult to be sure."

"Well, that's what you chaps are for, isn't it?" demanded Sir Charles. "If you're a Yard man, can't you take over? Have you got to leave everything to that fussy, interfering fellow?"

"Do you mean the Inspector?" Bobby asked coldly.

"Yes, I do," retorted Stuart. "Keen enough when it's a car you happen to have left parked for a minute or two, or if you're going a bit fast when you're late for an appointment, or something of the sort. In a case like this in my humble opinion, it's for you to take over. You should be responsible—senior officer on the spot and all that."

"Well, you see," Bobby explained mildly, "I'm not quite that, as far as he's concerned. I have no standing or authority outside the Metropolitan police area—no more than you have. Those responsible are the local police, who are under the control of the Joint Standing Committee, who are answerable to the Home Secretary through his Inspectors of Constabulary."

"Bureaucracy at its worst," Sir Charles snorted indignantly. "No wonder there's a crime wave. Everything divided up so that nobody knows anything. The baby handed round in turn, and most likely Jenkins left holding it in the end. I suppose it's no good my telling you what I was going to, any more than it would be telling that ass of an Inspector. Wynne has him safe in his pocket."

"I should be very glad to hear anything you have to say," Bobby told him, "and then to pass it on if it seems relevant at all."

"Well, I was going to tell you in confidence," began Sir Charles, but Bobby interrupted him.

"I can hear nothing in confidence," he said sharply. "In any event I shall have to let the Inspector know there was something you thought of telling me. You must please understand nothing can ever be said to a police officer in confidence, though we do know how to hold our tongues."

"Oh, well," grumbled a slightly deflated Sir Charles, "it's this, and you can tell anyone you like. I don't care. I'm dead sure Wynne fixed it so it should be me found that poor devil of a woman."

"Why should he do that?" Bobby asked.

"Spite," Sir Charles answered. "He has it in for me all right. Wanted to land me with all that infernal police questioning. Did I know her? What was I doing there? As if a man couldn't take a walk on his own land when he chose to. Couldn't face it himself, so handed me the baby to hold."

"I'm afraid I can't think that very likely," Bobby objected, still anxious to keep the other talking.

"You don't know Wynne," Sir Charles retorted. "There's something queer about the fellow, if you ask me. Close as a fish. No one knows anything about him—where he was educated or anything," and saying this, Sir Charles fingered, unconsciously perhaps, his own old Hareton tie. "If you've nothing to be close about—well, what are you close about?"

"Some people may simply prefer privacy," Bobby suggested—"even to-day, when to have your name in the papers seems to mean to most that God's in His heaven and all's right in the world."

"I don't know about that," grumbled Sir Charles, and repeated, "You don't know Wynne; I do."

"Mr Wynne did tell me you and he were not on very good terms," Bobby said, following his usual plan of encouraging people to talk, since even mere random chat is so often so enlightening. "Over this right of way, isn't it? Strayed from it, didn't we, I'm afraid?"

"Strayed my foot," retorted Sir Charles. "A dirty trick. Got it all worked out. Another dirty trick was the way he got my old aunt into giving him a lease that can only be cancelled by mutual consent. Which he jolly well won't give so long as he can go on paying practically no rent. As good as a freehold. The old lady was in such a panic to get everything fixed up and be off to Ireland after the Germans dropped a bomb miles away she didn't know or care what she signed. Only wanted to get away. There are letters to show she had no idea what she had agreed to; but my lawyers—they're no good, anyhow—say they were written so long afterwards that Wynne could plead she had simply forgotten. His blessed right of way cuts clean across the copse, too, so there's not much chance of selling for building. Did me down as well over that statue of his—the Atropos."

"Indeed. How was that?" Bobby asked.

"I found the thing," Sir Charles explained, "pushed away in an old barn by a farmer near here. His wife didn't like it— thought it brought bad luck. It had been there for years. Fine thing, I thought. I offered to take it off his hands—bad luck and all—and give him a fiver as well. The fool got boasting the same evening at the local about the fiver he was getting for what he called an ugly lump of stone. Wynne heard him, asked to see it, offered a hundred, cash on the spot, take it or leave it, statue to be delivered immediately, and gone it was when I went for it next day. Now he says he's been offered ten times as much for it and if he sells he'll give the farmer ten per cent. Easy promise when he has no intention of selling. Likes to look at it and remember how he did me down. Daylight robbery, if you ask me."

Bobby didn't ask him, but as by now they had reached the door in the wall round the Old Dower House grounds, he rang the electric bell Mr Wynne had pointed out. Fortunately it was in working order, as electric bells are not invariably, and that, Bobby thought, was in a way a tribute to the quiet efficiency with which he was beginning to associate Mr Wynne.

Sir Charles looked very much as if he strongly disapproved of this prompt call to the Old Dower House. Probably he would have made some sort of protest if he had been a little more sure of his ground. But Bobby, though he had listened with all due attention, had not been very encouraging, and Sir Charles contented himself with muttering something to the general effect that he supposed he had better get back and see what was going on, and if that ass of an Inspector had any more tomfool questions to ask.

With that he departed, and the close-growing trees and brushwood had hardly hidden him from sight before the garden door was opened by a rather frightened-looking, very subdued Sylvia.

"Isn't it dreadful?" she said. "Daddy's most awfully upset; he looks ever so ill. I wanted to send for the doctor but he wouldn't let me. Is she—is she really dead?"

"I'm afraid so," Bobby answered.

"But how could she? I mean in there where no one ever goes. . . . I mean like that, all by herself. Is it someone in the village?"

CHAPTER VI
QUESTIONS

BOBBY DID NOT attempt to answer these questions. Evidently the girl could hardly bring herself to believe that what she was told had happened could possibly be true. She began to lock the door again as soon as Bobby had entered, but he stopped her, saying:

"If you don't mind, I think it would be better if it could be left open for the time. Police officers are in charge, and they will want to see your father. He and I were near by when Sir Charles made his discovery."

"I'm so glad it wasn't Daddy," she said. "It would have been more awful still if it had been. I shall never, never dare go out that way again. I never did if I could help—it's so dark and damp and horrid."

They walked on to the house in silence, Sylvia trying her hardest to realize that what had happened had happened in stark, grim, actual fact; Bobby trying, and failing, to puzzle out any clear proof of connection between this unknown woman's death and the story of the stolen bank-notes still hidden somewhere in Twice Over. Through the open french windows Sylvia led the way into the room Bobby had been in before. Mr Wynne was sitting there, leaning back in one of the armchairs, looking pale and exhausted, as if still suffering from the shock of the discovery. Whisky and a syphon of soda-water and an empty glass stood on his desk. He looked up as Bobby and Sylvia entered. He said:

"I rang the police. Have they turned up? and a doctor? Have they found out who she is?"

"I left an Inspector of the County police in charge," Bobby explained. "It's for them to deal with, of course."

"I hope they will be able to deal with it adequately," Mr Wynne said. "I don't suppose they have much experience in this sort of thing. It was a dreadful shock. I've never had one like it. I saw plenty of dead men when I was serving in the army; but that was war—that was different. This is so—so personal. Happening on your doorstep almost. It'll be mixed up somehow with what you were telling me about?"

"I imagine so," Bobby agreed. "We must wait till we know more. At present I don't see how."

"No, no," Mr Wynne said. "If you are trying to recover stolen property buried somewhere, the last thing you would want would be to leave dead bodies lying about. Sylvia, get another glass, will you? I expect Mr Owen would like a drop of whisky. I know I felt I needed it," and he looked at the whisky bottle as if he were beginning to feel he would like another drink.

"Thank you very much," Bobby said. "I never take spirits during the day and never when on duty."

"Tea's ready," Sylvia said. "Shall I bring it in? I was just making it when you called."

She hurried away without waiting for an answer. As soon as the door had closed behind her, Bobby said:

"I think perhaps you ought to know, Mr Wynne, that Sir Charles Stuart told me that he was convinced you knew the dead body was there and that you were trying to make sure he was the one to find it."

"The devil he did," Wynne exclaimed angrily, sitting upright in his chair. "I'll have him in court for libel. There are limits. We don't like each other. Agreed. On bad terms. I don't care about that. And very likely he does feel he has a grievance over that lease of mine. Well, I say a bargain's a bargain, and I stick to mine, whether it turns out good or bad. All the same, I'll see my solicitors at once. What on earth does he think I should do that for? Does he want to make out I murdered the poor creature?"

"Oh, no," Bobby said. "No suggestion of that sort. I think what he meant was that you wanted to avoid all the questioning and so on, and having to give evidence—all that sort of thing."

"Oh, well," Wynne said, slightly mollified, apparently, "I daresay that's true enough as far as it goes. I lead a very quiet, retired life. It suits me. I'm quite content to potter about the house and garden, take a share in our village activities, and have a drink and a chat at the local sometimes. And there's always Sylvia." He paused, and again there showed that tender, smiling expression which so transformed him. "When she marries—not just yet, I hope—it may be different. I don't know. But how on earth does the man suppose I could tell he would be there, or that you would call, or that we should be taking a stroll together this afternoon through the copse? If he doesn't look out he'll be hearing from my solicitor."

"He may not repeat the suggestion to anyone else," Bobby remarked; "and of course, as made to me, it is privileged."

"Privileged?" Mr Wynne repeated, growing angry again. "Why? A thing like that?"

"A statement made to an officer of police with the presumed intention of helping the course of justice," Bobby explained; and Wynne said "Fiddlesticks," more angrily still.

Bobby made no reply. Mr Wynne sat and frowned, and his frown was not a pleasant one. It suggested a side to his character that had not as yet appeared—had had no reason to, for that matter. Bobby began to feel that Sir Charles was making an enemy of whom he would have reason to beware. Sylvia came back into the room, and with her entry Wynne's frown vanished. His eyes, that for the moment had seemed so cold and hard, grew tender again, and Bobby felt that any risk of incurring Sylvia's disapproval was not one her father would lightly run. She was carrying a tray with the tea, cake and a plate of thin bread and butter. She said:

"I did some scones this morning. I'll go and get them. They turned out rather well," and with that she put down her tray and disappeared, leaving Bobby wondering idly why, if that were so and the scones a success, he had seemed to detect a slight touch of disappointment in her tone.

"A wonderful little cook," Mr Wynne said, and as she went his gaze followed her with a deep, admiring affection. "Her mother over again," he said. "Bosses me, too, just like her mother. It was to please her I retired, but Sylvia does let me do a little on the side," and he smiled again—no hidden smile this time: one of open pride and affection. "Practically runs the house single-handed, except for Mrs Griggs, who is more bother than she's worth."

Sylvia, bearing her scones with her, had just returned, just in time to hear this last remark.

"Oh, no, Daddy," she protested. "She's very good indeed and a great help. I couldn't ever do without her. Daddy and she," she explained to Bobby, "have never forgiven each other since he complained she spilt coal all over the place when she brought it up from the cellar, so now he always does it himself, and she's not allowed in—in the coal cellar, I mean."

"Well, I don't spill it, anyhow," Wynne declared. Then he said in a surprised tone: "What's become of young Maxton? I thought you said he was staying to tea?"

"He's gone," Sylvia said. "He left a note to say he was sorry, but he had to," and Bobby was sure now that she was trying to make her voice sound as casual and her manner as indifferent as possible.

"What was that for?" Wynne asked; and he both sounded and looked much less disappointed than did his daughter. "The scones were to have been a special treat," he explained to Bobby. "We can't afford the cream and butter too often. Scrumptious when we get them, though," he added, smiling at Sylvia.

Sylvia returned the smile, though not with one of such radiance as some of those Bobby had seen her give before. He remembered the earlier use of the word 'scrumptious', and guessed this was a kind of private father-daughter joke. He asked:

"Did Mr Maxton know what had happened?"

"Oh, it couldn't be that," Sylvia exclaimed, looking startled. "Why should it?"

"He might have heard me 'phoning," Wynne said. "I don't know. I used the one in the hall, not the extension here. I didn't notice him. I was rather too excited, though, to notice much. He might have been there. Perhaps he thought with a thing like this happening we would want to be alone."

At this suggestion, Sylvia cheered up a little, though still not yet the radiant personality she had seemed previously. Bobby himself made no comment, but remembered afresh how closely the body found in the copse answered to the description given by Mr Wynne of the woman he had seen near, or leaving Maxton's cottage. Whether Wynne also had noticed this resemblance Bobby could not tell, but if so he had been careful not to draw attention to it. It was Sylvia who spoke first, saying:

"I don't think he need have rushed off like that, and next time I shan't make any scones for him," and she looked very severe and determined indeed.

"Well, anyhow, try one of them," Wynne urged Bobby, and Bobby, who had been eyeing the plate of thin bread and butter with some concern, doubtful if all of it provided more than one reasonable mouthful, accepted the suggestion and the offered scone, and found it merited all and more Mr Wynne had said—scrumptious indeed.

"Our own milk, cream, butter, eggs," Mr Wynne explained. "I rent a field from a farmer near by, and he looks after my two cows, so we aren't so badly off in that way, even if Sylvia does give half of it away."

"You can't help, can you?" Sylvia protested, "when you have lots and other people haven't. Daddy likes me to, really," she explained to Bobby, "only he pretends he doesn't."

Bobby said the scones were delicious, that Miss Sylvia certainly made good use of what she didn't give away, and that young Mr Maxton had missed something by his hasty departure—and privately he wondered if the scones were all that he had missed. Or avoided?

After that the conversation languished. Neither father nor daughter seemed in a mood for much more tea-table chatter. Not surprising, Bobby supposed, though he did wonder a little at Sylvia's unusual silence, for hitherto it had seemed no thought entered her mind that did not forthwith bubble out again in words. Possibly her silence was a result not only of the happening in the copse but also of young Maxton's hurried and unexplained departure. Mr Wynne was silent, too. Perhaps he was asking himself how much of the publicity threatened he could manage to avoid—an attitude as rare as admirable, Bobby told himself. Mr Wynne said:

"They must be finishing out there. That was the garden bell, and there's a policeman standing at the door."

"Inspector George," Bobby said. "The man I left in charge."

"I'll get another cup," Sylvia said. "I expect he would like some tea. You can give it him, Daddy. He'll want to talk," and she hurried away.

"I'll bring him in here," Wynne said. He got to his feet and then paused and said: "Sylvia told me she saw a light in the copse about eleven the night before last. I don't know if that can have anything to do with it. People do come prowling round there after dark, though eleven is a bit late. Lovers," he explained, and went on: "And last night I heard what I thought at the time was a cry—somewhere about eleven, too. I was reading in bed—a bad habit of mine. I got up to look. But it all seemed quiet and I went back to bed. Sylvia woke, too; but that may have been my opening my window."

He went out then through the french windows. The Inspector was coming up the path now. Bobby waited. Sylvia came back into the room with the cup and plate she had been to fetch. Bobby said to her:

"Mr Wynne tells me you heard something that woke you last night. Do you know what time it was?"

"It must have been soon after eleven," Sylvia said, "soon after I got into bed. I don't think I was properly asleep. Daddy says he thinks most likely it was him opening his window.

Noises at night always make me afraid it's burglars, but there was a light in Daddy's room, so I went to sleep again."

She put down plate and cup and went away again as Wynne came back with Inspector George. Wynne said:

"Mr Dowie has taken himself off without saying anything, and the Inspector has found a spade in the copse with Dowie's finger-prints on it."

"Checked," the Inspector said, "with same as left in room occupied at the Over All Arms."

"When did he leave?" Bobby asked.

"Last evening," the Inspector replied, consulting his note-book. "Eight, nine, ten, as reported various by Over All Arms staff. Took with him what he calls his treasure detector, as always done by him. Later, exact time or interval uncertain, reported various as before and unreliable, rang up to say he had been unexpectedly called away."

"Like young Maxton," remarked Wynne.

"Eh?" said the Inspector. "What's that?"

"Never mind just now," Bobby said. "Go on, please, Inspector. What about his luggage? If he had any. And his bill? He gave no other explanation?"

"None as reported," the Inspector replied, with one cautious eye still on his note-book. "Requested his things—nothing much except pyjamas, toilet material, so on—should be kept till called for, asked the amount of his bill, and promised to forward remittance immediately. Same not yet received. The girl who took the call said his voice sounded funny."

"As if someone were personating him?" Wynne suggested. "Sounds very funny indeed. And Stuart saying I knew where the body lay. He told Mr Owen that, Inspector. Did he say same thing to you?"

"I don't think I follow," the Inspector said, looking rather bewildered. "What for should he say a thing like that? And Mr Maxton?"

"Mr Maxton had called here," Wynne said. "Not the first time. Bought a new car on tick he wanted to show off. He left in what seems to have been a good deal of a hurry. He may have heard me talking to Jenkins on the 'phone, telling him what had happened, and thought he wouldn't be wanted. That's all."

"Not quite all," interposed Bobby. "I understand there have been stories in the village about his being blackmailed. Did you know?" When the Inspector shook his head, Bobby continued: "Mr Wynne told me earlier this afternoon that he noticed a woman leaving Maxton's cottage. There are points on which his description of her tallies with that of the dead woman."

"I didn't say actually leaving Maxton's cottage, did I?" Wynne protested. "If I did, I must correct it—'leaving or near' would be better."

"'Leaving or in vicinity of same'," suggested the Inspector, fingering his note-book.

"One moment," Bobby said. "About this spade—presumably Dowie hadn't it with him when he arrived? The Over All Arms people would have noticed it at once. Not an ordinary article of luggage. Looks as if he had either bought it subsequently or it belonged to a friend or assistant he was expecting."

"Yes, sir," agreed the Inspector. He sat down, opened his note-book at a fresh place, and then closed it again rather helplessly. "That means there's three as must be questioned. Mr Maxton and what call had he to leave in a hurry and why was deceased at his cottage? Mr Dowie ditto, and what about his spade and his dabs on it? And Sir Charles as found the body saying Mr Wynne here led him up to it purposeful like. And a suspicious-looking character, as stated by Sergeant Jenkins seen at the Over All Arms, but no complaint. Which is four." He opened his note-book again. "Four," he said determinedly.

"Five," said Mr Wynne bitterly. "You had better say five, Inspector. Sir Charles evidently means you to include me."

"Oh, well, sir," said the Inspector, uncomfortably this time. "Of course, if you say so."

THERE FOLLOWED a brief silence on this demand of Mr Wynne's that his name should be included in the list of those from whom explanations were to be demanded. Bobby was not sure that Wynne had intended or wished his suggestion to be taken as seriously, as apparently it was by the Inspector, now writing busily in his note-book. But, then, Mr Wynne was not a man whose thoughts, or whose intentions, could be read easily or quickly; and once again Bobby was not sure that that faint hidden smile of his had not flickered for one brief passing second behind his unmoved features. Possibly a smile of satisfaction at the prospect of having reasonable cause to send a solicitor's letter to a neighbour with whom he seemed on such bad terms. It was Wynne himself who was the first to speak, saying:

"Mr Owen here tells me what anyone chooses to say to a police officer is called privileged—license for libel, I call it. I'll see what my solicitor thinks."

"Very wise, sir, if I may say so," approved the Inspector, looking up from his note-book. "I always say the less talk, the better. There will be plenty." Then he looked at Bobby and said: "Do you think, Mr Owen, sir, you could stay on till Mr Kimms gets here? He's our C.I.D. chief. I'm sure he would like your opinion—what with people disappearing and no one knowing who she is or why, and talk starting already, and as like as not London journalists all over the place, making you say things you never meant."

"Yes, I know," Bobby said sympathetically. "All right. I've met Mr Kimms once or twice. Very efficient officer, too. Not that there's much to be done for the moment, till the routine stuff has been finished. Must lay the foundations first of all. Luckily neither Sir Charles nor Mr Wynne will disappear. The Over All Arms will have Mr Dowie's address, so it shouldn't be difficult to find him—unless it's false. If you have his fingerprints you can find out at once if he has a record—on tap at Central. There's the spade, too. That might help if you can trace where it was bought. Maxton lives here, doesn't he? Is he on the 'phone? If he is, he might be got hold of and told Inspector George would like to see him."

But Mr Wynne shook his head.

"His place—Hidden Cottage, he calls it—is a long way from here: two miles or more. It's right inside a small wood. Mr Jones, at Weston Fields farm, is his nearest neighbour, and I believe he has an arrangement with them to take messages for him. I expect if you rang them, they would send it on. I'll get their number."

He got up and left the room, so quickly and quietly the other two hardly knew that he had gone. Bobby said:

"You've found nothing to identify her by, Inspector? No papers or anything?"

"Not a thing," the Inspector answered. "Handbag missing. Question is—was there a hundred pounds in it, as reported in earlier case?"

"There's always that to remember," agreed Bobby.

"If she's the one Mr Wynne saw," the Inspector continued, "where was she between then and her visit to the copse, and why did she go there?"

"To wait for someone she expected, or else to watch who came," Bobby said. "That's fairly plain. She must have known something."

"Yes, sir," agreed the Inspector. "Only what? Doctor says he thinks she's been dead about twelve hours and he can't be more precise till he's made a closer examination." The Inspector paused, looked cautiously at the door, lowered his voice: "Mr Owen, sir, what do you make of Sir Charles saying Mr Wynne knew where the body was and led you and him up to it?"

Bobby was saved the necessity of replying by the return of Mr Wynne, a slip of paper in his hand.

"That's the Weston Farm 'phone number," he said as he gave it to the Inspector.

"I hope he hasn't done a bunk," the Inspector said. "Very nice respectable young gentleman, as far as we know, and must have a bit of money of his own, not having any proper job, Jenkins says, only writing books and such like."

"I think we've troubled Mr Wynne long enough now, don't you, Inspector?" Bobby asked, glancing at his wrist watch. "If he agrees, I suggest we let all arrangements made for to-night stand, in the hope that someone or another may turn up nosing after these buried pound notes. Possibly Rogers. He may have nothing to do with the murder, know nothing about it, and come along to-night as our information suggests he meant to. If he does it will probably mean he's innocent, and he may be able to put us on to the right man. Rogers may be the suspicious character reported at the Over All Arms. Having a preliminary look round. If, as is likely enough, he has been talking about the Post Office van robbery and part of the stolen stuff being buried hereabouts, one or more of his pals may have been trying to cut in ahead. I'll get on to our people at Central and ask them if they can learn anything of his recent movements. I'll ask them to send one of our chaps who knows Rogers—I think young Ford does—to wait at the Twice Over station and see if he can spot him arriving by train. Crooks always use cars nowadays, though. Plenty to do, Inspector, even if it's all mere preliminary clearing the ground. Will it be all right, Mr Wynne, if I come back later on, after dark, and slip into the copse by way of your garden door? I shall probably have one man with me, but not more, and meanwhile Mr George will be putting some of his men on watch on the other side of the copse. If anyone does come we must take care they don't get away."

"Of course; anything I can do to help you may rely on, anything at all," declared Mr Wynne in his quiet, confident way, and both Bobby and the Inspector expressed appreciation of such willing co-operation.

These preliminaries settled, the two of them departed. The interval before Mr Kimms arrived Bobby spent first in putting through a call to Scotland Yard, informing them there of what had happened, explaining that he had been asked to wait till Mr Kimms arrived to take over, adding that it was at present intended to carry on with the earlier arrangements in the hope that someone might appear in the copse on a hunt for the buried notes. If so, he would of course be held for questioning, and might be able to give valuable information. Bobby also asked that steps should be taken to verify the address given by the vanished Mr Dowie to the Over All Arms and now obtained therefrom. He asked also that Detective Constable Ford might be sent to keep watch at the Twice Over station.

After that, he and Inspector George had a hurried meal together and then retired—coffee accompanying them—to the private room Bobby had asked for. There they were presently joined by Superintendent Kimms, a tall, taciturn man whose prolonged silences appeared to be due either to deep, concentrated thought or else to a total absence thereof—Bobby was not sure which. In the war he had been a Regimental Sergeant Major, and possibly had come to rely too much upon established routine, which indeed is generally a very safe guide, even though at times it is necessary to throw it out of the window.

"An unholy mess," was the brief comment he made on his arrival, and then he sat down and waited for one of the other two to continue.

"All tied up somehow with what first brought Mr Owen here," Inspector George suggested; "and first thing, to my mind, is to concentrate on identifying deceased."

"Yes," agreed Kimms and waited.

"It may prove difficult," Bobby said. "A woman who tangles up with crooks may easily disappear without anyone worrying or coming forward to say anything. More prudent not to. A normal woman is sure to have friends or relatives to start inquiries sooner or later."

Mr Kimms nodded acquiescence and continued silent.

"To my mind," said Inspector George, "there's odd things about all five concerned, requiring explanation."

"Five's a lot," pronounced Mr Kimms.

"So it is," agreed Bobby.

"Too many by half," said Mr Kimms, and, stirred to un-wonted eloquence, added: "What I like is to find a straight line and stick to it."

Bobby agreed enthusiastically. Inspector George said: "Five straight lines in this affair."

Again Bobby agreed, but Kimms said with authority:

"None of 'em straight." He paused, and Bobby for a moment feared he was going to retire again into silence and thought—or no thought. Instead Kimms said: "Have to spend all night hanging round the copse." Again he paused, silent and meditative. Then, while the other two waited, unwilling, or too respectful, to break in on this contemplative mood, he said slowly: "Hope it doesn't rain," and Bobby perceived that when Kimms's silent thought blossomed into words, they were words of weight and wisdom.

After these exchanges, talk became brisker. Kimms was given a fuller account of recent events. He listened silently, but Bobby felt now that every detail was being assimilated in the slow-moving, ponderous, but effective machinery of Kimms's mind. The one question he asked was when Inspector George had finished his story. Then Kimms turned to Bobby and put the same one that George himself had posed earlier.

"What do you make," he asked, "of Sir Charles saying Wynne knew all the time the body was there but wanted him to find it?"

"Probably only neighbourly ill will," Bobby answered; "but to be remembered, all the same. Sir Charles himself suggested it might be Wynne trying to dodge the fuss and worry. Wynne does seem to dislike publicity."

"Even if so," said Mr Kimms, after giving this due consideration, "there's implications."

"So there are," agreed Bobby. "Not all of Mr Wynne shows on the surface. He told me that what Sir Charles inherited under his aunt's will didn't come to very much—three or four thousand at most after mortgages and death duties had been settled."

Kimms looked at George to indicate he was to answer, as being better acquainted with local affairs, and George said:

"A tidy bit, all the same—three or four thousand," and to himself he thought how nice it would be if he possessed even half that 'tidy bit'.

"But," Bobby objected, "he must be living at the rate of at least that much a year?"

"That's right," George agreed. "Very free-spending gentleman. Makes him much respected. What they said hereabouts at the time was that an uncle of his in America he didn't know much about had died suddenly and left him all his money."

"I've often heard of long-lost uncles in America with a million or two in their pockets turning up unexpectedly, but it's the first time I've come across one in real life," Bobby observed thoughtfully. "Just about the time of this first P.O. van robbery, wasn't it? At the end of the 1914 war, too, when everybody was thinking so much about the good days coming there wasn't much time to think of anything else."

"Oh, well," said George and looked startled.

"Implications there, too," pronounced Mr Kimms.

CHAPTER VIII
IN THE DARK

THE SOMEWHAT uneasy silence that followed on these remarks was broken by a knock at the door, and there appeared Sergeant Jenkins.

"Message from London, sir," he said. "Just received by 'phone. 'Re Detective Constable Ford, same detailed for duty at Twice Over station, as per request to hand. Re suspect Dowie, same not known at address given, being small boardinghouse. If fuller description received, further inquiries will be made as desired'."

"False name and address given," said George. "What for?" and, getting in first this time, he added: "More implications there, too."

"Further," Jenkins said, with a reproachful glance at his Inspector for interrupting him, "re Maxton. Information now to hand that same was seen in car on London Road, proceeding London way, about four this afternoon or a little later."

"Making a get-away and no time lost," said George. "I would never have thought it."

"Implications again," Bobby put in, scoring for the first time.

"Too many of 'em," said Kimms. "By a long sight," he added.

"That's right," agreed George.

Jenkins coughed to indicate he still had something to say. When they turned to him, he continued:

"Re deceased. Dr Harrison reports by 'phone he can place death of same as taking place not earlier than eleven p.m. and not later than two a.m."

"That reminds me," Bobby said. "Mr Wynne has since told me his daughter saw a light in the copse the night before the murder as she was going to bed. Last night Wynne himself heard a cry. Miss Wynne woke up too, but she went to sleep again. Wynne was lying awake reading. A habit of his. Doesn't amount to much, but it may work in later."

Kimms looked at his wrist watch and then at Bobby.

"Best get moving," he said. "Growing dark. Ready?" he asked George.

"All ready," George assured him. "All concerned warned to move to posts as arranged at nine-thirty."

"I'll drive round by the station," Bobby said, "and collect Ford as soon as the last train is in."

He was however a little late, and when he did arrive he found Ford waiting disconsolately outside a station being somewhat hurriedly closed for the night by a staff eager to get back to television. But he cheered up at the sight of Bobby and explained he had seen no one in the least resembling either the missing Dowie or the expected Rogers or anyone in any way of 'suspicious appearance'.

"The ticket collector said he thought they were all locals," Ford added and went on: "I had no instructions how to proceed. I was thinking of walking on to the village to report from there."

"Our next proceeding," Bobby informed him, "is to seek a certain copse where we shall sit all night in the most damp and uncomfortable conditions possible on the very slim chance of a certain badly wanted man turning up there. Which he won't."

"Very good, sir," said Ford, for, though young in the Force, he already knew full well that most of a detective officer's life is spent waiting in the most uncomfortable circumstances for something that never happens.

"Well, hop in," said Bobby, "and look cheerful."

"Yes, sir," said Ford, but obeyed only the first of these injunctions.

"Got your sandwiches?" Bobby asked. "What is a detective without sandwiches? Just a hollow sham," he answered himself.

"Yes, sir," Ford assured him. "Ham and beef, sir. And a thermos. Coffee."

"Good," approved Bobby. "Hot? Strong?"

"Yes, sir," Ford repeated. "Very. Trust the missus for that. And a drop of whisky in a pocket flask. Trust me for that."

"Bad," said Bobby, disapproving. "Coffee's a stimulant. Whisky's a soporific—all right before you go to bed when you expect a good night in, but not so when you have to keep awake."

Little familiar though he was with the roads in this neighbourhood, Bobby drove back by a circuitous route, so as to avoid passing through a village all agog with the news of what had happened and all on the look-out for fresh developments. Possessing as he did a good sense of direction, he managed to reach his destination without going too far astray. Some three or four hundred yards from the Old Dower House he parked the car in a conveniently dark spot by the roadside, whence he and Ford completed their journey on foot.

There were lights showing in the house, but nothing to suggest they had been heard. Making a circuit to the right, they reached the door admitting them to the copse and left

open as arranged. Here progress was more difficult, the darkness more complete under the close-growing trees. Near the
loganberry bush where the unknown woman's body had been
found Bobby halted.

"As likely a spot as any," he said in a low voice. "Bury what
you want to find and plant a loganberry bush on top. Easy to
remember, easy to find, and the only bush of its sort nearer
than Wynne's garden. Any implications there?"

Ford said he didn't know, and they proceeded to settle
down as comfortably—or uncomfortably—as circumstances
permitted. Slowly the slow moments passed, adding up as
they did so into hours that seemed to pass more slowly still.
The night was dark and as silent as night ever is when a faint,
chill wind rustles the tree-tops and the small things that love
the protection of night's cloak emerge to grow busy with their
private affairs.

In the distance the church clock struck midnight. Bobby
began to work out how many seconds, minutes, hours, had yet
to pass before their vigil could be written off as both useless
and completed. Ford had dropped off to sleep. Till now Bobby
had let him sleep, since that one should keep on the alert was
sufficient. But now he poked him in the ribs to wake him, for
a faint, cautious footstep was becoming audible, or so Bobby thought, but one coming from the wrong direction—that
of the Old Dower House, not from the side of the copse along
which the public footpath ran and whence access was so much
easier. Bobby hoped it was not Mr Wynne, come out to see
what was going on. Not likely, for Mr Wynne seemed an in-
curious man. But now the footsteps seemed to be passing to
one side, as if they had purposely left the right-of-way path or
else gone astray. All at once came an outbreak of shouting, of
electric torches flashing, of men running. Bobby began to run
himself. Someone ahead of him on the right-of-way path was
making at headlong speed for the unlocked garden door. In
spite of the delaying, treacherous darkness, the fugitive, Bobby, Ford close behind—all three of them—managed to keep up
an unchecked speed. Another man dashed out of the bush-

es just behind Bobby and joined in the chase, between him and Ford, whom collision with a tree-trunk had momentarily delayed. Presumably one of Kimms's men—or an accomplice or companion of the fugitive? Bobby was close upon the foremost runner now. Bobby could afford to run the faster, the less cautiously, since any obstacle or impediment should hamper or delay first the man in front. The garden wall loomed ahead, a faint shadow in the night. Bobby was now close upon the fugitive's heels, as the newcomer in the race was close on Bobby's. Of him Bobby took no heed; indeed, in the heat of the chase was hardly aware of him. Now Bobby flung out his hand and plucked at the other's shoulder. At the same moment the man behind Bobby, making a sudden spurt, was able to throw himself forward on Bobby's back. Taken by surprise, Bobby went down, his assailant on top of him, while the so nearly captured fugitive shot away in the dark.

"Got him," shouted Bobby's assailant.

"Got you," Ford panted, jerking him off Bobby. "Got the cuffs on him neat as one o'clock," he said, complacent, and to Bobby he said: "Not hurt you, has he, sir?" To his captive, he said: "Now, now; language like that won't help you."

Bobby thought he knew the voice in which the 'language' was echoing through the night air. He switched on his torch.

"Oh, you," he said.

"Take 'em off," bellowed the fettered victim, holding out his wrists.

"It's Sir Charles Stuart," Bobby said to Ford. "Lives at Over Abbey."

"It was him helped his pal to get away," Ford said, unimpressed, for he had never heard either of Sir Charles Stuart or of Over Abbey.

By this time Inspector George and one or two other of his men had arrived, and there was a babel of confused explanations before it became more or less clear what had happened.

"A lot of police barging about my land without a word to me," shouted Sir Charles, making his booming voice heard above all else. "Trespassers all of you."

"You've allowed a man to escape we very badly wanted to interview," Bobby told him. "A man who might have helped to clear up the murder last night."

"Take 'em off," roared Sir Charles once more, and in his wrath committed the indiscretion of kicking Ford on the shin.

"Ai-e-e," said Ford. "Ooo—now you've made me drop the key."

"Just like you, clumsy ass," Sir Charles snarled. "Here, one of you others—hurry up."

"I'm awfully sorry," Bobby said, while Ford searched diligently and without success, "but I'm afraid our London handcuffs are a different pattern from the local ones, and I don't think the keys fit."

It was some time before this information penetrated the bemused mind of Sir Charles. By then Inspector George and his men had stolen silently away, judging that this was a case in which swiftest departure was safest. Afterwards it was officially explained on more than one occasion, both verbally and in writing, that Inspector George had considered that his first and most urgent duty was to take all available steps for the pursuit, and, if possible, recapture, of the suspect who had so unfortunately escaped through the equally unfortunate but so understandable intervention of Sir Charles himself.

It was in the midst of the tumult and the shouting that a new figure had appeared—that of Mr Wynne. He came forward now.

"I was sitting up, wondering what was going to happen," he explained, "when I heard such a commotion I came out to see what it was all about." He paused to survey Sir Charles. "Isn't there some mistake?" he asked mildly, no sign of a smile this time, either secret or broad. "That gentleman is Sir Charles Stuart, perfectly well known all round here. I can answer for him as for myself."

"An unfortunate misunderstanding in the dark," Bobby explained, "and now the key has been lost, so we can't get the handcuffs off."

"How very awkward," said Mr Wynne, more mildly even than before.

"As soon as we can get a new one," Ford said, "the gentleman will be quite all right."

Sir Charles said nothing at all, so reduced was he. He simply stood in silence and looked at his outstretched fettered wrists.

CHAPTER IX
IRONICAL

THEY ALL BEGAN to move back towards the house, now with more than one window lighted up, so that it was easier for them to see their way. Ford was devoting himself with an almost maternal tenderness to the guidance of the handcuffed, handicapped Sir Charles. Wynne said to Bobby as they walked along:

"I saw someone running full speed through the garden past the house. Like a shadow. I shouted to him to stop, but of course he took no notice. I couldn't see who it was. Was it the man you were hoping to arrest?"

Bobby said gloomily that it was, at least he supposed so, and he told how he actually had his hand on the fugitive's shoulder when Sir Charles had so unhappily intervened.

"He has trespassers on the brain," Mr Wynne remarked. "Most unfortunate all round. I am afraid you have made an enemy."

Bobby offered no comment, and now Sylvia came running to meet them.

"Oh, Daddy," she cried, "are you all right? I heard you call out. Oh, Daddy, dear, are you sure you aren't hurt?"

"Quite sure," Wynne answered, with the new gentleness that always came into his generally calm, impersonal tones when it was his daughter he was speaking to. "It's all right, except that unfortunately a man Mr Owen hoped might be able to help him, escaped in the darkness."

"I've been so frightened," Sylvia said. "There was such a noise, and I woke up and you weren't there and, Daddy, you did say you wouldn't ever go out again late at night without telling me, and you didn't. Oh," and she grew silent as in the lighted study they had now all entered she turned and saw Sir Charles with his fettered hands held so awkwardly before him. "Oh," she said again, and was evidently not quite sure whether or no to believe her eyes.

"Sylvia," Mr Wynne explained smilingly to Bobby, apparently without noticing her sudden appalled, embarrassed silence, "Sylvia had a scare the other evening when she heard someone moving about after she had gone to bed. It was only me coming in again after a few minutes outside for a breath of fresh air and tumbling over a chair in the dark. But she made sure it was burglars."

Sylvia was still looking at Sir Charles with bewildered, incredulous wonder. He returned her gaze with such a scowl as can but seldom have darkened human countenance. He managed to recover the use of a voice from which an immense emotion had deprived him for the last few minutes.

"I insist," he said in little gasps, "on that key . . . being found . . . immediately."

"Flew right out of my hand," said Ford. "When you kicked me. Might be anywhere . . . pitch dark, too."

"Well, go and look for it, and don't come back till you've found it," Bobby told him, rather sharply; for Bobby had his own ideas as to where that key might be.

"Yes, sir; very good, sir; if it takes me till to-morrow morning," Ford promised and vanished.

"All of you—go—help," said Sir Charles hoarsely, pointing with his hands.

"I can't say I feel responsible myself," Mr Wynne said, "but I think we might all feel better for a drink. Sit down, both of you, won't you? I won't be a minute. Sylvia."

Sylvia, persuaded now that what she saw was factual, though inexplicable, had been hovering round Sir Charles for the last minute or two, anxious to do something but not knowing what, and, with all her sympathy, distinctly frightened by what can best be described as the muffled, smouldering ferocity of Sir Charles's scowl. Now she seemed a trifle relieved by her father's summons and followed him at once. Sir Charles managed to get out between his teeth in a barely audible mutter:

"You'll hear a good deal more of this young man, a—good—deal—" And what immeasurable threat did not lie in those last three words.

"I don't suppose it'll take the papers long to get hold of it; they'll run it in headlines a yard high," Bobby remarked. He permitted himself to smile broadly as he glanced at those so unfairly fettered hands. "Sort of story people enjoy telling when it's someone else. All over the place in no time. The papers will want to take snaps of you like that. I wouldn't let them if I were you."

Sir Charles received this excellent but possibly unnecessary advice in silence. It dawned on him, slowly penetrating through his red-hot, raging anger, that possibly other people might be more inclined to giggle than to flame into wrathful sympathy. Besides, all that publicity, and interfering newspaper-men poking about. An unattractive prospect. After all, there were things in every man's life . . . he began to look even a little afraid. He saw that Bobby was watching him closely, and the truculence faded slowly from his expression. Now, almost simultaneously, there appeared at the still-open french windows, Ford, holding triumphantly aloft the recovered key, and, at the door, Mr Wynne with whisky, a syphon of soda, glasses. Smiling benevolently, Ford released Sir Charles from his fetters and then stepped warily back, more than half expecting to have to ward off immediate attack.

"Say when, Stuart," Wynne called with almost equal benevolence as he began to fill one of the glasses.

"Yah," said Sir Charles, and banged out of the room.

"Now he'll go trampling all over the flower-beds the other chap missed," complained Wynne. "Why couldn't he wait and leave by the front door?" Then to Bobby he repeated: "Say when?"

But Bobby, too, declined to 'Say when'. The sooner he and Ford, he said, got back to London the better. They might even arrive in time to snatch a brief interval of sleep before going on duty again, and, in any case, no one should ever have a drink before starting on a long drive by night—or even on a short one by day for that matter.

Mr Wynne was in thorough agreement, and said so as he sipped thoughtfully his own whisky and soda—chiefly the former, Bobby noticed.

"I need a stiffener," Wynne said; and went on to express a hope that the whole thing would soon be cleared up and the culprit brought to justice. Bobby said the case was in the very capable hands of Mr Kimms, though the Yard would certainly be asked to help in tracing the vanished Mr Dowie, the departed Mr Maxton, the fleeing Mr 'Jolly' Rogers, if indeed it was he who had been their midnight visitor, as seemed most likely. And then there was also the even more pressing and important task of identifying the murdered woman.

"Ironical," pronounced Mr Wynne. "You came hoping to solve an old crime and you have instead a new one, and a worse one, on your hands. Ironical," he repeated.

They were in the entrance hall now where stood the 'Atropos', the holder of those shears which so short a time before had cut the thread of an unknown woman's life. From wherever she had been waiting, Sylvia appeared, a pale, nervous, frightened-looking child.

"Has Sir Charles gone?" she asked. "I didn't hear him. Oh, Daddy, isn't it all awful?" and she looked as if, had they been alone, she would have fled to the refuge of his arms for safety and for comfort, as she had been used to do when she was very small, and there had never failed to find them. "Oh, Daddy, suppose it had been you if you had been there that night."

"But it wasn't me and I wasn't there or anywhere near," Mr Wynne told her with a reassuring smile, "and the sooner you are back in bed, child, the better."

"Yes, Daddy," she said obediently.

Wynne unlocked and unbolted the front door and asked if they could find their way to where they had left their car and could he help? Bobby said that was all right. Unless it had been stolen—which wasn't likely—he and Ford could manage very well. Indeed, though dawn was still far off, the night now seemed less dark, for clouds had dispersed and the young moon and many stars were becoming visible. They had, too, their electric torches to show them the way, and as they went Bobby said:

"How is your ankle now, Ford?"

"My ankle, sir?" Ford repeated. "Where Sir Charles kicked me? Oh, much better now, sir, thank you; doesn't hurt any more."

"Had no trouble in finding the key the second time, had you?"

"No, sir; funny thing, sir," Ford said, a little uneasily. "There it was quite plain. Strange, isn't it? How first you can't see what you're looking for and then there it is, large as life."

"Very strange," agreed Bobby. "I suppose it wasn't in your waistcoat pocket all the time, by any chance? No, I thought not. Ford, you'll go far, I'm sure. But I'm not sure yet which way."

"No, sir; yes, sir; thank you, sir," said Ford; and added, anxious to change the subject. "Do you think, sir, by any chance that Sir Charles was in it all the time? But for him jumping on you the way he did from behind, you would have nailed that chap who was running, sure as eggs is eggs."

"Yes," agreed Bobby, "but there has been all this talk of hidden treasure in the copse. He could reasonably have been on watch, suspected us, been sure that's what we were there for, and when he saw us running, thought it was time he came in."

"And the other gentleman?" Ford asked. "He was there, too, and the young lady letting slip he had been out at night before."

"Yes, I know," Bobby said, and was silent.

"Tight-lipped gentleman," Ford said presently.

"Yes, I know," Bobby repeated. Then he said: "And Sir Charles came into a lot of money from a long-lost uncle in America just about the time of the Post Office van robbery; and did Wynne know where that dead woman lay and made sure it was Sir Charles who found her? Nothing much to go on yet; they couldn't reasonably be classed as suspect. All the same, we don't want either of them to take alarm and wander off on a voyage round the world—enough of one sort or another to track down in this thing as it is."

They had reached their car by now, and in it they drove back to town, both of them uneasy and thoughtful, for they both felt that they were faced with a problem as complicated as any the Yard had ever had to deal with.

"There's one thing, sir," Ford said, an envious eye on the driving-wheel that his fingers itched to get hold of—and was it not slightly beneath the dignity of a 'high up' to drive when a mere constable was there to take on this wholly subordinate job?—"whoever did that woman in, it doesn't look like it was Jolly Rogers. If it had been him, he would never have gone near the place again—stayed as far away as he could if he had known."

"There's that," Bobby agreed, still keeping up a mere crawl of forty m.p.h., though there was a perfectly clear stretch of straight road before them and sixty m.p.h. would have been wholly in order. "I said so myself to Kimms. But there's no telling. Murderers do strange things. A vague feeling that the body would be safer if better hidden. Or even strange ancestral memories whispering that the least you can do for your victim is decent burial. In any event, we must do our best to pick up Rogers. He probably has a good idea who she is, and very likely knows a good deal more as well."

CHAPTER X
THE 'BELL AND BOY'

SO, EVEN THOUGH the main investigation remained in the hands of the local force in whose territory the murder had been committed, there was still much, very much, for the London C.I.D. to do. More especially for those of its members who, unrecognized and unknown even to their uniformed colleagues, wander here and there in London's underworld, which is by no means confined to Soho, listening to gossip there, starting it here, keeping discreet eyes open all the time, and sometimes both eyes very hard indeed on particularly busy gentlemen, some days learning nothing at all, on other days obtaining valuable information entirely irrelevant, perhaps, to the particular inquiry on hand, but possibly contributing to the smothering before birth of highly undesirable enterprises.

In this way, gradually, on Bobby's desk, and in the file devoted to the Twice Over murder case, there began to accumulate quite a wealth of detail, all duly passed on to Superintendent Kimms, but of some of which the significance would be less immediately apparent to him than to his London colleagues. Then one day Kimms himself walked into Bobby's room.

"Hello," said Bobby.

"Hello," said Kimms, and there the conversation seemed to be stranded. "Getting nowhere," Kimms said presently, having filled the interval by filling his pipe, as Bobby had filled it by finishing the report with which he had been busy. "Too hard a knot," he announced.

"Shakespeare," said Bobby promptly.

"Sick of him," said Kimms. "Morning, noon, and night. Local dramatic society doing him, and my girl taking over from Miss Wynne. Giving it up. Shock?"

"No wonder," Bobby said. "Young girls and murder don't fit, and this was almost on her own doorstep, and her father in it as well. What about him?"

"Nothing wouldn't ever phase him," pronounced Kimms.

"Or, if it did, he wouldn't show it," Bobby suggested.

"Now, Sir Charles, he talks," Kimms said. "Loud and big."

"Not about handcuffs?" asked Bobby.

Instead of answering, Kimms collapsed into a silence that gradually changed to a slow, suppressed, muted laughter that shook his whole vast body from tip to toe.

"Maxton turned up yet?" Bobby asked when he judged this paroxysm had reached and passed its climax, and when, in response, Kimms shook his head and dried his streaming eyes, Bobby asked next: "Have you found anything to identify the dead woman with the one reported visiting Maxton regularly to collect money? According to Wynne, the dead woman was near Maxton's cottage earlier in the day. He gave a very accurate description of her."

"Must have seen her," Kimms agreed. "No one else did, as far as is known. Maxton's visitor seen by a good many, but descriptions vary. Tall, short, middle size; dark complexion or light; fair hair, dark hair; take your choice. Descriptions," he added bitterly. "Eh?"

"I know," Bobby agreed sympathetically. "No sign of the missing handbag?"

"None," Kimms answered. "If there was another hundred pounds in it—eh?"

"Might explain a lot." Bobby agreed. "Done any digging?"

"Dug up loganberry bush and all round. Nothing. Can't dig up whole copse."

"No," agreed Bobby. "Take bull-dozers to do the job, and cost more than anything you are likely to find. But that loganberry bush comes in somehow."

"Where?" said Kimms. "Eh?"

"Ah," said Bobby by way of variety.

"Jenkins," Kimms went on, "reports gossip re blackmail, re Sir Charles."

"Is there, though?" Bobby said, interested. "In what connection?"

"Women," answered Kimms. "Visitors. Young and pretty. Frequent."

"That's morals," Bobby pointed out. "Not crime."

"Older woman," Kimms explained. "Not young. Not pretty. Overheard using threats. Not clear re what or why. Sir Charles threw her out. Hard. Used violence."

"Might be a line to follow up," Bobby said, considering it. "If she ran one or two of the pretties and there had been some funny work. Possibilities there."

"Possibilities aren't evidence," Kimms retorted. "If your boys could get a line . . ." Bobby, adopting Kimms's technique, answered by an affirmative nod to indicate willingness to try. Kimms nodded in return to indicate thanks and appreciation and then said: "There's queer things go on in the West End."

"In the country, too, at times," Bobby retorted, willing to let the country share the discredit. "It does rather look though as if the blackmail yarn started about Stuart and then got tacked on to Maxton because of these mysterious visits and the hundred pounds business. We'll see if we can hear of Sir Charles being known anywhere in night clubs and places like that. Some of the Piccadilly girls might know of him. Probably a good payer if blackmail was thought worth trying, and a good payer soon gets known."

"Maxton too? Eh?" suggested Kimms, but Bobby shook his head.

"He would only be a casual, not a well-to-do regular," he said. "It's only good payers the women tell each other about. I've inquired about Maxton. He seems well known as a writer on country topics. Very popular with townspeople living in flats. Does the 'A Farmer's Wife's Diary' column. It runs in several big provincial city papers. His last book, *An Ignoramus in Arcadia*, did rather well. On the strength of it he's got a contract with a publisher for a new series of country books. He bought a new car the other day. The publisher provided the money."

"Fishy yarn?" suggested Kimms doubtfully.

"Oh, no—payment in advance, that's all. But he's left his brand new car in a Hammersmith garage and cleared out, and why the devil should he do that?"

"Ah," said Kimms.

"He may have hired another car," Bobby said. "You could follow that up, couldn't you?"

"Gazette?" asked Kimms.

"Oh, too early for that, don't you think?" Bobby asked in return. "If he got to know he was in the Police Gazette he might be off abroad or to the U.S., and that would rather do us. Difficult to make inquiries about a man who isn't there unless there's something very definite to go on."

Kimms nodded agreement and then said:

"Anything fresh about Dowie?"

"Only confirming what we know and have passed on to you already. Quite a lot of it, too. Know him like the palm of your hand, except who he is, where he lives, what he does, what he's up to, whether his treasure-hunting gadget is a fake or whether there is something in it on the water-diviner lines."

"Fake, ten to one," Kimms declared. "As per usual," he added.

"He was getting known in Soho pubs and cafés," Bobby went on. "Especially at the 'Bell and Boy' in Kinsman Street, Piccadilly. Sort of centre for respectables who like to think they aren't, and of very much not respectables who like to pretend they are. Queer sort of joint. They say if you only go there often enough you are bound to meet everybody in time. I don't know about that, but one report just in says Dowie was in real danger of getting beaten up on the general principle that no one would ask so many questions if he wasn't a police agent. One of our men tipped him off that asking questions in Soho was asking for trouble. After that he disappeared, only to turn up in Twice Over, where your chaps saw him leaving the copse in a hurry on the night of the murder. Before it took place, though, unless the doctor's made a bad bloomer."

"I wouldn't hardly expect that," protested Kimms, who still preserved much of the awe once so universally felt for the 'medicine man.'

"No, no," agreed Bobby, though he didn't. "Besides, for that matter, if it's Dowie, he might have gone back. The thing is, have these people vanished because they knew of, took part in, had some connection somehow, with the murder? All of them? That's hard to believe." Kimms here gave one of his customary nods of assent. "If not, how else are you to account for it?"

"Ah," said Kimms. "Needs it, too."

"Accounting for? So it does," agreed Bobby. "What it does suggest to me is a very tightly woven pattern with no loose threads."

"Ah," said Kimms again.

"But that also means," Bobby went on, "that if we can manage to find any loose thread, or rather to pick one loose, then the whole thing may come unravelled comparatively easily."

"Yes," said Kimms, but very, very doubtfully. "There's this Jolly Rogers chap, too. One of the disappeared."

"Common form with him," Bobby said. "He's on licence and up to now has reported regularly. If he does, we'll let you know and you can try to pick him up. Not yet, though. No proof he is the man I had nearly collared when your Sir Charles jumped on my back."

"Fishy?" said Kimms. "Pals? Eh?"

"What about lunch?" Bobby asked, leaving these suggestions unanswered. "It might help you to have a look at the 'Bell and Boy' for yourself. They put on a fair to average lunch at a more than fair to average price, but I might get it through the expense sheet."

"Both?" asked Kimms cautiously.

"Oh, yes," Bobby reassured him. "They know me there, and they've been asked to let us know if Dowie shows up any time. Nothing against him, of course; just a friendly question or two."

"Co-operative?" Kimms asked.

"Anyhow, they don't want to run any risk of finding us opposing the renewal of their licence," Bobby retorted.

"Ah," said Kimms; and therewith he and Bobby took themselves off to the 'Bell and Boy', to enjoy there a fair to average lunch at a more than fair to average price, and then, after it, they were joined for coffee by the Manager, who knew very well that important police officers did not visit his establishment without good reason.

"Sorry we've seen nothing of the gentleman you were asking about, Mr Owen," he said; "but there, you know what they say of us? Wait at the 'Bell and Boy', Piccadilly, long enough and sooner or later you'll meet the man you want. I won't say Mr Dowie might not have popped in and had a drink and gone again without being noticed. That might be, but no talk about discovering hidden treasure and no gadget to do it being shown. Confidence trick, to my mind, especially his get up being so different from the general run of confidence men and so like the general run of half-looney inventors."

"Well, he may turn up again," Bobby said; "but he does seem for the time to have vanished, and we should like to be sure he's all right, if only for his own sake. Don't forget."

"Oh, you can depend on us," declared the Manager, privately resolved that forgetting would take no longer than common decency required. "Vanishing seems quite usual just now," he went on affably. "One of our staff took herself off the other day without a word, and I can assure you, gentlemen, a first-class barmaid like her is hard to find—I mean one who knows how to jolly a man along and yet keep him at a distance, keep things going but know when to stop 'em, know when to bully and when to coax, how to listen and never to talk. Perhaps you knew her, Mr Owen? Mrs Field. Flossie everyone called her."

"Not that I remember," Bobby said. "Perhaps she's ill."

"I sent round to where she lives," the Manager said. "No answer, and no one seen her lately. Some of the staff said she seemed a bit quiet the last day or two, and there were some thought she had a second address, but none of them knew it. I didn't pay any attention. She was always a bit queer. She kept a tin of loganberries, of all things, on the shelf behind her. When she was told to take it away she said if it went, she went. Queer."

"Very," agreed Bobby. "And her name—Flossie Field? I think we might try to look her up, just to be on the safe side."

"Well, you don't think that she's run off with your Mr Dowie, do you?" the Manager asked, chuckling.

CHAPTER XI
LODGING OF CONVENIENCE

KIMMS WAS unusually silent, even for him, as he and Bobby started off for the address given them by the Manager of the 'Bell and Boy'. It proved to be that of a large, early Victorian mansion in North London, built solidly in an age that intended what it built to stand, and when, too, it seemed that since we had been told that the poor would always be with us, then it followed that an abundant supply of domestic help would likewise always be with us. Now this house of many rooms had been turned into furnished flatlets occupied by an odd diversity of swiftly changing tenants and looked as if it had had its last coat of paint, its last repairs done, some considerable time before the first world war. Kimms viewed it with marked distaste.

"Do you really think," he asked, "that this barmaid woman will have anything useful to say? I don't see where she's likely to come in?"

"I never think," Bobby explained. "Hard work, thinking, and too abstract for down-to-earth police work. I only try to notice facts and add 'em up till they seem to be getting somewhere."

"Such as . . . ?" asked Kimms.

"Such as," Bobby said, "a missing barmaid, name of Flossie Field. The same initials as those of Frank Farmer, the gangster in the P.O. van robbery case found dead in a ditch."

"Ah," said Kimms.

"That name of hers may mean nothing or a lot," Bobby added. "But that can wait. Something else. Barmaids, especially in a place like the 'Bell and Boy', get good money and could generally afford a better hole than this. Something was said, too, about another address, though nobody knew what it was, and this one does rather look like an address of convenience. Well, shall we see what we can find?"

The front door was open, and they entered a dingy, neglected-looking hall. On one wall hung a printed notice, warning tenants the door was locked and bolted every night at eleven p.m. sharp, that tenants creating a disturbance after that hour would be asked to go, that laundry must not be hung out to dry on landings or out of windows under the same penalty. There were various other severe regulations, culminating in a brief statement that rents must be paid in advance every Monday morning and that no credit was allowed in any circumstances.

"Very strict rules," said Kimms.

"Very," echoed Bobby and, throwing Shakespeare back at Kimms, he added: "Honoured in the breach or the observance?"

"Observance, this one," said Kimms, putting his finger on that one dealing with the prompt payment of the rent, and now it was Bobby's turn to say:

"Ah."

The 'flatlet' said to be occupied by the missing Mrs Field was No. 1, probably the dining-room in former days. Bobby knocked. No reply. He knocked again, with the same result or lack of it. He stooped to examine the lock. An ordinary Yale, and Bobby knew the technique of opening Yales without too much fuss. He knocked a third time, more loudly still. A woman was coming down the stairs from the upper region of the house, a much-made-up, shabbily smart woman who had once been pretty but was so no longer. At the foot of the stairs she stopped and looked darkly and angrily at the two men.

"Can't you busies ever leave anyone alone?" she demanded. "You've nothing on her; she's a decent girl. Cut it out."

Bobby turned, regarding her with extreme disfavour. There was nothing annoyed him more than being recognized as a policeman at first sight. What he liked, only it never happened, was to present his credentials and see result a look of extreme surprise and bewilderment. He tried to lay to his soul the flattering unction that no doubt it was only Kimms who had been so swiftly recognized, but something seemed to whisper to him that it was not so. He was tempted to retort that no doubt she had plenty of experience of busies in Piccadilly and St James's Street, but a little ashamed of it, he put that idea aside and contented himself with asking:

"Do you know Mrs Field?"

"She's a good sort," the woman answered. "No airs and always ready with a shilling or two when work's slack, as it is, with so few G.I.s about and amateur competition so strong. She paid the fare home and a bit over for a girl here when she didn't find the job any fun. It wasn't long before she was back, though—once the street has got you, it never lets you go."

"Have you seen her lately?" Bobby asked.

"Ask me another," she retorted. "I never tell busies anything. It isn't safe. You never know where they'll go from there. Bye-bye."

"One moment," Bobby said. "We have nothing against Mrs Field. She's been absent from work, and her employers are uneasy about it. So are we. I can't tell you why just yet, but we are."

"I'm not talking," was all the response this appeal elicited. "Keep off busies, that's my rule. Ask old Mother Grady if you like."

"Is she the landlady? Where do we find her?"

"In the basement. Private. She don't like visitors. I don't know why. When you want her you go to the top of the stairs and yell. If you say: 'Mrs Grady, can I settle up with you now,' she'll pop up like the demon king through the trap-door in panto. If you don't, she may take no notice—having no time to spare for the likes of tenants. Bye-bye," she said again, and began to hum a gay little tune. "Sounds jolly and friendly," she explained. "Fetches the men a treat."

She paused and looked at them, and her eyes were tragic, and then she went away.

"Makes you almost ashamed to be a man," Kimms said.

Bobby went to the head of the stairs leading down to the basement.

"Mrs Grady," he shouted, and when there was no reply he shouted again: "Mrs Grady, can I have a word with you, please? Police."

This last word was effectual. A sort of underground rumbling and grumbling ensued, rather like the threat of an eruption from some small underground geyser. Toiling up the stairs, wheezing, panting, grunting, came a stout, elderly, untidy woman, giving a general impression that she and soap had long since parted never to meet again. A faint odour of beer as she arrived seemed to impregnate the whole surrounding atmosphere.

"Police?" she panted as she got to the top of the stairs. "This is a respectable house, this is, and never no police and no call for 'em since I took over, and me as well thought of as any and well known to all."

"Quite so," interrupted Bobby. "I believe the occupant of your No. 1 flat is a Mrs Field, isn't she?"

"That's right," Mrs Grady assented, "and what might you be wanting with her? As respectable a lady as ever was, and if all tenants were like her and as punctual with her rent—"

"Yes, yes," interrupted Bobby again; "but she has left her work without explanation and her employers are worried, so we are making inquiries. Can you tell us when you saw her last?"

"She won't have done a bunk, will she?" inquired Mrs Grady anxiously. "The best tenant heart could wish for, and a month's rent paid in advance as regular as Christmas; never missed and due next Monday, too."

"There's no reason to suppose anything of the sort," Bobby assured her. "I'm asking if you can tell me when you saw her last."

"Not as I remember since she paid her rent last month and due again next Monday," Mrs Grady answered cautiously. "Not to speak to, anyway. I might have seen her in passing, so to say. I'm no snooper. Tenants mind their own business, and I mind mine."

"Were there any of your lodgers she ever seemed friendly with?"

"How should I know?" Mrs Grady demanded. "You can ask them yourself if you like. Nothing to do with me."

But she was beginning to look uneasy now, and she lumbered across the hall to knock at the door of No. 1 flatlet. It produced no reply. With much wheezing and grunting she lowered herself to her knees and applied first her nose and then one eye to the key-hole. Laboriously then she hauled herself to her feet.

"Can't see nothing, and no smell of gas," she said, "though I never took her for one to do the dirty on you same as that. Only you can't never tell with tenants, them being as they are, with never a thought for the good name of the roof that shelters them. I've known a girl come in, as jolly as you like, laughing and singing, and go straight up to her room and turn the gas on, no one knowing till all was over, poor dear, and the rent paid up and all."

"You've got a key?" Bobby asked.

"Same as obliged," Mrs Grady said. "If they bunk, they'll leave their doors locked sure as hell. No consideration for others, they haven't, and how can I get to clean up thorough if I've no key, or let the gasman in to collect. Not that Mrs Field ever used hers much. I've known her meter as empty as when last opened."

"Well, if you'll get her key, I'll take the responsibility of entering," Bobby said; and when he saw Kimms looking just a little doubtful at this proposed intrusion upon private property, he added: "If she's not there, I'll leave a note explaining and asking her to get in touch with her employers as soon as she can conveniently."

Mrs Grady hesitated, grumbled, saw how Bobby watched her, decided she had better comply, and, from under her voluminous skirts, fished up a bagful of keys. From these she selected one, and with it opened the door of No. 1 flat, taking the precaution of calling out before entering.

"Are you there, dearie?"

No reply coming, she went in, followed closely by the two men. It was a large, sparsely furnished room they thus entered. Two wooden chairs, two ancient basket arm-chairs, a table, an iron bedstead covered by an old rug, a rickety wardrobe, a strip of carpet, about completed the list. One corner of the room had been partitioned off to make a 'kitchenette', and here was provided also running water and a small gas cooking-stove—other less fortunate lodgers had to content themselves with a gas ring. Here, too, for the first time signs of recent use and occupation could be detected. A kettle on the gas-stove still had water in it. A box of matches lay near. On a shelf above stood a tin of cocoa and a packet of tea.

Bobby went back into the main room. He pulled away the rug that covered the bedstead and showed that beneath there was only the bare wire mattress, neither sheets nor blankets.

The chest of drawers contained only a few trifling odds and ends. In the wardrobe were none but articles of outdoor clothing. Bobby said to Kimms:

"She never slept or ate here—a lodging of convenience," and Kimms did not think it necessary to utter his customary 'Ah', of assent.

"If it was," Mrs Grady said earnestly, "it's such as I wouldn't ever have believed. Strike me dead if I ever saw any gentlemen visitors. Particular I am about that, as none can say the contrary."

"There is nothing more for us to do here," Bobby said, and added to Mrs Grady, "I shall be sending a plain-clothes man to make further inquiries and a closer examination of the room. He'll want to see some of your other lodgers. The rent is paid till Monday, you said? She may return to pay next month's or send it, perhaps."

"If she don't, out she goes," declared Mrs Grady, "such being the rule as must be kept, or where should we all be?"

"Where indeed?" agreed Bobby. "We must be off," and as they were walking to where they could get their 'bus back to the Yard, Kimms said:

"Hiding?"

"Who? Mrs Field, you mean?" Bobby asked. "If she were hiding she would hardly choose to work in a place like the 'Bell and Boy', where the story is that if you only wait there long enough you'll meet everybody you ever knew. No, not hiding, I think. Seeking perhaps, only what?"

CHAPTER XII
COMPLETE CIRCLE

KIMMS MADE no attempt to answer this question. His mind was busy with more immediate problems.

"Double life," he said suddenly.

"Looks like it," agreed Bobby. "You can get identification through the 'Bell and Boy' people, but it's fairly certain their missing barmaid and your murdered woman are the same. Certain, too, she must have been living somewhere else."

"Got to find it," Kimms said. "Can you help?"

"We'll do our best," Bobby promised. "Obviously it won't be far from Mrs Grady's place, and probably in a direct line with the 'Bell and Boy', so that she could stop off without going out of her way. To change her clothes, I take it. We can ask our chaps in the district to report any case of a woman vanishing they get to know of. The snag is that so many women take themselves off without our hearing—no reason why we should, very often. Leaving one man for another, or family row or something."

"Anything," agreed Kimms.

"Finding where else she lived is the next step, obviously," Bobby said, frowning at the problem presented. "Not too easy, perhaps. But until you have some idea of her background it's more or less working in the dark. Identification of Mrs Grady's lodger and the 'Bell and Boy' barmaid won't help much in itself."

"No," said Kimms.

After that they parted, Kimms returning to Twice Over and Bobby to his room at Central, where he put in hand the inquiry he had promised Kimms would be undertaken at once. Every boarding-house was to be inquired at, every porter at every block of flats questioned, plain-clothes men were to wander in and out of pubs and cafés on the chance of hearing some stray bit of gossip—gossip was always Bobby's favourite lead. All without result, as was also without result the look-out being kept for Maxton, for Mr Dowie no longer pursuing his interminable inquiries in Soho. Nor was even Jolly Rogers to be seen any longer in his accustomed haunts.

But then when Bobby was talking to a Divisional Superintendent about an entirely different case a passing reference was made to a recent 'breaking in' at a block of rather expensive flats much nearer the 'Bell and Boy' than was Mrs Grady's establishment.

"We can't get in touch with the occupant," the Superintendent was complaining. "Lady living alone and working somewhere in the city. A Mrs Meadows."

"Meadows," Bobby repeated. "Meadows, not Fields? No? Know anything about her?"

"Not much," the Superintendent answered. "Don't talk to me about iron curtains—give me a high-class block of flats like this Oxton Court for a curtain you can't get through. No one knows anything about anyone. Mrs Meadows lived very quietly in very good style. Rent of flat about three or four hundred or so. Very few visitors, as far as noticed. Out most of the time on her job, whatever it was. You know what some of these women in business are—always trying to get the edge on the men just to show they're as good or better."

"Yes, I know," Bobby said. "Forcible entry or key?"

"Oh, the old trick with the Yale," the Superintendent told him. "Tongue of the Yale forced back. The porter noticed it, but nothing to show when it was done. He rang us up, and Sergeant McGiven went along. He says the whole place was a shambles. Everything chucked everywhere."

"Looking for something," Bobby said. "I wonder what—money and jewellery, most likely. But it might tie up with the Twice Over affair. There's a man you remember—Jolly Rogers they call him; anything but jolly by nature. Thought of him? He rather specialises in that sort of thing—breaking in unoccupied flats by the Yale-lock trick."

"Oh, yes; we thought of him all right," the other answered. "But the last we heard of him he was reporting—on licence, you know—in Edinburgh. Of course, you can easy get from Edinburgh and back in twenty-four hours and no one know a thing about it. Difficult to get going when we don't even know if anything's missing. What's it to do with the Twice Over case? Kimms is handling it, isn't he? Not our pigeon. I haven't heard much about it."

"Well," Bobby explained, "here we have a missing barmaid—a Mrs Fields. You have a woman you can't get in touch with—a Mrs Meadows. Kimms has a dead woman not yet formally identified. And the address given us of the missing barmaid is one where she certainly never lived."

"I see. Yes. Well," said the Superintendent. "Rather thin tie-ups, but you never know. What's behind?"

"Also a man," Bobby went on, without attempting to reply, "seen in a Twice Over pub shortly before the murder. Reported as of suspicious appearance and might be Jolly Rogers, but only vague description, with—if Jolly Rogers it was—a lead from him, just recently released from gaol, to a pal of his, the Milkman, otherwise Charley Cream, who died in the same gaol a few weeks before Rogers's release, was probably concerned in the first P.O. van robbery, and may have known part of the proceeds were hidden in Twice Over and so back there again."

"The complete circle," commented the Superintendent. "Sounds as if there were a lot to uncover."

"Might be," agreed Bobby cautiously. "Add a retired gentleman who did not find the dead body and incidentally possesses a lovely happy little daughter. Also a somewhat free-living baronet who became mysteriously rich about the time of the P.O. robbery. Not to mention a rising young journalist, and an habitué of Soho with a treasure detector gadget, both of whom have retired into obscurity forgetting to leave their addresses behind them. And there you are."

"Thank Heaven I'm not," said the Superintendent devoutly. "You may like that sort of thing, but give me honest-to-goodness, down-to-the-ground police work."

"Got your car?" Bobby asked. "How about giving me a lift to this Oxton Court? I've been over the missing barmaid's flat. I would rather like a look at Mrs Meadows's. Mrs Meadows, Mrs Fields. And a dead gangster, name of Farmer. Quite a coincidence in names. Quite bucolic. Precious little to see where Mrs Fields hung out—or rather where she didn't. But I might spot something at this other place to show if the occupiers were the same."

"An eye for detail," said the Superintendent, half enviously, half smilingly. "Well, it counts," he said.

They started off accordingly; and at Oxton Court were assured by the porter in charge that there was no fresh development, that no suspicious characters had been noticed anywhere near, that no word, no sign of any sort, had been received from the still missing Mrs Meadows. The damaged lock on the flat door had been replaced by another. The key to this was in the porter's care, and with it he admitted them to the flat, remaining himself at the open door, whether as a measure of precaution, out of curiosity, or from a sense of duty.

Much of the 'shambles' reported by the police on their first visit had been sorted out into tidy heaps and carefully examined to make sure it contained no useful clue or information about either the tenant or the intruders. But the whole place remained as impersonal as an hotel suite. It had been comfortably, even expensively, furnished in a conventional Tottenham Court Road style, the only sign that the occupant was a woman being a complete absence of comfortable armchairs, and a certain care that seemed to have been taken to arrange the colour scheme. There were no books. On the walls were a few engravings, generally sentimental representations of children and animals. Even some of these had been taken down and thrown on the floor. No letters seemed to have been delivered. No newspapers either.

"All her interests outside," said the Superintendent. "No private life, if you see what I mean. Bleak sort of place it must have been. Looks more homely in a way now it's all upside down. Just for sleeping and eating. Sort of hermit's cell, but with all modern comforts."

"A dedicated life," Bobby said slowly. "Dedicated to what?" He neither expected nor received an answer. He pointed to the mantelpiece. "See that?" he said.

"You mean that tin of loganberries?" asked the Superintendent. "Why? What about it? She probably fed out, but if she did eat at home it would be tinned stuff. Boiling an egg is about the limit in cooking for most women when they're alone."

"Yes, I know," Bobby agreed. He added: "Mrs Meadows and our missing barmaid both seem to have had a liking for loganberries—a tin on the mantelpiece here and one kept well in view of all customers at the 'Bell and Boy'. Rather odd."

"Well, yes, in a way," agreed the Superintendent, but not as if he really thought it mattered. He went across the room, picked up the tin and gave it a shake. "It's not been opened," he said. "Can't have been anything put inside."

"Mrs Meadows wasn't no barmaid," the porter interrupted with a touch of indignation in his voice. "Barmaids don't run to Oxton Court, they don't, and Mrs Meadows was a real lady and no mistake. Had a mink coat, she had."

Finding this conclusive, the Superintendent nodded in agreement. Bobby was either less impressed or else more interested in the tin of loganberries. He was staring at it with concentrated attention, not so much thinking as waiting for thought to come.

"Can't say I see much here to help," the Superintendent announced.

"No, there isn't," Bobby agreed, waking from his meditative trance. "That's what's so interesting, isn't it?"

He removed his attention from the loganberry tin and wandered abstractedly into the other rooms: the bedroom and kitchen. Both these presented the same scene of overturned drawers, ransacked cupboards, of a busy and intensive search that seemed to have missed nothing—a chaos imposed, as it seemed, upon a meticulously tidy, carefully maintained background and made to seem even more chaotic by the sorting and examining that the police had carried out without attempting to put things back in their original places. He returned to the sitting-room, to the patient Superintendent and the watchful porter. He began to look through a small pile of papers that had apparently come from the upturned drawers of a small writing bureau.

"Nothing personal there," the Superintendent told him. "No letters, no addresses; only receipts, bills—that sort of thing. Anonymous," he said with sudden irritation. "Where do you go when there's nowhere."

Bobby made no attempt to reply. He wandered through the flat again and then went back to where the Superintendent was waiting, now a trifle impatiently.

"There's one thing, if you notice," Bobby said to him and paused, staring hard at the other, as if challenging him to reply.

"There are a lot of things I notice," was the prompt retort, "but none that seems to help much."

"That's just it," Bobby declared, looking pleased, as if this was the very answer he had hoped for. "Nothing to help. Which means, I take it, that whoever broke in here broke in for that very reason. To remove everything that could in any way be any help, especially anything that could throw light on her past life or real identity."

CHAPTER XIII
HIDDEN COTTAGE

ON BOBBY'S DESK next morning was a note from Edinburgh. It contained the information that John Rogers, known as 'Jolly Rogers', convict on licence, had left the address from which he had reported. It asked further if London wanted him brought in? If so, was there any specific charge on which he could be held? To which Bobby sent a reply explaining that there was at the moment nothing definite against Rogers, but it was believed he could give useful information that might help in the investigation now going on into a recent murder. If he could be located he might perhaps be induced to talk. There was even a chance that Rogers might have some idea where a part of the loot from the first Post Office van robbery still lay hidden.

Not that this possibility was considered very likely by Bobby's colleagues, some of whom were still inclined to think of him as too imaginative and fanciful for so matter-of-fact and prosaic a job as police work.

"Spent as soon as got," one of them said. "A hundred a night in the West End is nothing to 'em when they've brought a big one off—and then betting. A hole without a bottom."

"One of the gang," Bobby reminded him, "had his head blown off almost immediately afterwards. We never knew why, but before he had had time to do much spending. And there's the chance that Charley Cream—another of them, only he got caught—stowed his share away and Rogers, who was in gaol with him, got a hint where. It might be at Twice Over, where one of them came from."

"Well, it's an interesting case," admitted the other. "Plenty for us to do, though, without opening up the old jobs. I hope there won't be any more murders on the way."

With that he departed, half believing that Bobby Owen was going to bring it off again, even though it seemed at present that there was so little to go on.

"Except tinned loganberries," he added to himself with a chuckle; for already the tale of Bobby's interest in tinned loganberries had become known and caused a certain amount of amusement.

Later on there came a 'phone call from Twice Over, where Mr Kimms had established temporary headquarters at the Over All Arms.

"Information just received," said the distant voice—not that of Kimms, who disliked the telephone and seldom used it, "that a light was seen at Mr Maxton's place, Hidden Cottage, last night. No one there now, and no sign of breaking in, but Mr Kimms is thinking of effecting entry. As our inquiry overlaps yours, Mr Kimms wondered if you might think it advisable to be present. Will you let us know if you agree?"

"Oh, yes, I agree," Bobby answered at once, strongly suspecting though that Kimms, a cautious soul, still a little surprised that he had reached so high a rank in the force, still a trifle unsure of himself, was anxious for the moral support while 'effecting entry', of the presence of a London 'high up'. For 'effecting entry' into private premises is a procedure requiring ample justification.

So time and place were duly settled and then the telephone went on:

"I am to inform you also that the identity of the murdered woman with Mrs Fields, Mrs Meadows, and the 'Bell and Boy' barmaid has been fully established. 'Dabs' coincide, and the Assistant Manager of the 'Bell and Boy' identified the body at once. A report is in the post. Mr Kimms says he doesn't suppose it will surprise you much."

"No, only puzzles me a bit more," Bobby answered. "All these disconnected leads ought to get us somewhere—that is, if we ever do get there."

"To the dead woman's murderer or to recovery of the P.O. pound notes. Or both?" asked the telephone.

"Both," Bobby said, but without much conviction, and with that their talk ended.

The case was sufficiently important—and more than sufficiently interesting—for him to feel justified in putting aside all other work for the time being. Soon therefore he was on his way to Twice Over and then, in company with Kimms, to Hidden Cottage. This, well deserving its name, was situated two or three miles from the centre of the village in the midst of a small wood. Access to it by wheeled traffic was almost impossible—and in bad weather sufficiently difficult even by foot—though close by was a footpath running between a neighbouring farm and the road where now Kimms parked his car. Even from this path, however, owing to the lie of the land and a close-growing thicket, the cottage was almost invisible, so that some of those who habitually used the path could not have told its exact position.

Originally it had been intended for a gamekeeper's residence at a time when the owner of the land had wished to provide good shooting for himself and his friends. But the war had left little money to spare for such aristocratic luxuries as game preservation—or paying gamekeepers, for that matter—and the cottage had become vacant. Then it had been occupied, repairs and some structural improvements carried out, by one of the more swiftly rising lights of post-war literary London. It had been his intention there to retire to commune alone with nature and his soul. But presently he had discovered that cocktail parties are perhaps more truly inspiring, and that, for literary London, out of car reach, is out of mind. He had therefore been deeply grateful when Martin Maxton had offered to take the cottage off his hands, and had done his best to show it by two brief but highly flattering references in Heights, that well-known periodical, to Martin as a 'coming man'—and to be so mentioned in Heights is equivalent in the more intellectual circles of London to being awarded the D.S.O. in the army. For Maxton, the cottage had provided a cheap and convenient headquarters to return to after his frequent visits to other parts of the country in search of material and for making that close and patient observation of nature on which he did in fact base much of his work. Indeed, his initial success—modest enough—had been his book 'Hidden Cottage', from which, and not the other way round, the name had been derived.

To it now Bobby and Kimms were drawing near, and Kimms said, pointing to a thicket which at least was visible enough.

"Behind there."

"Easy to pass without seeing it," Bobby remarked. "It's been given a name that suits it. But suits it for bird-watching and that sort of thing or even for quite other activities there would be no one to notice?"

"Ah," said Kimms.

He led the way round the thicket and through some further trees to where before the cottage a sergeant and a constable waited, sitting on a veranda. Kimms nodded a greeting; they put their cigarettes away and stood up; Bobby, examining the lock, agreed there was no sign of forcible entry.

"No reason for it," he commented. "Anyone could open a lock like that with a hair-pin."

Kimms gave a nod of agreement to Bobby, and, to the sergeant, one of permission to begin operations. The door was soon opened—though not by means of a hairpin—and then the sergeant stood back to allow the two senior officers the first look. It showed them just such a chaos, just such a scene of violent, hurried search, as had been presented by the Oxton Court flat.

Every one of the four rooms—the cottage had the usual layout, two rooms downstairs, kitchen and scullery, two bedrooms upstairs, one of them now converted into a bathroom—had been thoroughly and completely ransacked. Tables and chairs had been overthrown, drawers and cupboards emptied, the divan bed turned upside down, books and papers tossed aside, clothing—not much of it—thrown into a heap. Even the bathroom had not been spared; and later it was noticed that the rain-water tank from which it was supplied had been emptied to make sure there was nothing there. Yet Bobby thought that beneath all this he could still distinguish a former care and well-ordered tidiness. Crockery, much of it broken, was clean. Washing up had evidently been done before the cottage was left. The cleaning rags had been washed out, the cooking utensils properly cared for, the linoleums covering the floors well kept. And these small points Bobby noticed with interest and attention, since it was his belief that such details threw much light on character, and character much light on the problems presented to him.

There was something else that he remembered. Those who lead irregular and lawless lives generally, almost invariably, show a comparable disregard for order in their daily existence. Not only do they dislike and shirk the discipline of society, but also they deny that imposed upon us by the routine of daily life. Some few there are to whom this does not apply, some whose daily life seems as regular and well ordered as that of any city clerk, and these are the most formidable and dangerous of their kind.

"Someone must be wanting to find something pretty badly," Bobby said suddenly, leaving these abstract considerations for the time.

"Yes," said Kimms. "Only what?" he asked and clearly expected no reply.

The sergeant, who was also the local finger-print expert and who had been busy with his powder and his brushes and the rest of it, came up and said:

"There's some dabs I've found look to me uncommon like those I got from Mr Dowie's room at the Over All Arms. Of course I can't be sure till I've tested them."

"Queer bloke, Dowie," said Kimms. "Suspicious."

"Battledore and shuttlecock," said Bobby. "Clues tossed to and fro from one to t'other."

"No straight line," Kimms said. "If only—" And he lost himself in a vision of how easily and quickly a solution would be arrived at if only such straight line would kindly present itself.

As there seemed nothing more that could be done at the cottage for the present, the sergeant and constable were left in charge to clear up as far as that was possible, and Bobby and Kimms began to walk back to where they had left their car. It was, or would have been if their thoughts had been less busily engaged, a pleasant way they thus followed along this winding woodland path through trees bright with their autumn tints, and then presently they caught sight of someone approaching. A good way distant still, but Kimms had had a momentary glimpse through an opening in the trees, giving him a clear view.

"Miss Wynne," he said. "To meet Maxton?"

"He's not there and hasn't been for some time," Bobby said. "More likely she's heard about us, or been told I'm here again, and wants to know why."

"Her and him," Kimms said. "Everyone knows."

"Mr Wynne doesn't altogether approve, does he?" Bobby asked.

"He won't stand out," Kimms said. "She's all the world to him and Heaven, too."

"A cold, reserved man," Bobby said. "But not to her?"

"No," said Kimms.

They had halted as they talked, and Sylvia was near now, coming with her quick, light, dancing step, and all about her lay the varying rays the sun sent down through the overshadowing foliage of the trees. A veritable incarnation of the spirit of youth and joy she seemed as she came towards them like a morning in May, and yet to Bobby came the thought that the first beginning of a hint of approaching griefs was with her, like a following shadow of which she was neither quite aware nor wholly ignorant. She had seen them now where they waited. For a moment she stood still, and it seemed as if her glance went past them to see if any other was in sight. Then she came on, her step quicker and her clear bright eyes with an odd little look of determination in them, as much as to say: Yes, you're two big men, but I'm not a bit afraid of you.

"I thought I might meet you," she said, now with a touch of rebuke in her voice. "People are saying such things, I had to know."

"What things?" Bobby asked.

"Nothing's happened to Mr Maxton, has it?" she asked in return, without answering him.

"Not that we know of," Bobby told her. "Why? Is that what's being said?"

"Yes. Only I knew it couldn't be true, but I had to be sure," she replied. "I expect it was just you being here again, and then what happened to that poor woman is so awfully upsetting, isn't it?"

"It is indeed," agreed Bobby, "and so is Mr Maxton's going away without warning. He didn't say anything to you, did he?"

"No. Why should he?" she retorted with just the faintest touch of sharpness in her voice.

"What were people saying that was so silly?" Bobby asked.

"Oh, it was just stupid," she answered, and when Bobby still waited, pressing for an answer as it were, silently demanding one, she added: "It was Mrs Griggs from the village; she said he had been found dead where he lives, and of course I knew it wasn't true."

"No, it isn't true," Bobby said. "His cottage has been entered in his absence and searched, and we would like to know why. That's all."

CHAPTER XIV
PERTURBED MR WYNNE

As perhaps had not been far from Bobby's intention, for he knew that a touch of temper loosens the tongue as effectively as wine is said to do, there was unusual asperity in Sylvia's voice as she retorted:

"Well, that's horrible, isn't it? Somebody pawing all your things all over. I do hope you find out who it was."

"Do you remember ever hearing Mr Maxton say anything about a Mr Dowie?" Bobby asked. "He's been staying at the Over All Arms."

"The man they said was trying to find the old monastery church plate?" she asked in return. "Daddy says it's all rubbish. I don't think Mr Maxton ever said anything about him—I don't remember if he did. Why? You don't think it was him, do you?"

"Oh, no," Bobby said. Now they were all three walking back to the road. "But we have reason to believe that Mr Dowie visited Mr Maxton. They left here about the same time, so possibly they left together."

"I shouldn't think that at all likely," Sylvia said, and she was beginning to look a little worried. "I'm sure they weren't friends. Martin—Mr Maxton would have said something."

"Mr Wynne," Bobby went on, "mentioned that you saw a light in the copse behind your home late one night shortly before the murder. Do you think it could have been Mr Dowie busy with his treasure-hunting?"

She shook her head without answering in words. But her cheeks showed a slightly heightened colour, and for Bobby, watching her closely, that was enough.

"Could it have been Mr Maxton?" he asked. That tell-tale colour deepened, but she was still silent. "I think it was, wasn't it?" he asked again.

"He's most awfully silly," she said; and Bobby, taking this for an admission, pressed her no further.

They had reached the road by now. Sylvia had left her bicycle there, leaning against a tree, near the police car. She hurried to it. Kimms called an offer to take her and the bicycle back to the Old Dower House. She did not seem to hear. At any rate, she did not answer. She mounted and rode away as quickly as she could, and the two men watched her in silence till a turn in the road hid her from sight.

"Frightened?" Kimms said. "Why? That light she saw? Before the murder, though."

"Maxton may have been back in the copse but shown no light," Bobby said.

"Um-m-m," said Kimms. "Well, now then. Search. Buried pound-notes or monk's hidden treasure? Two lots of 'em on the job. Clashing? As they would. Is that it? Eh?"

"Might be," Bobby agreed. "Worth keeping in mind, but no more than a possibility. One strand making up the knot we have to unravel, but all pure theory at present. No solid foundation of fact to build on, and what we want is facts first of all. Theory from facts, not facts from theory."

"Spade found," Kimms said. "Not traced. Fact."

"Yes, there's that," Bobby agreed, and thought to himself, but did not say, that it was a pity Kimms had been so prompt to start digging under and around the loganberry bush at the scene of the murder. A pity, too, he himself had not thought to warn Kimms that many archaeologists—as he knew, but Kimms perhaps did not—maintain that where a hole has once been dug the resultant disturbance of the soil can always be recognized, even though centuries have passed. "Any suggestion of anything being buried would naturally mean providing a spade," he added.

"Might have been for a grave," Kimms said. "No telling. Eh?"

"Oh, well, yes," Bobby said, a little startled by this suggestion and not much liking it.

They had been standing by the car as they talked, or rather as Bobby talked and Kimms made his brief comments. Now they took their places in the car and drove off, soon passing Sylvia, who had stopped to chat to a passing woman from the village and who kept her back resolutely turned to them as they went by. Soon they were at the Old Dower House, and Bobby suggested it would be a good opportunity for a chat with Mr Wynne, still so much, it seemed, in the forefront of all these happenings. But Kimms had an appointment to meet his Chief Constable at the home of the chairman of the Joint Committee, and had no idea of offending two such dignitaries by keeping them waiting for the sake of what he privately called a desultory chat with Mr Wynne.

"Never get anything out of him," he said by way of explanation or excuse. "Misses nothing. Says nothing. Not quite human."

With this diagnosis, unusually full for Kimms, Bobby was in complete agreement. And he was more than willing to make his visit unaccompanied. It was his experience that people talked much more freely to one than to two. Naturally, when a formal statement had to be taken, a companion was necessary—at the mouth of two witnesses shall it be established.

So, alighting here and waving farewell to Kimms, he walked briskly up the rhododendron-lined avenue to the house, where in answer to his summons, it was Wynne himself who came quickly to the door and who, seeing who it was, there stood in silence, not answering Bobby's greeting, for once his habitual calm entirely deserting him.

"Have you . . . is anything . . . ?" he asked at last, stammering a little. "Sylvia isn't here," he said.

"Why, what's happened?" Bobby asked quickly, surprised in his turn.

"Someone was in the house when I got back," Wynne said. "I've been in town all day. I think the telephone wire must have been cut. I couldn't get through. Sylvia isn't here," he repeated.

"I saw her a few minutes ago," Bobby said. "She was up the road not far away. She was talking to someone."

"Oh, that's all right, then," Wynne said. He put his hand up to his face; and it was for all the world as if he were replacing the mask behind which he habitually hid himself but that for the moment had slipped aside in his fear that ill might have come to Sylvia. Even that brief split second of time had been enough, though, for Bobby to glimpse the almost terrifying passion of fear and anger that had raged within him at the mere suspicion. Now it was gone, now he knew that she was safe, and in his ordinary level, somewhat monotonous tone he went on apologetically, "Stupid of me, but for the moment I half thought—" He broke off his sentence. He resumed: "Someone has been in my study. The door was locked."

"Did you see anyone?" Bobby asked.

"No. The front door was open when I got back. I thought Sylvia must be somewhere about, and I sounded the gong to let her know. There was a sort of scuffling at the back of the house. I went to see what it was, and of course when I found the study door locked I knew something was wrong. I ran round through the kitchen. The study windows were open, but no one was there. They must have made a quick get-away into the copse at the back. I tried to 'phone, but couldn't, and then I heard your knock." Now as he talked he began to lead the way through the hall where the Atropos presided and on to the study Bobby had seen before. "I don't like it," he said over his shoulder.

"Do you know how they got in?" Bobby asked.

"No; just walked in, perhaps," Wynne answered. "It wouldn't be the first time Sylvia has run out and left the door open. Goes to the shed for her bicycle and forgets to come back to shut the door. She's a careless child. I must give her a good scolding," he added with a fond smile that hardly promised a scolding of any great severity, his voice indeed now tinged with that warmth—that glow, so to speak—which came so strangely into it whenever he made reference to his daughter. "It's all just as it was," he added as they entered the study.

"Nothing missing?" Bobby asked, glancing round the room, where at first sight no sign of disturbance showed.

"They've been at my desk," Wynne said; and when Bobby made a step forward he could see that one drawer was wide open and that another had been pulled out and emptied on the floor. Wynne opened a third drawer. "There's some money here—or was," he said. "No, they've not found it. About a hundred pounds in pound notes, but it's not been touched. Nothing much to be done, is there? I suppose it is hardly a criminal offence to walk into a house by the front door and then out again without taking anything?"

"No," Bobby agreed. "No, but there may be a tie-up. I think that is more than likely. With the murder. I can't imagine how."

"Nor can I," Wynne said in his impassive way. "Disturbing and annoying. I don't pretend to like it. I was alarmed. I thought a thief might have got in and that Sylvia had interrupted him and been attacked. I half expected to find her knocked out and pushed into some cupboard out of the way. Stupid, no doubt. Fortunately she can't have been in."

"Something of the same sort has been happening elsewhere," Bobby commented. "Mr Maxton's cottage has been entered and thoroughly ransacked. He is still away, so whoever it was had plenty of time and no risk of being interrupted. No telling if anything is missing till we can get in touch with Maxton."

"Maxton's place, too," Wynne repeated incredulously. "But that's mere lunacy. Lunacy," he repeated and went on: "I did just wonder for a moment if it could have been Maxton here. Trying to get to see Sylvia without my knowing. I don't understand it," he repeated, and he looked really worried, that customary, aloof, untroubled demeanour of his deserting him for the moment, as it was so apt to do whenever Sylvia's name was mentioned.

"In London, too," Bobby continued. "We believe we have identified the murdered woman with a Mrs Meadows, reported missing. The flat she occupied has also been entered and most thoroughly searched. No telling if anything was taken, but nothing whatever found to throw any light on her personality or her past. That suggests, of course, that it was the murderer himself, and that his aim was to remove everything of the sort."

"Yes, I can see that," Wynne agreed. "But surely not here, or at Maxton's place. A murderer would never risk returning, would he? I'm sure I shouldn't. I should keep as far away as long as possible."

"You are sure no valuables have been taken, no papers of any sort?" Bobby asked again.

"I'm pretty certain none at all," Wynne assured him. "Anyhow, my wall safe's not been disturbed. Behind that picture," he said, indicating one hanging on the wall near the french window. "I keep anything important either there or at the bank. Not that there's anything much in it at the moment." He showed a brown-paper parcel, lying on a chair near. "I've paid four thousand—guineas—for that this afternoon," he said. Bobby regarded the brown-paper parcel with a respect seldom accorded to brown-paper parcels. "That's what I've been in town for," Wynne resumed. "Stamps. Unless I'm badly mistaken I can keep those I want and sell off the rest by degrees to show a good profit. The advantage of paying cash down. Most people can't resist a good fat roll of crisp, new bank-notes. If the man I bought from—it was his father's collection, I knew him slightly—had employed an expert to sort it out and then sold separately, he could have got two or three times what I gave him. But it would have taken a year or more and waiting your chance—and taking it. When I began to cover the table with bundles of a hundred one-pound notes, more than he could resist."

"Very interesting," Bobby said, and indeed found it even more so than his tone suggested.

He looked vaguely round the room, expecting to see some signs of Mr Wynne's own collection: whole rows of stamp-albums, perhaps. Mr Wynne noticed that wandering eye.

"Oh, I keep mine upstairs," he explained. "Too bulky for here." He indicated the brown-paper parcel again. "Only the cream of the collection," he explained. "The rest is coming later."

"I don't think," Bobby said, "I had realized stamp collections could be so valuable, but I daresay they make a good investment."

"None better," Mr Wynne assured him. "Stocks and shares, outside your control. Slumps, take-over bids, other people's skill and knowledge—all kinds of unpredictable factors. With stamps you depend on yourself alone. No income tax either. Capital gains. I estimate my collection upstairs is worth a hundred per cent more than it cost me, and that should make a very substantial addition to what there'll be for Sylvia when I've gone." And, with these last words, there came again into his voice that warmth, that kind of inner glow, which seemed always to be there when he spoke of his daughter.

"I can understand that," Bobby remarked as he rose to go. "Needs very good judgment, though—knowledge as well. Brains. I'm afraid I should soon find myself in Queer Street."

"Oh, well," Mr Wynne said; and was that aloof, impassive man susceptible, if to little else, at least to the very common, almost universal weakness of vanity? It seemed so, for surely that was a touch of gratification, of pleasure, which flickered and passed across his usually unmoved countenance. "Well, you see," he went on, "before I retired I was a buying agent in the City," and once again that strange, almost imperceptible smile hovered for a moment as a shadow on his lips and was gone. "So I got plenty of experience. Buy or sell for anyone, anywhere, any time, anything. Always on commission. I took no risks. Studied the market, too. Very important. Some city folk still remember me, and it's known I pay cash down, so when people want to realize in a hurry they often come to me. Money on the table, that's my ace of trumps."

"A very nice ace of trumps, too," Bobby said smilingly. "One we in the police can't play, unfortunately. But I mustn't forget what brought me here. You mentioned once that Miss Wynne saw lights in the copse late at night, shortly before the murder took place. Do you think it possible it might have been Maxton?"

"Maxton?" Wynne repeated. "Why Maxton specially? No, I don't see what he could be doing there at that time. It was Stuart I thought of at once. I knew his mania about trespassers and then all those old stories of church plate and so on buried by the old monks. Yes, definitely. I remember very well thinking it would be Stuart busy chasing probably entirely imaginary trespassers away. Of course, a mere passing fancy. I never gave it a second thought."

"We should very much like to know who it was and what he was after," Bobby remarked. "One thing more. You remember the loganberry bush where the murder took place? Dug up now. Mr Kimms made a thorough job of it. Sir Charles was very angry, I believe, as his permission hadn't been asked. I must say he seems an extremely touchy gentleman, very strong on his property rights. Have you any idea whether that bush was an offshoot from your garden or if it's the other way round and they are its progeny?"

"I'm afraid I can't say; no idea," Wynne answered; and this time his smile was broad, as if he thought it a very wild sort of question. "I don't even know when I noticed it first. Probably planted there as a kind of rallying point. Perhaps lovers wanting somewhere definite to meet. Or it might be for children planning a raid on Stuart's precious blackberries—anything."

"Yes, I daresay," Bobby agreed. "Something like that, anyhow. Not that it matters much," and soon after he took his leave.

CHAPTER XV
CHARACTER SKETCHES

IT WAS IN a thoughtful and troubled mood that Bobby walked back to the village. Links there must be, he was convinced, between these three breakings in and the murder, and yet it was difficult to imagine what possible 'tie-up' there could be. Rogers had seemed the obvious intruder both at the Old Dower House and at Hidden Cottage, but not at Oxton Court. There the object had clearly been to remove every clue to the identity of the occupant or her background, and that did not seem likely to interest Rogers so greatly as to make him ready to run the risk of interruption and arrest in such suspicious circumstances.

"Someone who knew a bit, though," Bobby told himself. "Novices aren't generally up to dealing with Yale locks. I wonder if Maxton is? Journalists pick up odd bits of knowledge sometimes," and with this reflection he went on at a brisker pace to the Over All Arms, where he had left his car and where Mr Kimms had established temporary headquarters. Kimms had not yet returned, and Sergeant Jenkins, left in charge, appeared to have been keeping a somewhat anxious look-out for Bobby.

"The Super told me he had dropped you off at the Old Dower House," he told Bobby. "I tried to ring you, but I couldn't get through."

"Anything fresh turned up?" Bobby asked.

"Well, sir, it's just that Sir Charles has been on the line. Very impatient gentleman. He was wanting Mr Kimms to go to the Abbey immediate. I had to say he couldn't, being in conference, so then he said you would do, if you'll excuse me repeating it, sir, and to come immediate."

"Me?" exclaimed Bobby, surprised. "Why? How does he know I'm here?"

"Oh, well, sir," Jenkins explained, "in a manner of speaking, everyone knows. Saw you come, and now they're all telling each other you're here. Very keyed up, sir, they are, murders being uncommon rare in our neighbourhood and something to talk about. Vicar says there hasn't been such a thing in Twice Over for more'n three hundred years, which is a tidy bit, and if you ask me, sir, I could do with it if there hadn't been one for another hundred and more, all of us being run clean off our feet."

"Yes, I know," Bobby said sympathetically. "Murderers never stop to think of all the work they give other people. Very kind of Sir Charles to say I would do, but he'll have to do without instead. It's in Mr Kimms's hands, and very capable hands, too. Not for us at the Yard—unless asked," he added, keeping his voice under strict control, lest it might be thought he was asking to be asked.

"Well, sir, as far as that goes," Jenkins went on, "when I rang the Super about Sir Charles being on the line, he said to say if you could spare the time he would be much obliged, murder being a thing we haven't much experience of, and Sir Charles very touchy and impatient and best to keep in with when same can be."

"Oh, of course, if Mr Kimms says so," Bobby answered this plea, trying as he did so to make his voice sound more reluctant than reluctance itself. "We are certainly interested at the Yard—what with identification established, and the chance of recovering some of the stolen P.O. van pound-notes. One of the gang murdered immediately afterwards too. We would like to clear that up, if possible. All very intriguing, if only we could make even a guess at the connecting link. There must be one. Don't you think so, Jenkins?"

"Oh, yes, sir," promptly agreed Jenkins, who in fact had never thought about it at all, since in his opinion thinking was for the 'high-ups', who were paid accordingly, and not for sergeants and constables, who weren't.

"That's all right, then," decided Bobby, now trying to pretend to himself that he had been in some doubt whether to fall in with Mr Kimms's suggestion. "The Abbey's not much out of my way, and I'll let you people know if Sir Charles has anything interesting to say. When your Super gets back, tell him Mr Wynne says he found an intruder in his house, but nothing was taken. He tried to ring you, but couldn't get through either. Looks as if the 'phone wire had been cut—and looks as if Maxton's visitor had paid a visit as well to the Old Dower House. I'll send a full report as soon as I get back to the Yard. A difficult man to understand—Wynne, I mean. Well liked here, though, isn't he?"

"I don't know as I would say liked exactly, sir," Jenkins replied with some hesitation. "Respected more, if you see what I mean. Comes in here for a drink of an evening and sits and watches, never speaking unless spoke to, just sitting and watching. Mr Harris—he's the landlord—says it's like a cat watching mice at play, but too well fed to want to pounce, only you know he may. Now, that young lady of his—a treat for sore eyes, she is, always a smile and a happy sort of look to her, as if nothing ever could be wrong anywhere."

"He seems very fond of her," Bobby remarked.

"That's right, sir," Jenkins agreed. "The apple of his eye, if you see what I mean." He paused, reflected, and then, a little pleased with the phrase, repeated it: "The apple of his eye, and nothing he wouldn't do for her."

"Miss Wynne was on her way to Maxton's cottage when we met her," Bobby went on. "Apparently she had heard he was there again, and wanted to be sure. Is there supposed to be anything between them, do you know?"

"Nothing official like," Jenkins answered. "More like walking out together only for being gentry as don't; but sweet on each other, as all can see. But young they are, especially her, and Mr Wynne has money, and Mr Maxton—very nice young gentleman. Every one's a good word for him—but no proper job. Only writing and such like, and not even proper books—guides to places, same as they send you free from the seaside. So you can't wonder if Mr Wynne doesn't like it too well, if you see what I mean. But she'll get him all right if she wants him, same as she would have the moon, if wanted and he could get it for her."

"Yes, I know," Bobby said. "No sign of Dowie turning up here, I suppose? We've got a photo of Maxton now, and at the Over All Arms they gave you a good description of Dowie, didn't they? Tall, pale, shambling sort of walk and squeaky voice and big nose? One of the best we've had. I don't want to use it yet, though, or the Maxton photo either. Too much publicity too soon might drive them both further underground. What about Sir Charles Stuart? What can you tell me about him? Popular, isn't he?"

"Oh, yes, easy to get on with unless rubbed the wrong way, as happens. You know where you are with him, and if there's more nieces in his family than Vicar thinks ought to be—well, nothing he can do about it. Vicar says when he's at outs with both gentlemen—with Mr Wynne for never

showing at church and with Sir Charles because of his nieces, though such may happen to any man and no fault of his,
as Sir Charles would do and be done with it and Mr Wynne
wouldn't either, but only remember. I don't know what he
means, in a manner of speaking."

"A bit complicated," Bobby agreed. "Mr Wynne is certainly
an unusual sort of man. Difficult to know what to make of him.
He gives me the idea, when I'm speaking to him, of having a
sort of secret joke he wants to smile over but won't, for fear of
having to explain. Puzzling. I expect there's a lot of talk and
gossip going on?"

"Talking their heads off, all of 'em," Jenkins agreed, "as you
can't be surprised at with them two gents finding the corpse
hand in hand in a manner of speaking. But Mr Kimms says to
take no notice—gossip it is, and as such to be treated."

"Gossip," Bobby told him, "is often important. I've sometimes thought it could be called the intuition of the common
man."

"Yes, sir," said Jenkins, looking slightly dazed at this pronouncement.

"Which means," Bobby added, "never neglect it."

"Oh, no, sir, never," agreed Jenkins, still a little bewildered, and then in a gallant effort to hold his own, "Not as you
get much chance, with all of 'em running to tell you the latest
as you've heard fifty times before."

"Well, I'll get along to the Abbey," Bobby said. "A waste of
time, probably, but you never know. Many thanks, though, for
the very interesting character sketches you've given me."

"Yes, sir; certainly, sir," said Jenkins, pleased; but once
again more than a little baffled, for he did not know he had
done anything of the kind.

"Know your man," Bobby went on, but speaking as much
to himself as to Jenkins, "his character, his disposition, how
he is likely to behave, and you're half-way there. Worth more
than all the cigar ash and magnifying glasses put together."

"Yes, sir," repeated Jenkins, not so much dazed now as
worried, for he thought Bobby's eye was fixed on him with a

severe and challenging gaze, "which is same as often said by me to the missus. Cigar ash, if any, as isn't here, is what you want, I tell her."

"Well, I'll be off," Bobby repeated; and this time really went, much to the relief of Jenkins, who later on confided to his 'missus' that the London man talked funny like, but did talking funny ever bring in your man? And Mrs Jenkins told him to hurry up and eat his supper and get to bed, before being called out again, as was more than likely.

It was still fairly early when Bobby drove up to the Abbey to be at once conducted to what Sir Charles called his 'den' known also as 'study', though no studying was ever done there, or as library, though there no book was ever opened. It was a big, badly lighted room, crowded with heavy mahogany furniture of the mid-Victorian period. Most of it had been pushed aside, apparently, as if to get it out of the way. An incongruous roll-top desk, introduced by Sir Charles himself, was probably the only addition since first furnishing. In one corner a footstool was lying on its side, very much as if it had been kicked there in a moment of impatience. A commonplace room, Bobby thought, untidy, not well cared for—a carpet that needed sweeping and chairs and tables that had known no polish for years. There was a faint smell of alcohol in the air, but all in all little or nothing to give much idea of the personality of the occupier. On the walls were paintings, cosy, friendly productions. Bobby eyed them with appreciation. He knew that now these were slowly creeping back into auction-room favour from that nadir of contempt to which informed criticism of the day has been so busy condemning them. And on the shelves round the walls were long, serried rows of books that again for many years had known no other touch than the flick of the domestic duster or a whisk of a passing feather brush.

Though so different in every way from the room at the Old Dower House, yet there remained one point of resemblance. The rather prim tidiness of that, the rather conventional bachelor neglect of this, both served to prevent anything emerging in any way likely to give a clue to the occupant's real personality. True, at the Old Dower House there was to be felt the impress of a powerful, yet secret and withdrawn personality, while here there was only a suggestion of a commonplace temperament unable to impress itself on its surroundings, accepting them, with no impulse to do otherwise.

Sir Charles himself—big, burly, red-faced as ever—was standing near the window, hands thrust deep into pockets, looking impatient and out of temper.

"Oh. it's you," he grumbled as Bobby entered. "Where's Kimms? You're the London bloke, aren't you?"

"I am," Bobby said tartly, not much liking this greeting. "I understand you have information to give. I hope that is so. I am here at some inconvenience, and I have no time to spare. Wouldn't it have saved time if you had simply rung up?"

CHAPTER XVI
CONTINENTAL TRIP

SIR CHARLES GREETED these remarks with a formidable scowl. For a moment, indeed, he seemed inclined to make an equally tart reply. Then apparently he changed his mind. Probably Bobby's manner did not suggest that tart retorts would be received with any noticeable meekness. So instead Sir Charles opened a small cupboard and produced whisky and soda-water.

"What about a drink?" he said.

"Thank you, no," Bobby answered with decision. "I never drink on duty and I never drink when I'm driving. May I hear what it is you wish to tell us?"

Sir Charles put down the bottle from which he had already begun to fill a glass. He was looking very surprised. For any one to refuse a drink—first-class pre-war whisky too—was almost outside his experience, varied though that was.

"Oh, well," he grumbled. "There's such a lot of talk going on, you don't know what to believe. Is it true you want to know what's become of that young blighter, Maxton? Because, if you do, he's in France."

"France?" Bobby repeated. If that was so, it was going to make things very difficult. "Are you sure?" he asked.

Sir Charles moved over to his roll-top desk. He fumbled for a moment or two and then produced a letter.

"There you are," he said. "Read that; read the postscript. That's what counts with women—the postscript. You can bet your last potato on that."

Bobby took the proffered letter. It was addressed to 'Boy-o', from an hotel in Paris, and was signed simply 'Joey'. The body of the letter contained the information that 'Joey' had had a good passage, that the hotel wasn't too bad, but not quite what 'Joey' was used to, and that she was 'moving on' next morning. The postscript ran:

"Whoever do you think I met on the boat? Give you three guesses? But you never would. That nice young Marty Maxton. Such a charming boy. He said he was expecting to make a long trip—a travel book. All the go, he says, and he's cashing in. So thrilling."

"Who is Joey?" Bobby asked when he had read this.

"A niece of mine," Sir Charles stated, staring hard at Bobby, and clearly on the look-out for any reaction produced by this statement. Bobby's impassive face showed none. "Calls me 'Boy-o'. Always has. Baby talk. Did it in her cradle, and keeps it up."

"Is she a friend of Mr Maxton's?" Bobby asked, ignoring these touching reminiscences.

"They met when she was on a visit here. They would. Trust Joey to meet any young man anywhere near. Maxton didn't mind. Infernal young blighter."

Bobby was beginning to see light. He remembered hearing mention of Sir Charles's 'nieces'. It seemed possible that, the 'visit' having terminated, 'Joey' was trying to play Maxton as a card for a renewal thereof. Possibly again with a view to matrimony and a vision, should that prove boring, of alimony in the distance.

"Is the young lady to be trusted?" he asked doubtfully.

"Well, I don't see why she should be lying," Sir Charles answered equally doubtfully. "'Charming boy' indeed. She knows I can't stand him. Gives himself airs, and he's nothing but a cheap, penny-a-liner journalist. Lives in a tumble-down cottage you can hardly find—five bob a week, most likely. Look. I don't want Joey's name mentioned. That's really why I didn't 'phone. You might as well use the public crier as the 'phone in this hole."

"Is Miss Joey likely to be long away?" Bobby asked. "It seems a bit of a coincidence that she should happen to meet Maxton like that."

"Coincidence my foot," retorted Sir Charles. "Got it out of him when he was meaning to cross, and took care to be on the same boat so as to be able to tell me. Get anything out of anyone, she would. She won't be away long, I don't expect. Gone to see her step-father and get some money out of him. He's French. Look. All this talk going on. Can't you do something to stop it?"

"Dominion over palm and pine? Yes," Bobby answered. "Dominion over life and liberty? That's easy. Dominion over wagging tongues? That's different. What are they saying?"

"You don't suppose they say it to me, do you?" Sir Charles snapped. "It's got round that you came down here about that big P.O. robbery there was years ago. Kimms seems to think he's on something to do with it. The stuff they got away with buried near here, perhaps. Oodles of it, apparently, all cash. Well, it does happen I made a big killing on the Stock Exchange about the same time. Nothing wrong in that, is there?"

"Matter for congratulation," Bobby assured him. "Every City man's favourite dream. I am sure you could easily satisfy Mr Kimms if you cared to. He would certainly appreciate it."

"I thought you might help if I put all my cards on the table," Sir Charles said moodily. "It's Wynne started it all. Done me down two or three times already—that Atropos statue and the lease trick—and now fixing it so I should be the one to find that poor devil of a woman's body. I wouldn't put it past him to have done it himself. God knows why."

"I wouldn't say that to anyone else," Bobby remarked. "Might lead to serious trouble. I think I've told you so before."

"Oh, I know, I know," growled Sir Charles. "But I'll swear he knew. He always knows. Sits there, all eyes and ears, and hardly ever speaks, but always ready to drop in a word to turn things the way he wants. I can't stand the fellow. How the devil he managed to have a girl like Sylvia, I don't know. Even Joey calls her a sight for sore eyes, skipping along the way she does, as if no one ever had a care in the world. And Joey hasn't much use for other girls—too competitive, I suppose. So I gave her a drink or two, and then she was happy, too, and so was I," and he finished with a grin that made Bobby feel he would rather like to push it down his throat.

"Did it last?" Bobby asked.

"Our being happy?" Sir Charles asked in his turn. "Well, it never does, does it?"

Ignoring this question, to which he felt many replies could be made, all different, Bobby went on:

"Mr Wynne tells me he very seldom uses that copse path. Damp and overgrown in places. It seems, though, that Miss Wynne saw a light there the night before the murder. None on the murder night itself. Mr Wynne told me that at the time he thought it might have been you on the look-out for trespassers."

"Just what he would say," Sir Charles grumbled. "A word in season, that's him, and next thing you know every one has heard it and no one knows who started it. No need to ask how he got his money. Buying agent, he says. Doing people down more likely, same as he did me."

"Isn't there some story of the old monks having buried the monastery treasure in the copse?" Bobby asked. "People seem to have started looking for it again recently—or else for the pound-notes from the P.O. robbery, if that's got about, too. Trespassing, of course, and very annoying."

"Well, I have been keeping an eye on the place," Sir Charles admitted. "But not at night. Break your neck as likely as not, tripping over roots and brambles, or getting your eyes scratched out. All tommy-rot about the monastery treasure, though if it is there, it's mine. Treasure trove. If anyone's really looking for it, you can bet your last potato it's Wynne himself, trying to do me down again."

"Well, we should very much like to know who was showing a light there the night before the murder, and why," Bobby said. "I'm accepting it as true. I don't feel if Mr Wynne had invented the story he would have said it was Miss Sylvia saw it. She would always tell the truth, and if she didn't anyone could tell at once."

"Wouldn't know how to lie even if she wanted to," Sir Charles agreed grudgingly, resentfully almost, as if unwilling to make any such admission in which he sensed there lurked somewhere a rebuke to others.

It was, Bobby felt, an unconscious tribute to the kind of aura of a joyous and completely integrated integrity which seemed to accompany Sylvia wherever she went. He found himself wondering, a little uneasily, how life would deal in days to come with one who seemed to find in it only sunny hours. He noticed that Sir Charles was looking at him with some curiosity—uneasiness, too, perhaps—as if wondering for his part what had plunged Bobby so deep in thought. He got to his feet to go, and Sir Charles's relief was almost palpable.

For many reasons, most of them accumulating on his desk at the Yard, Bobby was anxious to get back to town, but he decided, he must first discuss with Kimms the implications of Maxton's reported visit to France. The comment made by Kimms, now returned from his conference, was characteristic. It consisted of the one word:

"Awkward."

"Very," agreed Bobby. "Nothing like enough to apply for an extradition order on. We could ask to be kept informed if anything is heard of Maxton and if he registers anywhere in his own name. But nothing much else, for the time anyhow."

"No," said Kimms. "That boat meeting. Put-up job?"

"Oh, yes," Bobby agreed again. "That's fairly clear. Prefabricated, as the business people say. But why and who by? The

Joey girl? Her postscript shows she was trying to use Maxton as a prod to Stuart. But was Maxton using her to let us know he was out of our reach? If he was, why? Just cocking a snook at us? That would mean he is the murderer? Or would it?"

To this question, when Bobby paused to let the other reply, Kimms returned his favourite observation, only more drawn-out than usual.

"Um-m-m-m," he said.

Bobby nodded in full agreement. The two men sat and looked at each other. Then Bobby said:

"I had quite a long chat with Stuart, trying to weigh him up."

"Get anywhere?" Kimms asked.

CHAPTER XVII
FIVE FOR CHOICE

IT WAS A question Bobby found difficult to answer, so he lapsed into a silence as complete as that in which Kimms sat ruminating. Indeed, it was Kimms who spoke first. He said:

"Chap on the run? The one we want?"

"Yes, I know," Bobby agreed. "As a rule, but not always. Fear, not guilt, perhaps. But there are other things against him. Woman answering dead woman's description reported seen by Wynne near Maxton's cottage. Faint flavour of black-mail about it, too."

"Confirmatory evidence," Kimms said. "Strange woman seen by others making regular monthly calls, but descriptions differ."

"Descriptions always do," Bobby remarked. "Nothing except Wynne's story to suggest connection with Mrs Field. She certainly had more money than she got at the 'Bell and Boy'. That would hardly have paid the rent of her Oxton Court flat. And why her sort of double life, and what for? And what was her extra source of income?"

"Maxton?" Kimms suggested.

"There's nothing to suggest that he had any money be-yond what he earned as a writer," Bobby objected. "And that wouldn't be much. It's only the very tip-top ones who make money, and they don't always. Still, we know nothing about his background. Have to make inquiries. His friendship with Miss Wynne was no secret, apparently, and Mrs Field may have known something to put a stopper on his hopes in that direction."

"Wife?" suggested Kimms.

"Eh? Whose? Maxton's?" Bobby asked, rather taken aback by this flight of the imagination. "Well, I suppose youngsters do make fools of themselves with barmaids at times, but that does not seem to explain either her double life or where the money for it came from. Why, too, did she insist on keeping that tin of loganberries in plain view on a shelf behind the bar at the 'Bell and Boy', and another such tin in her flat, and then meet her death by a loganberry bush? There must," said Bobby, with a kind of angry exasperation, "be some meaning to it all, if only we could hit on it."

"Loose ends," said Kimms. "The whole case. Got to tie 'em up."

"Got to make 'em meet first," Bobby retorted. "I don't know that I see young Maxton as a killer."

"All may be," Kimms said. "You, me—anyone."

"That tin of loganberries," Bobby repeated. "I can't help thinking that in it there lies the key to it all. And Sylvia Wynne, does she come in somehow?"

"No," said Kimms firmly.

"Oh, I didn't mean that," Bobby said. "My feeling is that if she wasn't what she is, this might never have happened. I don't know. Wynne worries me. There's that sort of imperceptible smile of his, as if he knew it all but wasn't telling, and it amused him. You've noticed it?"

"No," said Kimms, even more firmly than before.

"He's a man so secret you feel he must have something to hide," Bobby continued. "Not much to take into court, I grant you." Kimms grunted acquiescence—emphatic acquiescence. "And if Stuart is right—as I think he may be—in believing that Wynne knew the position of the dead body—well, how did he know?"

"If," said Kimms. "Ifs aren't evidence."

"No," agreed Bobby. "But 'ifs' do at times turn into pots and pans for tinkers and detectives, too. Stuart himself became suddenly rich soon after the first big P.O. robbery. He has his explanation pat, but I can see the shadow of an 'if' there, too. My reading of his character is that he might kill in rage or fear, while Wynne, I think, would kill very quietly, but only in cold blood—only if he had to, all risks calculated. Then in the background Mr Dowie, and was the treasure he was looking for not the legendary one the old monks are supposed to have buried, but the cache of pound-notes from the P.O. van?"

"Yes," said Kimms.

"There you are, then," Bobby said; and at the 'there,' he looked rather moodily, with very little idea in his mind of where to go from this 'there'. "About the most puzzling case we've had to do with since those Old People's Home murders. Thank goodness, I had nothing to do with that. It's almost certainly one of those five, though."

"Which?" said Kimms.

"All lined up for you to make your choice," Bobby told him, scowling at the five as he spoke, as if they were actually ranged before him in their own persons. "Wynne; and why is he so secret, so knowing, with that tiny smile you never see till it has gone?"

"Gone?" repeated Kimms, and meant how can you when it's gone, but did not say so.

"Stuart, and why so suddenly rich?" Bobby went on.

"It happens," said Kimms, and meant 'but never to me'.

"Maxton," continued Bobby; "and if he's innocent, why in France?"

"Ah," said Kimms, and meant 'he's my man'.

"Mr Dowie," Bobby continued; "and what was he after with his treasure-hunting gadget?"

"U-m-m-m," said Kimms, and meant he didn't think Dowie was worth bothering about.

"Not forgetting," Bobby concluded, "Jolly Rogers, and how much did the Milkman tell him in gaol? Oh, and Miss Wynne. A delightful little person in herself and a pleasure to watch, like a dawn in May; but has she been a kind of catalyst to change the way things had to happen. And there's a very nice little set-up I'm leaving you to handle."

"Thanks," said Kimms, and meant the opposite.

"Oh, we'll do our share," Bobby promised him. "I'll try to pep up our inquiries at our end, and if we manage to dig up anything, we'll call you pronto."

"Thanks," said Kimms, but in a slightly different tone of voice.

"Well, I must be off," Bobby said; and then, as he got to his feet there came a knock at the door and Sergeant Jenkins appeared.

"Sir Charles on the line," he announced. "Says suspicious-looking stranger found in copse near scene of murder. Is detaining same and now awaiting your arrival to take over. Requests immediate action."

"O.K.," said Kimms. "Tell him so. Coming?" he asked Bobby, who nodded assent, and as he had left his car just outside the inn entrance, in this they drove to the Abbey, only to be greeted with the disappointing news that the captive had made his escape.

"I had him safe," Sir Charles explained. "By his arm—you can't wriggle out of your arm. He was quiet as a lamb. He knew he had better. Took me off my guard, a twist and a wriggle and he was off like a shot and out by the garden door where I had brought him in. Too quick he was for me, and not a man around to help; only the maids all squawking their heads off."

"Middle-aged chap," Bobby said. "About five feet four. Square head. Square, heavy build. Grey, bloodshot eyes; thin sharp features; long nose; two front teeth missing; prominent ears. Wearing dirty raincoat and soft hat over eyes. Is that right?"

"How the devil did you know?" demanded Sir Charles, opening wide his mouth.

"I suspected it might be a man recently released from prison," Bobby explained, though he hated having to give explanations that took away all glamour from any little attempt at swanking he might be tempted to make. "Bad record," he went on, as he watched Sir Charles's mouth close again. "The Old Dower House was entered earlier, though no one was seen. Mr Kimms and I both thought it was probably the same man."

"Ah," said Kimms, who hadn't thought anything of the kind, but was now deciding that anyhow he soon would have. "'Phone?" he asked, and without waiting for assent went off to use it where he had seen it lying on a table in the hall.

"Well, what did the fellow want, if he was at Wynne's place as well?" demanded Sir Charles, without noticing this. "Why Wynne, too?"

"That's what we should like to know," Bobby said. "If you had been able to hold him, we might have got something out of him. We may still, if we can bring him in. That's what Mr Kimms is trying to arrange now. He'll probably go underground, though, and it may be days before we can pick him up. Could you tell me exactly what happened?"

"Unders—he does odd jobs here, makes himself generally useful, or says he does—was going home when he noticed this fellow hanging about by the copse path. I had warned him to let me know at once if he saw anything suspicious, so he came back and told me, and I went out to see for myself. Well, there this fellow was, poking about just where it happened. I collared him. He tried to put up a fight, but that game didn't last long, and I took him along here to wait for you. Where I slipped up, though. Took me off my guard, he did, and off like hell."

"Too bad," Bobby said.

"May get him yet," said Kimms, who by now had returned from the 'phone.

"Looks to me as if he might be the man you want," Sir Charles said. "If you know him, you ought to be able to get him all right."

"Get him, question him, let him go," said Kimms moodily. "That's all."

"Nothing much to hold him on," Bobby agreed. "Not yet. But he might talk."

Sir Charles expressed a strong opinion that there was plenty to hold him on. Bobby said the thing was to get a magistrate to think so. Kimms expressed his appreciation of all Sir Charles had done. Outside, driving away in their car, Bobby said:

"It must have been Jolly Rogers Stuart collared; but why did he let him go again?"

"Think he did?" Kimms asked.

"That's the idea I got," Bobby said. "Stuart's the sort of man to stick to what he's got. There's someone signalling us," he added, as he stopped the car.

"Him," said Kimms.

CHAPTER XVIII
ALIBI

FROM THE DARKNESS now swiftly gathering in the shadows by the wayside there emerged a hesitating figure—that of Jolly Rogers—and approached the car.

"Ah, you," Bobby said. "Jump in."

"I dunno as—" began Jolly; but Bobby cut him short, repeating an invitation that sounded very much like a command, and one Jolly obeyed, though very much in the manner of the animal-trainer who places his head in the lion's mouth without being too sure either of the lion's temper or his own courage. "What's the big bloke up there been saying?" he asked somewhat anxiously, as he settled himself in the back of the car.

Bobby, driving on, made no reply. The distance to the Over All Arms was not great, and soon they were there. They all three alighted, and Jolly, looking less and less every minute like his nickname, was ushered within.

"I could do with a drink," he said as they entered.

Bobby gave the expected order, and as soon as they were in the room where Kimms had established himself, supplemented it with a cigarette and said:

"We've been looking for you."

"What for, guv'nor?" Jolly asked. "You've nothing against me. Has the big bloke—"

"He caught you in the copse, didn't he?" Bobby interrupted. "What were you doing there?"

"Just having a dekko. Spot marked with an X," retorted Jolly, his natural confidence fast returning under the combined influence of beer and cigarette. "That big bloke, he's a wrong 'un himself, for all his coming the swell the way he does."

"Is that why he let you go?" Bobby asked, careful to show no surprise at this statement and relieved to notice that Kimms, too, had received it with the same equanimity—but, then, Bobby had long ago realized that it took much to disturb Kimms.

"In a manner of speaking, it was," Jolly admitted. "Did he let on? Took him all in a heap like when he saw I knew, but I didn't wait to talk it over. Saw my chance and took it, and I heard him shouting away behind me, but I didn't hear him running any. I hung around a bit, and I saw you coming, so I reckoned I might as well ask what sort of a yarn he had been pitching."

"Never mind that just now," Bobby said. "Why do you call him a wrong 'un?"

"Well, I don't know as I did ought to say," Jolly answered, looking even more cunning than usual. "Might be putting you off, and you would be saying I done it of purpose."

"This is a murder inquiry," Bobby reminded him sternly. "We know that before his death Charley Cream talked to you about the first big P.O. van robbery, and we know that after your release you boasted he had given you information about where some at least of the stolen money was still hidden."

"Shooting off my mouth, guv'nor, that's all; strike me dead," protested Jolly.

"Probably what Charley Cream told you referred to the copse here," Bobby went on. "Not much help in itself. You couldn't dig up the whole copse. But you were seen near it shortly before the murder."

"I've an alibi, guv'nor," Jolly interposed; and when Bobby seemed but little impressed, for his opinion of alibis was that, like pie-crusts, they were made to be broken, Jolly added earnestly: "A genu-ine, true alibi, guv'nor, what stands up along of so being," and as he said this he looked a little surprised himself, as though such a thing as an alibi of truth was so rare he could hardly believe it himself. "Straight, guv'nor, I didn't know nothing, except that the Milkman, all wandering like and out of his mind, kept on about tinned loganberries, and none I asked knew what that meant—only some sort of password. So I come down here to see if anyone knew anything about tinned loganberries, which they didn't, only thinking me being funny; but then it was in all the papers about her as was done in being found near a loganberry bush, but where it all fits in is more than none can tell, and me with no thought in my mind, only the reward as was offered for recovery of the stuff, and no harm in that, guv., now is there?"

"None," Bobby agreed; "no offence in the world if that were all. No, don't go yet," he added as Jolly scrambled to his feet. "Got a good deal more to tell us, haven't you? Let's look at it another way. There's the Milkman's story, and if you can find out a little more you may be able to get hold of the hidden money—if it exists. So you start asking questions, and you hear there's a barmaid at the 'Bell and Boy', who keeps a tin of loganberries in full view of all customers, but no one knows why, and she won't say. That fits in with what Charley Cream told you. You visit the 'Bell and Boy' to see if you can get anything out of her. You don't, but she gets out of you, or hears in some other way that it's Twice Over you're interested in. So she follows you here. That doesn't suit you. You don't mean anyone else to get those notes, but if she has some idea of their exact position, she may be induced to tell. Did you try, and if you did, what happened next? Or did she tell, but claim too big a share, perhaps—and, if so, again what happened?"

"For God's sake, Mr Owen, sir," Jolly protested. He had become very pale. He took out his handkerchief, twisting it uneasily between his hands. When Bobby did not speak, but only watched him, he went on: "There's my alibi. You can't get over that. You check up, Mr Owen. That's all I say. It's straight, it is. I caught the last train that night, and a gent, in my carriage, just us two, was took bad. Soon as we got in I called the railway blokes, and me and them we got him out, and they sent him off to hospital. You ask them; they'll remember—can't help it. You got to accept that."

"If proof of identity is satisfactory, yes," Bobby agreed. "We will go into it carefully, of course."

"I don't hold with murder," Jolly insisted, finding Bobby's tone less warm than could have been desired. "I never did. A bloke's got to live, hasn't he? And if no one won't give him a job along of his having made a mistake once, what's he to do? But murder's a thing as never brings luck, not even if you get away with it for a time. Not me, Mr Owen, sir," he said, gathering confidence as he talked, but still anxiously watching for any sign to show his story was winning credence. "It's right I came along because of hearing there was a lady seeming interested like in what the Milkman told me before he popped off, but him never saying nothing about no ladies, which same is always best kept out when it's business, and me reckoning I had to know who she was and what she wanted, and if maybe we could do a deal. Most like," he concluded, "there's no money buried there at all and never was, only poor old Milkman wandering like."

"Whether the money was there or not," Bobby said, "it's where a woman was murdered."

"There's my alibi," Jolly repeated, clinging to it like the shipwrecked sailor to his raft. "No getting away from that. And if you ask me, it was that there Dowie bloke did her in. What was he messing about for, as I saw with my own eyes—him and that dodge of his, like what they used for mines in the war, as is different?"

"Mr Dowie?" Bobby repeated, a good deal surprised at the sudden introduction of this name; "what do you know about him?"

"Asking questions," Jolly said with some resentment, for this was an activity of which he did not approve, associated as it was in his mind with the unwelcome methods of the C.I.D.

"He did use to claim it was him found the stuff what was lifted from Wilbraham Hall up north and left behind, only buried, it being too heavy to take when pressed, but safe as houses till this Dowie bloke figured out where it was—him and his dodge. May have been the way it happened here, like you said, Mr Owen, sir, only him, not me, meeting the lady and doing her in because of not wanting to split with her, and it was him bought a spade. In all the papers that was. Shows he meant to dig and knew where—only she was there first, so he had to split or else the other thing. And got no alibi, either, has he? Mr Owen, sir, not forgetting the Superintendent. You pull him in and see."

"Got to find him first," remarked Kimms, but all the same obviously impressed by Jolly's eloquence.

Bobby was silent. It had to be admitted that the provisional theory he had put forward could apply just as well to Dowie as to Jolly, who for his part had certainly shown an unexpected nimbleness of wit in adapting it so quickly to divert suspicion from himself to the vanished Dowie.

"Done a bunk, has he?" inquired Jolly sympathetically. "Daren't face it, as he would if innocent and a straight alibi like me," and his complacent smile expressed now his complete confidence that he had fully established himself in the eyes of his two interrogators.

"Tell me more," Bobby said abruptly, "about these questions you say Dowie was asking?"

"Mostly," explained Jolly, "about stuff hidden after lifting, like he had a notion that when a bloke did a job he just buried what he got all nice and tidy, waiting for him to come along and dig it up. Reaping where others sowed, if you ask me," Jolly concluded disapprovingly.

"Did he seem to know about you and the possible hiding-place of the stolen Post Office notes?"

"He might have," Jolly admitted. "Only human nature when you've been inside, where you never get a drop, to get a bit tiddly when you do come out, and easy to let slip more than you ever meant." Jolly paused for a moment to shake his head at this unfortunate but so understandable human weakness.

He resumed: "Only he got it all mixed up some way with what them old monks and such like used to hide away along of there being no banks in them ancient days. He had a book telling all about it."

"A book?" Bobby repeated. "Do you know what it was called? Who wrote it?"

"I never take much notice of books, only when they're spicy," Jolly answered. "Some sort of guide-book, I think he said."

Bobby glanced at Kimms to see if this had registered. Kimms indicated by a nod that it had. Bobby said:

"Well, all that's very interesting, though I don't know that it takes us much further forward. If your alibi stands up, you're all right, of course; and we will go into it at once. What sort of response was there to Mr Dowie's inquiries? Was he taken seriously? It sounds to me as if he were heading for trouble."

"That's right," Jolly agreed. "Some of the boys wanted to beat him up—not bad like, just enough to teach him as you shouldn't want to know too much about other blokes's business. But some of 'em said to wait and see what he can do with that dodge of his. If it's the goods—O.K., take it over. I stood out. I'm running straight now. Reformed, and if you can help me to get a good job, Mr Owen, sir, you'll never hear no more of me."

"What do you call a good job, and how long would you keep it?" asked Bobby, who had heard this story too often to be much impressed by it. All the same, he gave Jolly an address, and told him if he meant what he said he would be given all the help possible. But Jolly, who knew that address of old, shook his head and murmured something about 'no sympathy, no understanding', and Bobby, who had expected nothing else, went on: "There's one thing more. You called Sir Charles Stuart a 'wrong 'un'. Why? Birds of a feather know each other? Is that the idea? Or do you really know something about him? Oh, and don't lie."

CHAPTER XIX
DIAMONDS

A CERTAIN HESITATION was apparent before Jolly answered this question. One might have surmised he was considering, with some uneasiness, how far he could go without incriminating himself. Bobby waited. Kimms looked at him, clearly wondering why he did not speak again. But Bobby never hurried a witness. He used to say that silence was often as eloquent as speech. Jolly, apparently making up his mind at last, now began to speak, but slowly and with evident caution.

"It's like this," he said. "If he got them diamonds for Fatty Veale on the straight, why does he? That's what I say."

"Does what?" Bobby asked, more than a little taken aback by this sudden introduction of mysterious diamonds into a case already sufficiently baffling.

"Does what I'm telling you of," retorted Jolly, "letting Fatty Veale have 'em instead of going where more would be give but questions asked."

"Who is Fatty Veale?" Bobby asked. "I've never heard of him. Do you mean he's a fence?"

"Well, I wouldn't quite go for to say that," answered Jolly, a little shocked by the use of such blunt language. "It's only that he don't ask questions. If you've the goods, he's got the money, and no more said. No office neither."

"Post Office never reported diamonds missing," Kimms interposed, as bewildered as was Bobby by all this about diamonds.

"Which I never said," retorted Jolly, rather pleased at having so evidently puzzled his two interlocutors. "Nothing to do with it, no more than the new-born babe."

"You haven't told me yet who this Fatty Veale is?" Bobby reminded him.

"Everyone knows that, unless not knowing anything at all," Jolly told him severely, and clearly he now placed Bobby with those in the latter category. "Hatton Garden, like the other blokes, but no office. If you want to sell diamonds and such, and no questions asked, you wait till you spot him having a cup of coffee somewhere and you go and sit at the same table and he don't take no notice, so you put what you have on the table and he names his price, take it or leave it, which you take it, his price being as good as any and better'n most, but a lot less than if it was all on the straight. Smuggles 'em abroad again, if you ask me."

"How do you know all this?"

"Ain't much I don't know when things are moving," Jolly grinned. "And warned him there was talk of a job being done on him, so him, grateful like, and wanting a trustworthy bloke, same as me, ten bob, he paid me regular to sit around handy like, all ready for funny work, if tried. Which I did till put inside, all on account of a bit of bad luck as might have happened to anyone."

"I don't see where all this comes in," Bobby said, but he was looking worried. "What we are working on is who killed Mrs Field and why, and if her murder is in any way tied up with the supposedly buried Post Office pound-notes." He took out his wallet, produced a ten-shilling note, looked at it rather regretfully and passed it across the table. "Sure you've told us all you know?" he asked. "But remember, you are not in the clear till we've tried out that alibi of yours. If it doesn't hold water you won't be long in hearing from us again."

"Hold water?" repeated Jolly, looking really hurt. "Why, guv., it would hold the whole At-a-lantic Ocean."

Therewith he departed. And when he had gone Bobby and Kimms sat for a long time in silence, till at last Kimms broke it by saying aloud:

"The more you know, the less you know."

"Very true," said Bobby, much impressed by this profound observation. "What do you make of all that?"

"Ah," said Kimms. Then he said "U-U-m-m-m," and Bobby nodded his agreement.

"If," he said, half to himself, half to Kimms, who anyhow wasn't listening—"if it's jewellery or something of that sort the crook has to get rid of, he's almost bound to go to a fence, and the fence of course takes the lion's share. Pound-notes are easier, but when you get into the thousands and tens of thousands, there are difficulties. No one takes their numbers, but bank officials can sometimes identify them by private marks and so on; and if they are deposited in bulk, it may easily attract attention, especially after there's been a big-scale robbery. It might give a very useful lead. Or even if we heard that a possible suspect was splashing money about in a big way, always putting down chunks of pound-notes—that again might be a useful lead. And to avoid the risk, some such dodge might be used as buying diamonds on the black market and then selling 'em again."

"Any lead better than no lead," observed Kimms, whose attention had now been caught; and Bobby agreed, and said it was time he got away back to town.

It had grown too late, however, for anything more to be done that night, so he went to bed instead. Next morning the first thing he did, after his usual preliminary glance through the reports and correspondence waiting his attention, was to send for Ford, the young C.I.D. man, who already had been of some help in the case.

"It's the Twice Over murder," Bobby said when Ford appeared. "Jolly Rogers comes into the suspect class. So do several others, for that matter. Jolly claims an alibi. Common form, of course—they always do; but this time he seems confident and says it can be supported by reliable independent witnesses. His story is that on the night of the murder he came up from Twice Over by the last train. He says a man in his compartment was taken ill and that when the train arrived he called the railway people. Check up."

"Very good, sir," said Ford, and departed, and Bobby put another mental good mark against Ford's name.

So many would have asked questions, required more detail, wanted a full description of Jolly, and so on and so forth. Ford had simply accepted his orders, and was content to think out for himself the best way of implementing them.

Satisfied then that this question of the alibi was in good hands, Bobby rang up the City Police force and asked if anything was known of a certain Fatty Veale—a question which seemed to produce a good deal of interest and even excitement at the other end of the line.

"Have you got anything on him?" demanded the telephone hopefully.

"It's only information about him I want, if you've got any," Bobby explained, and the telephone registered resigned disappointment. "His name has cropped up rather vaguely in the Twice Over murder case—not our pigeon exactly, but it does seem connected in some way or another with the P.O. van robbery we've opened up again."

"Yes, I know," the distant voice replied, sounding still more disappointed, "but Fatty Veale isn't likely to have been mixed up in that. Not his line of country at all. Black market and smuggling—especially diamonds and that kind of thing—is his speciality. If it's diamonds, put us wise and we'll follow up. If it isn't, you can probably wash him out."

"One of the suspects in the Twice Over murder seems the connecting link," Bobby said. "There are diamonds in it, too; but no idea how or why. May all come to nothing. If you hear anything fresh about the chap, let us know."

"O.K.," came the prompt reply. "Got your hands full with that Twice Over business, haven't you? You and the local boys."

"You're telling me," retorted Bobby, who always boasted that he could speak three languages fluently—English, French, and American. "An awful snarl of a case."

The telephone told him that a little intellectual exercise in straightening out snarls would help to brighten wits that probably needed it badly; and Bobby was too dispirited even to try to think of an appropriate and sufficiently cutting retort. He simply hung up. Another disappointment for the telephone.

For a time Bobby sat in silence, wondering a little how to set to work to brighten wits that did indeed at the moment seem as if they required a bit of extra polish. Then he applied himself to the routine work needing his attention, and did it badly enough, since all the time his thoughts were elsewhere. Then came lunch—a late lunch—and afterwards he went on to the office of the 'Morning Daily'—a building so enthusiastically up to date when erected that already it seems more old-fashioned than anything from the Victorian era. There he asked for a journalistic acquaintance of his, a Mr McKie, more generally known as Sandy Mac. Fortunately he was available, and he appeared at once.

"Come to papa to help you out," he greeted Bobby cheerfully. "Just tell me what it is and consider it done."

"You've heard about the murder of a woman at Twice Over?" Bobby asked.

"Now, don't tell me there've been sensational developments?" McKie implored. "Such a cliché. We haven't been running it at all. Too many women getting themselves bumped off just now, for one thing. Common form almost. And then I've been away, so there was no one to work it up. It could have been," he added reflectively, "if I had been on hand to do it. Needed someone with the right touch."

"Modesty was always your most marked characteristic," Bobby observed.

"Yes, I know," McKie answered, seriously, even regretfully. "Well, what's the trouble?"

"I didn't say there was any," retorted Bobby. "And I'm not playing Lestrade to an all-wise, all-knowing private eye."

"That's me," said McKie complacently. "Go ahead."

"Can you tell me anything about a Martin Maxton? A journalistic free-lance, apparently, and writes books about the country."

"Maxton?" McKie repeated, and his manner changed perceptibly. "Why? What about him? You don't think he's the unknown murderer, do you?"

"For goodness sake," Bobby said irritably, "don't go jumping to conclusions like a flustered landlady who sees the gallows before her if one of our chaps calls to make some routine inquiry. I simply want any information you can give me about Maxton and his background and so on."

"Well, I can't," McKie answered, not at all pleased by being compared to a flustered landlady. "I don't think anyone can. He's a bit of a mystery man. Blew into Fleet Street some years ago—I couldn't say when exactly—and started sending in his stuff, like several million others. It all went back, of course; and then by some accident—Lord knows how or why—some of it got into print, and that started a weekly series: 'Nature Study in London Squares' it was called, I think. Ran quite well. Now he is entered for the Best-seller Stakes."

"Country Boy Makes Good," Bobby commented. "Ordinary success story; is that all?"

"Success stories aren't ordinary," retorted McKie. "And I never said he was a country boy. But it was his walking in his sleep that really gave him his start."

"And what on earth," demanded Bobby, exasperated by this new twist to the affair, "has walking in your sleep got to do with it?"

CHAPTER XX
THE SLEEP-WALKER

MCKIE HESITATED. He did not seem to wish to answer, and he looked almost imploringly at Bobby, as if he hoped Bobby might just possibly say, 'Oh, well, never mind', and yet knew well that would not be, nor could. And still Bobby waited with his air of inexorable patience that indeed McKie had seen before. McKie said:

"Oh, well, I suppose you would dig it all up anyhow, so I may as well tell you what I know, and then you'll get it right. I was there at the time, you see."

"At the time of the sleep walking?" Bobby asked.

"That's right," answered McKie. "There was a lot of talk. 'The Man with a Past', some of them got to calling him. Occupational disease in our job, thinking in headlines."

"Suppose," Bobby suggested, when McKie seemed inclined once more to lapse into silence, "you tell me what on earth you are talking about. For instance, what walking in your sleep and having a past have got to do with Maxton's getting a start?"

"My dear innocent," retorted McKie, beginning to recover himself, and inwardly hoping that this last word would cut as deep as had Bobby's recent 'flustered landlady', "it all meant publicity," and now this last word was uttered with the reverence, the awe, due to that strange, lime-lit, capricious god whose will and whim have come to rule so much of human destiny.

"Why the publicity?" Bobby asked. "Walking in your sleep isn't so rare as all that, is it?"

"No, but always something uncanny about it, don't you think?" McKie asked in his turn. "Something not quite—right. What is it takes control and works the body perfectly when consciousness isn't there? And when it ends up in what seems like a try at suicide—well, what do you make of it?"

"Why not start at the beginning?" Bobby suggested. "Then perhaps I may be able to make something of it?"

"It was when his stuff was first attracting attention," McKie answered in response to this appeal. "One of the 'Announcer' blokes had the bright idea of taking Maxton on the staff, so as to keep his stuff exclusive to them, and another 'Announcer' bloke thought he was just another of the cub reporters every paper has to take on now and then to oblige somebody's aunt, try out, and sack. Routine. But he did know in a vague sort of way that Maxton was a country boy, so he gave him an assignment to cover a big West-country agricultural show that was on at the moment. I was there to cover the musical festival being held at the same time so the farmers could park their wives out of the way while they got down to the pigs and the cows. Maxton being just a cub reporter on his first—and probably last—assignment, the office booked a room for him in a small cheap hotel right outside the town, and in the middle of the night Maxton walked out of the hotel in his pyjamas. There was a canal running at the back of the hotel, and next thing Maxton was in it. Luckily some wandering night-bird saw him and he was fished out in time. But he acted as if he didn't want to be—fished out, I mean. Afterwards he claimed he must have been still asleep; he didn't remember anything about it. The police claimed that was rather a stiff yarn. They claimed finding yourself in the middle of the night in a canal instead of in your bed would wake up the most hardened sleep-walker that ever was. So they ran him in for attempted suicide, but Maxton got hold of a doctor or two and they talked a lot—induced self-hypnotism and Lord knows what. Anyhow, the jury disagreed, the police dropped the case, and that was that. But it didn't stop the talk; that went on all right. Our job in Fleet Street may be writing, but what we really like is nice spicy libellous talk."

"Yes, I know," Bobby said. "What sort of talk?"

"I don't know exactly. On the 'Macbeth-hath-murdered-sleep' line. There's always been a sort of ravaged look about Maxton, a way he has if you're talking to him of suddenly seeming to lose contact with what you're saying and staring past you at something that isn't there and never was. Some chaps put it down to drink, but it isn't that. Drink doesn't give anyone that sort of look."

"I met him once," Bobby said. "I can't say I noticed all that. He looked nervous, worried. Well, struggling journalists often do."

"Was there a girl, name of Sylvia, knocking about anywhere near at the time?" McKie asked.

"Yes; why?" Bobby asked in some surprise. "Miss Wynne. Have you met her? Where?"

"The office sent me to try to bribe Maxton to leave the 'Daily Announcer' and sign up with us," McKie explained. "Said if anyone could talk him over, it was me. Nothing doing. Maxton didn't want to leave the 'Announcer'. They had given him his first chance and he had a contract. You knew he was living alone in an old cottage, in the middle of nowhere, miles from anywhere?"

"To get material for his nature-studies, I understood," Bobby remarked.

"Not him," retorted McKie. "No writer worth twopence ever wants more material than he can find in the London library."

"Don't go to the ant, go to Fabre instead," commented Bobby. "That the idea?"

"Who is Fabre?" asked McKie, and without waiting for a reply, he went on: "In my idea he's living alone because he's afraid of living alone and wants to get over it. I left my car in the village, and in case I got lost going back, as I had done coming, Maxton walked back with me. We ran across a girl in the village. I shall always remember her. God knows why. You could see a dozen prettier girls in Fleet Street any day. It was something about her—something she carried with her like an aura. Happiness. It was like she had so much of it, it just overflowed all round her. Turned Maxton into quite a different sort of chap—into the ordinary, everyday bloke you felt he was meant to be if something hadn't happened. There wasn't any more of that looking over his shoulder, as if there might be something there he didn't want to see. Sort of gave you the willies to watch—as if you might see it too. He may have a past, but he has a present, too, and I don't believe his present has murder in it."

"There's murder in someone's present," Bobby said grimly, "and we've got to find out whose."

"Well, if you go asking more questions about him up and down Fleet Street he'll be done for," McKie said. "No one likes suspected murderers. Publicity's fine, but it can be overdone. Besides, I've told you all about him, and I know more than anyone else. What's put you on him?"

"The last information we've had," Bobby said, "is that he was seen on a cross-Channel boat going to France."

"Run off?" McKie asked. "I suppose that does look bad. Makes things difficult, too. You can't try your celebrated technique of getting 'em talking, and if they talk, they tell. One of the nurses at the hospital where they took him after the canal business told me that when she asked him how it happened, he said he had a debt to pay, and somehow the way he said it frightened her. You don't think the dead woman at Twice Over—"

"Could be that debt," Bobby completed the sentence when McKie paused. "Possible, of course; but, then, anything's possible in this affair."

"Maxton's under contract to deliver his new country book quite soon," McKie said gloomily. "I don't see why he should go running off like that. The publishers told our literary bloke that Maxton had sent in half his new stuff, and they think it so good they are planning to splash it. They'll be left high and dry if the second half doesn't turn up to date. All their next season's schedule knocked endways. He had a special advance from them, too, on the strength of it, for a new car. Not a thing they would do for every author."

"He doesn't seem to be making much use of it," Bobby remarked. "It's in a Hammersmith garage under close observation in case it's claimed."

He got up to go then, but McKie spoke suddenly.

"You are reopening the killing of one of the gang who brought off that first big P.O. van robbery, aren't you?" he asked.

"Well, I wouldn't say that exactly," Bobby replied, "but we are not forgetting it." He paused then, wondering if McKie too saw the possibility, however vague, of some connection between that half-forgotten, far-distant tragedy and this debt young Maxton had said he owed, and that perhaps had now been paid in full at midnight by the side of a loganberry bush in the Twice Over copse? Changing the subject abruptly, Bobby said: "Did you ever happen to hear of a man named Dowie in connection with Maxton?"

"Dowie?" McKie repeated. "No. Why? Who is he? Another suspect? Never heard of him. You know that girl I told you about. Maxton was pretty badly hit—anyone could see that. Perhaps she turned him down, and that's why he's taken himself off to France—broken heart and all that, and nothing else matters a damn. What do you think of that for a theory? You know, I can't help remembering her and the way she seemed just a sort of living joy scattering it all round. Not quite natural, somehow. Riding for a fall. You felt life's not like that, nor meant to be."

"Or else exactly what it was meant to be if we hadn't messed it up," Bobby retorted.

But McKie shook his head doubtfully, and went on to suggest that in common decency, now that he, Sandy McKie, had given Bobby, as pal to pal, so much highly important information, the least Bobby could do in return was to promise a twenty-four hour 'exclusive' tip-off if and when there was any fresh development. Bobby replied by reminding McKie that he had done no more than his duty as a good citizen, and McKie said "Nuts", and anyhow he wasn't a good citizen, he was a journalist. So Bobby said he fully recognized the distinction, but he would promise that if and when lollipops came to be handed round, McKie might be sure of getting one—an undertaking for which McKie seemed little grateful.

Therewith Bobby departed, and as soon as he was back in his room at the Yard he rang up Messrs Dickens and Defoe, Maxton's publishers, to ask if they had any news of Mr Martin Maxton, who might, Bobby explained carelessly, be able to throw a little light on some small matters of detail.

It appeared that nothing had been heard, and that McKie had in no way exaggerated when he described the firm as worried. They sounded, indeed, almost panic-stricken. They had planned the whole of the coming season's campaign round this one book. The first half was already in print, and if the remainder didn't arrive in time they would, said the scholarly voice at the other end of the line, 'miss the bloody 'bus'. They only hoped that Maxton hadn't met with any accident. Even his friends were getting anxious. A Mr Dowie, for instance, had only a few minutes since been ringing up to inquire, and had seemed quite worried when told no communication had been received from the missing author for some time.

"Authors are so irresponsible," sighed the scholarly voice. "A necessary evil in our job. If only we could do without them!"

"Did Mr Dowie give his address?" Bobby asked, and was told no, but learned in reply to further questioning that it was a long-distance call.

A slender clue indeed. Bobby asked to be informed at once if any similar inquiry was received, then rang off, and at once rang up the Post Office to ask if the place of origin of a long-distance call just made to Messrs Dickens and Defoe could be traced. He received a promise that every effort would be made to do this, and then some time later, indeed not till he was beginning to think of going home, did he get the information that the call had come from Applegarth in Holmshire, and Bobby expressed gratitude for such a prompt reply, while inwardly wondering if it would prove of the slightest use. Still, information was always information, and then, the name of Applegarth seemed somehow vaguely familiar.

But he was not destined to be allowed to depart homeward yet awhile, for Ford appeared, looking very pleased with himself.

"About that alibi of Jolly Rogers, sir," he said. "I thought you would want to know at once."

"Yes, of course," Bobby said, sitting down again. "Go ahead."

CHAPTER XXI
LEGEND

"WELL, SIR, IT'S this way," Ford began, but speaking hesitatingly, as if he felt some difficulty in expressing sufficiently clearly what he wanted to say. "In my view Rogers's alibi is cooked all right, but I'm not sure it wouldn't go down with a jury; I can't put my finger on any obvious flaw. All of the railway staff on duty that night remember a passenger shouting from a carriage window that there was a man taken ill and to get a doctor at once, just how Rogers said. But I couldn't get any description. Whoever it was seems just to have faded away, ghost-like. The railway people didn't even know whether he was tall or short or fat or thin."

"I suppose they were all too busy with the sick man to give the other a thought," Bobby commented. "What about the sick man? He ought to be able to say."

"Yes, sir," agreed Ford. "But he died soon after they got him to hospital. Heart failure."

"That's bad," Bobby said. "Bad all round. No chance of a satisfactory identification, then?"

"No, sir, none at all that I can see. I suppose Rogers might be able to produce some sort of evidence that he was really there. More likely he'll get a pal to swear he saw Rogers that night and Rogers told him all about it, and expecting as much to be done for him when needed. I rang up Twice Over to ask if anyone of Rogers' description was seen leaving by the last train. No one was."

"Negative evidence," Bobby said. "We need a positive statement before we can either break it or accept it as an alibi of truth and consider Rogers cleared. What about tickets?"

"None issued to London by that train," Ford answered; "but Rogers may have had a return, though none seems to have been collected. There was a lot of bustle and excitement, of course, and Rogers could claim it had been forgotten or lost. In my view he could give a prompt answer to any objection raised."

"It does seem the perfect alibi," Bobby agreed. "Which may be because it really is genuine. But it also seems just a little too pat, and one doesn't associate Rogers with anything genuine."

"There's one thing, sir," Ford continued, "that did strike me. Is Rogers likely to have slipped away like that? Not so much of the modest hero about him, in my view."

"No," agreed Bobby, considering this suggestion carefully. "No. I think you've got something there. No. But he knew all about it, apparently?"

"It was in all the evening papers next day," Ford said. "I checked on that. And a par. in two or three of the morning papers the day after. Putting things together and picking up a bit of gossip as well would soon give Rogers enough to make his story stand up. At least, that's my view."

"Yes, I suppose so," Bobby agreed. "I don't think at present we can do more than keep him under close observation. You have his address, I suppose?"

"He left this morning," Ford answered. "Not notified any change to us so far. Hope he's not gone underground."

"Well, do your best to bring him in—for questioning only, of course. Make that plain. On the face of it he seems as likely to be guilty as any of the others. And certainly not in character for him to slip away quietly. I should have expected him to fuss about telling everyone all about it, making himself the central figure of it all." Here Bobby paused and began to show signs of going into one of those profound and prolonged meditations which had come to be known as the 'Bobby Owen trance'. But this time he came out of it quickly. He asked: "Can you think of any good reason why Rogers should want to make a quick get-away?" Ford looked puzzled and shook his head. Bobby said: "Well, have a try. One thing did occur to me. But never mind. Too obvious, perhaps. Did you get a list of what the dead man had in his pockets?"

"Much the same as usual," Ford replied. "Handkerchief, keys, ball pen, cigarettes, lighter, small pocket diary, pen-knife. Two ten-shilling notes in waistcoat pocket and nine and six in silver and copper in trousers. Wrist watch."

"One thing missing," Bobby said reflectively. "Yes. Isn't there?" Ford, a little puzzled, did not reply. He was not sure what Bobby meant. "One thing nearly every man carries," Bobby continued, and Ford looked at him interrogatively, but got no response. "It might be the explanation," Bobby said, more to himself than to Ford, and then went on: "There's Mr Dowie staying at the Twice Over pub at the time of the murder; he was seen near the copse shortly before it happened; then he disappeared and all trace of him was lost. Now I've heard of him at Applegarth in Holmshire."

"Do you think it might be him the murderer?" Ford asked doubtfully. "It was before it happened he was seen . . ." and he left the sentence unfinished, sub-consciously unwilling for attention to be diverted from Jolly Rogers, his own pet suspect, in whom indeed he was beginning to take a kind of proprietary interest.

"Dowie could have gone back," Bobby pointed out, "but the copse-murder side of it all is Mr Kimms's pigeon. Our business is the supposedly buried P.O. notes, which may never have been buried at all, or if they were once, been lifted years ago. Dowie seems to have heard something about it. I want to know what and how. It might give us a lead. And I've a feeling, too, he may be able to give us a lead as well to the killing of one of the gang that's never been cleaned up. I'm writing to Applegarth to ask their help, and I'll ring them in the morning to hear what they have to say—if anything. I spend half my time ringing people up—detection by 'phone," he added gloomily. "It gets you nowhere. You need the personal touch, so I may go up there myself to-morrow, and if I do I shall want you, so report to me first thing, in case."

"Very good, sir," said Ford briskly.

The reply from Applegarth next morning—a Saturday— when Bobby got his call through, proved to be non-committal and, in Bobby's opinion, unsatisfactory. No trace in it of the burning energy—restlessness his critics called it—that always consumed Bobby when he had a case of this kind on his hands. No one answering to the description of Mr Dowie was known to the Applegarth police, said the distant voice from Applegarth, and added that not much that went on in Applegarth was unknown to the Applegarth police. Bobby said he was of course fully aware of that. Applegarth promised that 'all possible steps would be taken', and Bobby, most unfairly, detected in this reply a devotion to the second-hand cliché that inspired in him no confidence in Applegarth efficiency.

However, he had made his plans beforehand. If he and Ford set off at once they could reach Applegarth—a six or seven hours' drive if you weren't afraid of using the accelerator—before dark and return on Sunday, in time to be on duty again by Monday morning. Not much time in this schedule for sleeping or eating, but C.I.D. men have often to regard sleeping and eating as purely subsidiary and incidental.

"Only mind," Bobby added severely to Ford, when he saw that young man's eyes beginning to glisten at the prospects thus sketched out—for Ford's fixed belief was that he had missed his vocation in joining the police and that he had really been intended by nature for a racing motorist, driving endlessly at record speed round and round a closed circular track. An odd ambition, perhaps, but it was his. "Only mind," Bobby repeated, still more severely, "you aren't going to hog all the driving—turn and turn about and fair shares."

"Yes, sir; of course, sir," Ford answered meekly—but with mental reservations.

In due course they started, in due course they arrived, in due course, between start and finish, Ford managed to 'hog' fully three-fifths of the driving, for Bobby was too often plunged deep in thought, reviewing mentally the whole history of the case, noting afresh those small, possibly significant, details that might in the end add up to a solution, to remember exactly when the change-over was due.

The Applegarth Chief Constable had been duly warned by 'phone of Bobby's arrival, but had little information to give, and was plainly inclined to consider the Yard man's rush from London more as an attempt to beat the London–Applegarth speed record than as serious police work.

He was emphatic also that none of his men knew anything of an Applegarth resident possessed of a treasure detector, and he ventured to think there wasn't much about the town and its inhabitants that he and his men didn't know. But of course the matter 'would be borne in mind', and Bobby, again most unfairly, concluded that a mind so apt to express itself in secondhand clichés was also a second-rate mind.

"Of course," the Applegarth man pointed out, "here we are at the hub, so to say, of a number of roads radiating from four of the biggest towns in the county, and none of them far away. Easy to come here to ring up anyone you didn't much want to know your address."

Bobby agreed, expressed his thanks for help given, and departed. But he knew that police do not take—and have no reason to take—much interest in such local eccentrics as inventors of treasure detectors. Whereas they are always worth a paragraph, or even a column in a local newspaper. So from the police station he proceeded to the office of the 'Applegarth Evening Times'.

As it was a Saturday afternoon, he found it closed, but he was able to get the address of one of the staff, a Mr Upton, who lived close by in the High Street, where he combined his journalistic activities with the much more lucrative occupation of a retail tobacconist. The shop was easily identified by various adapted journalistic slogans placarded in the windows, such as 'First with the cigs' and 'All the baccy that's fit to smoke', and it had the air of being a prosperous little concern. So Bobby entered, explained his errand to the brisk, business-like-looking woman behind the counter, and was thereon shown into a room behind, a combination of office, store-room, and snuggery. Here Mr Upton was accustomed to entertain the magnates of the town, and thus pick up what he liked to call the 'inside story' of local affairs. At the moment he appeared to be busy with the books of the business. But he seemed quite willing to push these aside as he waved Bobby to a chair and offered him a cigarette.

"Anything we can do," he declared. "But I hope it's not urgent. We don't appear again till our first late extra special Monday noon."

Unfortunately, however, his answers to Bobby's questions soon made it clear that he had never heard of Mr Dowie and knew nothing about him or of his treasure-seeking activities.

"Not an Applegarth man," Mr Upton declared with decision. "If he 'phoned from here he must have stopped off going somewhere else. If he were local we should know of him. Always a story in treasure-hunting, always worth a bit of space. There is an old legend about jewels of untold value hidden where Applegarth Castle stood till it was pulled down last century. Very old story everyone had forgotten till Marty Maxton cooked it up again in one of those Fresh-Air books of his."

"Oh, yes, I know," Bobby said, carefully concealing his interest—even his excitement—at this casual reference to the vanished Maxton. "I've heard of him. The book made a big hit, didn't it? I suppose you couldn't put me in touch with him. I've always been interested in these buried-treasure stories."

"Nothing in 'em," declared Upton. "If a woman dropped a brooch or something of the sort when she was out for a walk, that was good enough for a start. But Maxton built this one up a treat. Found all the required trimmings, or else invented them. I don't know which. Love-lorn page of lowly birth and high-born-maid cruel-tyrant papa was bargaining off to a pal. Love-lorn page serenades at night. High-born maid drops him a casket of jewels to cover runaway overheads. Page buries the treasure, goes away to arrange for the get-away, returns next night and shows a light to signal all is ready and will she join him pronto? But tyrant papa is there first, so page gets buried as well as the casket of jewels, which the legend claims is still there—and very likely it is if it ever was. But that's another story. Maxton told the old tale wonderfully well. Inspired him, so to say—set his imagination on fire, as if he were the page himself and had lived all through it again. We got permission to reprint it in our Weekly Supplement, and we had to reprint two or three times to meet the demand. It may be it's that your man—what's his name? Dewey? Dowie?—has got hold of."

Bobby was silent, staring at Upton with an odd intensity of vision that Upton did not understand, did not like. It seemed, he thought, to indicate that in this tale Bobby had found a significance plain to him alone, and what that might be Upton could not imagine. He broke the silence, saying abruptly:

"Anything wrong?"

"No, no," Bobby answered. "No. Why should there be?"

"Well," Upton grumbled, "you were staring as if you could see something that wasn't there. Same trick Maxton has. I saw him twice when we were getting his permission to publish. A haunted man, my wife called him, though generally like anyone else. Only he isn't. If you want to get in touch with him, the Holmford 'Grand Universal Hotel' might be able to tell you where he is. His sister is the manager's wife, and one of our staff saw him there the day before yesterday, I think it was."

CHAPTER XXII
GRAND HOTEL

BOBBY WALKED AWAY from Mr Upton's establishment in a mood of mingled doubt, surprise, bewilderment. Impossible, he told himself firmly, that this old-world tale of the lovelorn page, his nightly serenades, his tragic end, should throw any light on the problem of the barmaid of the 'Bell and Boy', her double life, and her tragic end by the loganberry bush. Yet somehow it ran about in his mind that it did, or rather would, if only he could see through the obscurity in which it was veiled. But he knew he would never dare suggest any such association to Superintendent Kimms, whose practical, competent mind would certainly be highly allergic to such flights of fancy. Surprising, though, that Maxton, seen on his way to France, should next be heard of, and so soon, in this northern English county. Easy enough, of course, in these days of aeroplanes, to get back again from Paris within a couple of hours or so of arriving there. A bit of a rush, though, all the same; and what object could there have been? Laying a false trail? It looked very much like it; and then again it had to be asked—and very seriously—'What object?' More than a little bewildering, too, the way in which, in this almost unique case, following the trail to one clearly indicated end seemed so often to result in arriving somewhere entirely different.

"Like going gunning for wild duck and bringing home a basket of fish," he grumbled to himself.

Only at present neither wild duck nor fish were in his bag.

He went on to collect Ford and the car, explained briefly to the former what had happened and that their next visit would be to the 'Grand Hotel' at Holmford, a prospect which made Ford look serious, for though he was fully prepared to tackle burglars and cosh-boys and such small deer, a 'Grand Hotel' in a big town like Holmford sounded a trifle intimidating. Indeed, on arrival they found it showed every intention of trying to live up to its name, and even more so.

Rooms safely booked for them both, however, and Ford happily busy in the hotel garage, making sure that the car was in good order and re-fuelled after their long run—Ford viewed hotel garage-men with a jaundiced and suspicious eye—the first thing Bobby did was to ring up the Holmford police headquarters both to let them know of his arrival and to ask them to report it to London. Until he was more sure of his ground here he did not wish to risk a direct communication from the Yard to the hotel prematurely betraying the purpose of his visit. It might result in a complete silencing of all tongues, for hotels are as sensitive to visits from the police as is a woman out in tearing wind and rain to her make-up. Then he sent Ford, happily returned from the garage in the sure conviction that all was well with the car, to get a drink at the bar and to get on terms with the barman—or barmaid—while Bobby himself would try to have a chat with the receptionist, a young lady who had seemed just a trifle more affable and a little less aloof than are some of her kind. But this time there was with her in her office, talking to her, another woman—older, but still young. They both looked up as Bobby came to the office counter, and the instant that he saw this second woman Bobby knew who she was.

The resemblance was striking. Even if he had not been warned that Martin Maxton's sister was here, he would have known her at once. The dark, brooding eyes were the same, the cast of feature was the same, the same loose, sensitive mouth. She had, too, something of that air of nervous apprehension, that hint of strange hidden memories ready at any moment to spring to life, which others had said they had seen in Martin, though Bobby himself had not. But, then, Sylvia Wynne had been there, and beneath the sunshine of her presence such signs, if they had real existence, might well have melted away.

There was something else even more surprising, more significant, too. Not only had he recognized her at sight—but, then, he had been forewarned—she also had instantly recognized him, and as instantly been afraid, as Maxton also had known him and also been afraid. Yet in his memory, trained as it was, there remained no recollection of either of these two, striking though both were, both in manner and in personal appearance. And somehow Bobby felt at once it would be no good trying to beat about the bush with her—necessary rather to go straight to the point.

"I am trying to get in touch with Mr Martin Maxton," he said. "A matter of business. I think you are his sister?"

"Yes," she said. "Yes." She spoke with some effort, and she had one hand against her breast, as if to still the beating of her heart. "He is not here," she said. "You had better see my husband, Mr Toosoon."

"I should be glad to later on," Bobby said; "but this is rather a personal, one might say a family matter. You will naturally know more about your brother than he does," and at that Mrs Toosoon grew even more pale and her eyes more terrified. Bobby produced his official card. "A matter of business," he repeated. "Private business."

"Yes," she repeated. "Yes." She came out of the office and began to walk away. "I will tell Mr Toosoon," she said over her shoulder.

"If you prefer it," Bobby said, and followed her through one door marked 'Private' and down a passage to another door, marked 'Manager'.

It opened on a small office. It was unoccupied. She left him there and hurried away, with such flurried speed, indeed, it had rather the air of a panic flight.

"Hysterical, not very stable mentally," Bobby said to himself, and then he thought that here perhaps was another of those tiny, apparently insignificant details that might have to be fitted in before the pattern he was weaving, or trying to, could be called complete.

He looked carefully round the room in which he had been left. But offices are impersonal things, and this one offered him no such clue to the character of its occupant as he was wont to look for. Then a tall, dark man in a dinner-jacket came quickly into the room. He had an authoritative, busy air—the air of a man with the chief direction of a big business and control of a large staff.

"What is the trouble?" he asked, a nice mingling in his tone of unease, resentment and the touch of deference due to anyone who was an hotel guest, even for a night. "Mrs Toosoon is very upset. Something to do with her brother? We don't know anything about him."

"I am sorry if Mrs Toosoon is disturbed," Bobby said. "I trust quite unnecessarily. I am anxious to get in touch with Mr Martin Maxton. In connection with the murder of a woman at a place called Twice Over. You may have heard about it?"

"I saw something in the London papers," Mr Toosoon answered with a slight suggestion in his voice that only Holmford things did he find of much interest. "What's it to do with Martin? Anyhow, we can't tell you anything."

"Our information is that he was here very recently," Bobby answered. "He left where he lived near Twice Over immediately after the murder. He seems to have told no one where he was going. We think he may be able to help us check up on times in a way that might be exceedingly useful."

"I don't see what we can do," Toosoon protested. "He only stayed the night here. He always says his business is with residents, not with transients—people with roots in the places he's writing about. You may take it he's mooching about somewhere, getting material for his next book. He may be anywhere—Holmshire, Yorkshire, Lancashire, anywhere; and the more out of the way and old world a place he can find, the better he likes it. He wrote columns once about a village he found up on the Yorkshire fells of about a dozen cottages and everyone in the place with tales going back to the Pilgrimage of Grace, or the wars of the Roses, or further. Took him a month, he says, to get them talking. It may be something of the sort this time. We don't know."

"Well, if you do happen to hear from him," Bobby said, "you will be sure to let him know—won't you?—how necessary we feel it to ascertain if he can tell us anything useful. In fact, he must be found as soon as possible, or certain steps may have to be taken."

The nature of such steps Bobby deliberately left vague, having a well-founded belief that the vague is also both impressive and disturbing, since so many meanings can be read into it. But somehow he did not feel that this accustomed effect was being produced on Mr Toosoon. Perhaps the manager of an hotel—a Grand Hotel at that—has too much experience of those who arrive in style and depart by night to be much impressed by anything short of a receipted bill.

It was now too late for anything more to be done that night. So Bobby expressed a hope that before he left in the morning he might be able to have another chat with Mrs Toosoon, and so retired to bed. But next morning, when he and Ford were having an early breakfast, Mr Toosoon came to their table; with him a companion whom he introduced as Dr Laper, and who at once gave it as his professional opinion that Mrs Toosoon, whom he had just examined and who was an extremely highly strung woman, had sustained a severe nervous shock and was in no fit condition to undergo further questioning.

Bobby said he was indeed sorry to hear it and he hoped no further interview with her would be found necessary. Probably, suggested Bobby, Mr Martin Maxton would soon be letting them hear from him, and he added, laughing lightly at the absurdity of the idea, that even if he were deliberately keeping out of the way—and why on earth should he?—he would soon be 'picked up'. In case the meaning of this technical term was not fully understood, Bobby explained it, and explained, too, that there wasn't so much as the smallest farmhouse, the most isolated cottage, that was not in the purview of a local police officer.

"A well-policed country," Bobby claimed. "People would be astonished to know how much we get to hear one way or another, even though we have to be jolly careful to keep it to ourselves."

Mr Toosoon made no comment on these remarks. Instead he and his companion drifted silently away. So Bobby paid the bill and went out to the garage, whither Ford had preceded him and was now snugly established in the driving-seat. But this was a bit too much for Bobby, who sternly ordered him to remove himself elsewhere, and indeed almost determined to stay at the wheel the whole of the return journey without allowing Ford to so much as lay a finger on it again. But then he reflected that this would be both extremely fatiguing and rather cruel. So Ford was allowed his 'fair share', in compliance with the great political slogan of the day.

CHAPTER XXIII
'THE HANGOVER'

MONDAY MORNING found Bobby at his desk as usual, rather pleased to think that but for the entry in his diary and the others to be made presently in his expense sheet, his foray into the North Country need never have been noticed.

Not that he was quite sure it had been fully worth while, even though it had confirmed his suspicion that Maxton had not only laid a false trail to France, but was now deliberately keeping out of the way. Why? However, that was for Kimms to follow up, if he decided to do so. Bobby's own aim had been to track down the elusive Dowie, whose visit to Twice Over might—or might not—indicate that he held some sort of clue to the whereabouts of the stolen pound-notes, the more immediate concern of the Yard. That would mean, of course, that it was these notes, and not the legendary and probably apocryphal treasure of the monks of Over Abbey, for which he was searching, and that his treasure-detector gadget was merely camouflage to hide his real purpose. Not much progress had in fact been made, Bobby told himself, and this was a conclusion Kimms also expressed when unexpectedly he turned up to exchange views and theories with Bobby.

"Dead end, eh?" he said. "Dead-end kids; that's us," and then he sat back to hear what comment, if any, Bobby had to make.

"No more breakings in your way?" Bobby asked.

"None that we've heard of," Kimms answered cautiously. "What I say is, there's more going on than we know of."

"Very likely," Bobby said. "I have the idea myself of a secret, hidden dance. Partners always changing and figures always different, but perpetually in the centre of it all the form of a dead woman, the barmaid of the 'Bell and Boy'."

Kimms contemplated this picture for some time in silence. Then he uttered the single word:

"Loganberries."

"I know," Bobby agreed. "Two tins and a bush. Some sort of sign or signal that Mrs Field was waiting for, and that meant a rendezvous at midnight by the loganberry bush in Stuart's copse. But with whom and what for?"

"Nought to show," said Kimms.

"You are keeping an eye on Stuart?" Bobby asked. "He's still a possible."

"He's putting it about," Kimms said moodily, "that those breakings in were us, wanting grounds to do it openly, so done instead on the quiet trying to work up evidence. Hints it means we're after Mr Wynne or Mr Maxton. As is so, but not more than others, including him."

"An open field," Bobby agreed, "with Dowie still missing and Rogers now reported working in an East End café, but exactly where not known yet."

"His alibi," Kimms said. "Strong."

"Water-tight," Bobby agreed, "except for one small pin-point of a leak."

"What?" asked Kimms, and, growing verbose, added: "Where?"

"Slipping off unnoticed, the way he did," Bobby explained. "Not in character. I should expect him to stop there, telling everybody all about it and how quick he was to call assistance. And I would rather build my case on character than on clues. Clues deceive, character stays true. But you have to relate character to motive, and of motive we are hardly sure yet. Difficult, too, to get character across to a jury."

"Impossible," was Kimms's grumbled comment.

"There is one thing, though," Bobby continued, "that would be in character all right and at the same time explain why he got away as fast as he could. I'll put it to him as soon as we find him again. If it holds, he's out."

Kimms looked rather sad at this possibility and then said: "Dowie?"

"Wanted, too," Bobby agreed. "For questioning, but it looks as if he will be more difficult to find. Awkward when suspects do the vanishing trick with nothing definite to hold them on and no local ties to work on. Wynne and Stuart do stand pat, thank goodness. There's been nothing unusual to notice about either of them?"

"Not about Mr Wynne," Kimms said. "He goes on just as usual—makes you feel somehow he's above it all. Holds his nose, so to speak, when it's mentioned, and tries not to let that young lady of his know anything about it." He paused, looking brighter somehow, as people always seemed to do whenever Sylvia was there, or even when her name was mentioned. "Stuart," he resumed—"Stuart's been going up to town more often than usual, but nothing in that; only one of my men says when he's had a drop more than enough he starts telling what he would do if any attempt's made to search his place. Only it wouldn't matter if we did, there being nothing there."

"Does that mean once there was?" Bobby asked, but not with much conviction. "Diamonds? You remember that yarn?"

"No known connection," Kimms said. "Keeps me awake at night trying to find one."

"There may be none to find," Bobby said. "Hidden cache of diamonds, perhaps? Oh, well, you never know. When he runs up to town, is it car or train?"

"Car."

"Does he stop the night?"

"Generally. Stays at the 'Magnificent' in Mayfair Square. Likes to tell you that. Swanky place."

"None more so," Bobby agreed. "Might do no harm to do a bit of observation on him. When you're in a fog you've got to—well, grope."

"Grope," said Kimms as he rose to go—"grope is the word."

Fortunately, keeping a discreet watch on Stuart's movements during his visits to that extremely imposing, smart, and expensive hotel, so justly named the 'Magnificent', was a problem presenting no great difficulty. The chief house detective there—he had a responsible and busy job, since to 'work' the 'Magy' was the ambition of every top-level 'con' man—was a former C.I.D. Inspector, Summerson by name, under whom Bobby himself had served in earlier days.

Nor was it very long before interesting information came through. For later in the week Sir Charles duly appeared, booking a room for two nights, and the following day Summerson called up Bobby.

"That client you asked us to keep an eye on," he said. "You remember? He's just taken a taxi to the Hangover Club, Notting Hill, so now it's up to you to look after him, if you think he needs it."

Bobby didn't—at least, not in the sense Summerson intended. Summerson had evidently jumped to the conclusion that the Yard's interest in Stuart sprang from a benevolent desire to protect him from the wiles and schemes of the 'con' men. In Bobby's opinion, however, Stuart was well able to take care of himself in that respect, nor was he wealthy enough to be worth the attention of the really high-ranking crooks—those pointed out, from a respectful distance, by their admiring confrères, just as at a London cocktail party the heavyweights of the London literary world are pointed out from afar by their awestruck admirers. It was that tale of the once-again-vanished Rogers about the surreptitious sale of diamonds in Hatton Garden cafés that still lingered in Bobby's mind as possibly having some connection, though for the life of him he could not imagine how, with the rest of these strange and doubtful happenings. But, considering all things, Bobby decided the information might be worth following up. Sir Charles was still one of the principal suspects, and one could never tell what unexpected lead might not turn up in the most unexpected quarters. All the same, Bobby knew he would have to go himself, even though there was, as always, plenty of desk work claiming his attention. No use sending anyone else on so vague an errand, one he could hardly explain to himself—merely to 'grope', indeed, to adopt the mot juste Kimms had managed to produce.

By now it was that useful interlude, the luncheon hour, though to Bobby the luncheon hour and luncheon were two entirely different aspects of reality, the former sacrosanct, the latter often forgotten or ignored, or else reduced to a thoughtful cigarette and a meditative cup of coffee, calculated both to stimulate the intellect and to keep at bay the secret dread of Bobby's young life—that of growing fat.

So first he noted in his diary that he was going out to lunch, added the exact hour, since every policeman as soon as he joins the Force is taught the importance of keeping a precise record of his movements, and soon was alighting at Notting Hill Gate station. As it happened, he had never before had occasion to visit the 'Hangover', famous as it was at the Yard for the dexterity with which it broke the law, ignored regulations, and yet managed to preserve a fascinating façade of respectability. Even the very name suggested respectability—though respectability with a difference. It was a favourite resort for dashing young men who yet had not the least intention or desire to get into serious trouble; for the shadier kind of sportsman; for 'con' men who were apt to think of the 'Hangover' as the place where to hatch out the eggs laid at the 'Magy'. Many a big betting coup had been planned at the 'Hangover'. Many stories, too, were told of the big sums there lost and won at cards, and it was whispered that the champagne provided by the club included a very special brand, heavily laced with brandy, as a contribution towards lessening prudence in play.

This interesting institution was situated not far from the station, in a terrace of late Victorian houses, once the habitat of a rather prim and smug, above all prosperous respectability; but now, forlorn in lack of paint and repair, only too clearly on their way with ever-increasing acceleration to a general state of slumdom. Even the 'Hangover', money-maker as it was reputed to be, had not escaped this general air of melancholy and decay. But that was only the whitened sepulchre idea in reverse. Inside all was 'gaiety, gas, and glitter'. For the proprietors, with no intention of spending one penny more than necessary on the outward appearance of premises they knew might well be closed down at almost any moment, yet spared no expense within in conditioning visitors and members alike to such an atmosphere of careless wealth as would make them ashamed to think even once before spending. A subtle touch Bobby, observing all this with his quick, trained eye, was much inclined to admire was that in the room where he was asked to wait hung three or four large Landseer paintings, striking a most reassuring note of faithful watch-dogs, wholesome country sport, happy, simple Victorian days.

There was already one other occupant of the room, presumably also waiting for a club member. He was sitting in a big armchair, his back to the door, and the only notice he took of Bobby's entry was a quick look round. Then he picked up a newspaper lying near and became immersed in it. To Bobby's fancy there was something rather hurried, even furtive in these movements. Someone who knew him, perhaps, but who had no wish that the recognition should be mutual.

But before Bobby could investigate further—for he did not like to be known and yet not to know—the club secretary came bustling into the room; outwardly suave, amiable, more than willing to help his good friends of the police in every way possible; inwardly sadly afraid that the inevitable, long-awaited hour of doom had struck and that warning of notice to close was looming dark on the horizon—though what it was in particular the police had found out was a bit of a puzzle. An immense relief, therefore, to find that all Bobby wanted to know was if a certain Sir Charles Stuart was a member and, if so, was he at present in the club?

With a conscience for once perfectly clear, the secretary replied that the name was entirely unknown to him and was certainly not on their roll of members—a roll, the secretary added, kept with the most meticulous care. But—for his attention had in no way been drawn to the third person present: the occupant of the big arm-chair—he did not notice the abrupt start that gentleman made at the mention of Sir Charles's name, or how the newspaper he was reading then dropped abruptly to the floor. These things, however, Bobby did notice, for it was some such reaction he had been half inclined to expect.

CHAPTER XXIV
DOWIE TALKS

No SIGN OF the interest this trifling incident had aroused in him did Bobby allow himself to show. He stood silent and thoughtful—'moonstruck' was how the club secretary described it to himself, and began to hope that though all policemen were dangerous, this one was less so than most. And now perhaps he would go away, a consummation devoutly to be wished, thought the club secretary, who once upon a time had been an actor, till professional jealousy had driven him to adopt a more lucrative profession.

But if Bobby was silent, it was only because there had come back into his mind, and with renewed force, the problem of Sir Charles Stuart and his diamond-dealing transactions with 'Fatty' Veale, which surely did demand some sort of explanation. More groping in the dark? But then what was all detective work but groping in the dark, with sheer luck presiding over what the groping might produce?

"If there is anything else—" murmured the club secretary. He coughed apologetically. "Anything at all—"

"Ah, yes," Bobby said. He paused and took a turn or two up and down the room. "You see, our information—" he began again, and again paused, leaving the exact nature of that information both doubtful and, he hoped, disturbing. Abruptly he said, and rather loudly: "And Mr Veale? Is he a member? Is he here?"

"Mr Veale?" the club secretary repeated, looking a little dazed by this sudden and unexpected change of objective. "There is a Mr Veale," he admitted cautiously, afraid to deny what the police might know. "A very popular gentleman. I only wish all our members were like him. I think I saw him in the smoking-room. He may be lunching here—he often does."

"Ah, yes, yes," Bobby said. "Yes," and he took mental note that this time there had been no reaction from the armchair. Suddenly he went to stand by the fireplace, directly opposite the armchair, looking down at its occupant, who, taken by surprise at this sudden and unexpected movement, stared up at Bobby in return.

Someone Bobby had never seen before—of that he was sure. But equally certain was it that that someone knew him. And yet a vague touch of the familiar in the man's appearance. A tall, shambling, pale-faced man, almost completely bald, with a great Roman nose and small, light blue eyes that seemed to stick out of his head, a wide mouth with irregular, discoloured teeth.

It was a catalogue that he noted, that seemed to tease him with a hovering certainty that it ought to bring with it recognition, and yet refused to do so. Almost without meaning to, he made a swift decision.

"Good day," he said. "I didn't see it was you, or I would have spoken before."

The other squirmed—it is the only word to describe the kind of uneasy twitching that seemed to result from Bobby's steady scrutiny. But Bobby had hoped, not for squirming or wriggling, but for some verbal response that would give him a clue to the man's identity. None came. Bobby waited, still keeping up his grave and expectant contemplation of the armchair and of the plainly increasing uneasiness of its occupant. So also was evidently the uneasiness of the club secretary. He coughed discreetly and said:

"The gentleman is not a member—a visitor."

"I know," Bobby said; and so he did, now he had been told, and looked still more severely at the armchair. "Well?" he said, and managed to make the word sound not so much a question as a threat.

The other got to his feet and tried to look defiant, not too successfully.

"I expected to meet a gentleman here," he said. "I can't wait any longer," and he stooped and picked up the small suit-case—it seemed heavy for its size—that had been standing on the floor near his chair.

But now Bobby felt he had been given the clue he had been hoping for. They might, of course—he and this stranger—be waiting for different club members who had not yet arrived. But that would be coincidence, and Bobby kept always a wary eye on coincidence. Worth taking a risk, especially since, even if he were wrong, no great harm would be done. The time to mention names, he felt, had come.

"Oh, Sir Charles is sure to turn up before long," he said. "For that matter, I want to see him myself, as soon as I can get round to it. One or two bits of information he might be able to give us that could help. I think you could, too, perhaps. But we can't talk here. Should you mind coming back to Scotland Yard for a chat?"

The idea was plainly unwelcome—more than unwelcome. A glance towards the door suggested hopeful contemplation of instant flight. Another glance towards Bobby suggested reali-zation that flight would not be permitted.

"I can't. I mean to say—" he began, and paused. Bobby's expression was growing ever less and less encouraging. "What for?" he demanded wildly.

"Mr Dowie," Bobby said, venturing now on using the name. "There was a murder at Twice Over, and you were there. It took place in a small copse which you were seen to leave but to which you may have returned. You disappeared, and we have been looking for you ever since. These are things that need explaining."

Dowie collapsed on the nearest chair.

"This is incredible," he panted. "You can't really . . . you don't mean you think . . . you can't," and now his rather thin voice had grown to what was nearly a scream.

"I'm not thinking or supposing anything," Bobby retorted sharply. "Except that we don't want to have a scene here, do we? Or do you?" He picked up the small, heavy suit-case. "This your treasure-detector gadget? We'll ask the hall porter to get a taxi for us, shall we? Second time I've gone wild-duck shooting and brought home a basket of fish instead. One never knows. Come on."

He jerked the collapsed Dowie to his feet, escorted him into the hall, where the porter eyed them curiously but quickly procured the desired taxi, within which they were soon on their way to the Yard. Neither of them spoke. Bobby was waiting. Dowie was evidently trying to collect his scattered wits, to control his shaking nerves. Once back in his office, Bobby began without further preliminary than the ritual offer of a chair—accepted—and a cigarette—refused.

"Now, Mr Dowie," he said, "I would like you to feel that this is nothing but a friendly chat to clear up things a little—puzzling, worrying things. But probably you know that you needn't say anything if you don't want to. The choice is entirely yours, and in any case there will be no question of a written statement—certainly not till you've had more time for consideration. In this affair, too, there's the further complication that it's a double inquiry. Here in London we are chiefly concerned—how it all began—with the recovery of very valuable stolen property. The Twice Over people are concerned chiefly with the murder that took place there recently. The two inquiries continually interlock. A scent picked up here may lead there, and vice versa. Now, first of all, do you care to say why you chose to disappear immediately after the murder of Mrs Field?"

"Because," explained Dowie resentfully, but with voice and nerves now under better control—"because if it hadn't been her, it might have been me."

"How do you mean?" Bobby asked, not quite knowing what to make of this unexpected reply. "Do you mean you were threatened? Who by?"

"I don't know, I was taken entirely by surprise," Dowie answered. "And I didn't disappear. That's nonsense. I simply went home. That's all."

"I see," Bobby said. "But about this threat you say was made? What actually happened?"

"I was exploring," Dowie told him. "A small wood. I had reason to believe articles of considerable value might be buried there. I was attacked from behind. I heard and saw nothing. I was flung violently to the ground. A man knelt on me. I was quite helpless. He put a cord round my neck. He tried to strangle me. Three times."

"Three times," Bobby repeated.

"Three times," Dowie said once more, and now he was very pale and there were little drops of perspiration on his cheeks and forehead. "Three times I was as good as dead. Three times I died and three times I was allowed to come back. Then I was told to go and keep going and never show myself there again. So I went home."

"You didn't mention this to anyone at the time?" Bobby inquired, and not without sympathy for the man who had had so terrifying an experience.

"I was much too upset," Dowie replied. "All I wanted was to get home. When I did I went to bed. I've only now felt able to get about again. Besides, I don't mean my invention or any details of it to become public till I have proved its value. If I did, I should be exposed to every sort of misrepresentation and slander, even ridicule. Nor have I thought it wise to patent it. Others might then discover the principle on which I worked."

"Your invention is a kind of hidden-treasure detector, is it?"

"A precious-metal diviner," Dowie corrected him. "I'm not much interested in these old stories of hidden treasure, of gold and silver hidden by monks at the time of the Reformation or by Cavaliers during the Civil Wars. Dug up again, most likely, if they were ever there at all, or else the locality too vague. Take too much time to cover. In the grounds or in the neighbourhood, or something like that, is about as near as these stories generally get. The emanations from gold and silver are much weaker than those from water. Water is a moving, lively thing of bubbling energy. Its emanations can be felt almost at once. For gold and silver one must wait till the manifestation has time to show. Especially silver. Silver is very inert. Gold comes between. Not so lively as water, much more so than silver. Gold is beginning to be used in medicine because of this active quality it possesses."

"I see," said Bobby, slightly overwhelmed by this torrent of information and rather inclined to the belief that it all belonged to the realm of what is now called science fiction. "What about valuable documents—wills, title-deeds, so on?" he asked. "If they were hidden, could your machine smell them out?"

"Hardly," Dowie answered, smiling a little at the simplicity of such a question. "Paper is totally inert. Only water and the precious metals are active. I am not sure about jewels. Diamonds, especially. Further experiment is needed. Of course I except the radio-active substances. They belong to a different order."

"Very interesting," Bobby repeated; and he asked himself if this casual passing reference to diamonds had any significance. Probably not, he thought. "One more question. If you don't attach importance to old-world legends of buried treasure, why were you exploring the Twice Over wood? There's such a legend there."

"Hasn't it occurred to you," Dowie asked, still faintly superior, "that to-day the practice of burying gold and silver and such-like still continues?"

"Well, no," Bobby admitted; "I can't say it has."

"If you cared to examine accounts of the many recent burglaries," Dowie instructed him, "you would soon notice that articles of value taken are often buried in convenient spots till a suitable opportunity occurs to remove them."

"Oh, I see," Bobby said, feeling suitably rebuked. "It does happen, but not, I think, very often. But you said you needed fairly precise indications. Burglars don't leave those, do they?"

"Which is why I decided to get them for myself," Dowie answered. "I came to London and made careful, cautious inquiries in the Soho district and elsewhere. I soon found there was an undercurrent of talk about Twice Over and articles buried there. It all appeared to originate with a man recently released from prison. I made up my mind that I would visit Twice Over and look round for myself. As soon as I saw the small wood there I knew that would be the place, if any. And it wouldn't take long to try it out. It was almost entirely covered with thick undergrowth, bramble chiefly, where no digging could have been attempted for many years. I bought a spade and concealed it so that I could begin to dig the moment my indicator registered. But then I was attacked in the brutal manner I told you. I must have been watched."

"I can guess by whom," Bobby said. "But go on."

"As soon as I felt fairly fit again," Dowie resumed, "I wrote to Sir Charles Stuart. It was his land, and with his support and co-operation it would be safe to continue. I was to have met him for consultation to-day at the Hangover Club."

"You rang up a firm of publishers recently, didn't you? To inquire about Mr Maxton?"

"Well, it was clear it must have been Maxton who attacked me," Dowie said. "No one else knew. I thought it prudent to warn him that this time I should not be alone. I had been to see him to inquire if he had any reliable information about an account he had published of jewels buried somewhere in Holmshire. If he had, it might give me another useful field for experiment. I found the story was largely his own invention. Embroidered out of all recognition. Most unscrupulous."

CHAPTER XXV
DEAD END

THAT WAS ALL Mr Dowie seemed prepared to say, nor did Bobby attempt to press him further. Always was it best, or so Bobby thought, to allow a witness time to think over what he had said, to wish he had said more here and less there, to allow his memory time to remind him of details he had forgotten. Then, when the investigator, on his side, had fully considered what had passed and followed up any leads given, questioning could be resumed, more formally, perhaps, and sometimes with surprising results.

For the present, therefore, Bobby contented himself with writing out a full report of his interview with Dowie, together with his own comments, to add to the rapidly increasing dossier of the case. A copy was to be made at once and sent to Superintendent Kimms, and with it Bobby sent a letter in which he managed to make it clear that if Kimms so wished he would be willing to run out some afternoon to Twice Over and talk over these developments and what deductions could properly be drawn from them.

It was a hint the badly puzzled Kimms was quick to respond to.

"Dead end," he said gloomily over the 'phone when he rang Bobby up within an hour or two of the receipt of report and letter. "Local Press getting nasty. Bad for discipline. I mean to say when men see their chief as good as called a nitwit."

"Call a Press conference," Bobby advised. "Fashionable thing just now. Tell 'em nothing; but lots of drink. Anyhow, police and Aunt Sally; same thing. I can spare to-morrow afternoon, if that'll do. Suit you?"

Kimms said it would, and so it was arranged. Next morning, though, there was a fresh development. Ford appeared to report, not without a touch of complacence, that Rogers, missing for some days from his usual haunts, had now been traced and was at the moment waiting below, to be interviewed, if Bobby so wished.

"Seems," Ford explained, "that his old woman has taken him back. She didn't like it when, just before his last stretch, he tried to strangle her, and only let up at the last moment, when she was as good as dead. To teach her to sing, he said."

"Why?" Bobby asked. "Was she threatening to give him away to us?"

"That's right," answered Ford. "He was bringing home stolen stuff, and she told him to stop it, or else. But after he put a cord round her neck and pulled it so tight she's hardly sure yet she's really alive, she got out. Now she's running a small café down Hoxton way, and that's where he is. Sort of odd-job man and chucker out, but kept at arm's length on account of that strangling affair. Must have been touch and go."

"Did he make any fuss about coming with you?"

"No, sir; trotted along like a little lamb. Very confident. Kept telling me no one could break an alibi when it was true."

"That much is true, anyhow," Bobby agreed. "But I want proof. Only his word for it at present, as far as I can see. Bring him in, though, and we'll hear what he has to say. There must be clear evidence one way or the other, and I think I can see how to get it—or near enough."

"Yes, sir," said Ford, more than a little puzzled, since, for his part, he could see no possibility of obtaining any such definite proof.

"Old man's got something up his sleeve," he confided to a passing colleague he met in the corridor outside, and the colleague said the 'old man' generally had, and Bobby would have been excessively annoyed if he had known, as he never would, who was the 'old man' in question.

Even if Bobby had not been warned beforehand, he could scarcely have failed to notice the self-confidence that fairly oozed from Rogers as Ford brought him into the room. For self-confidence was not as a rule very marked in those members of the criminal class who from time to time appeared in this room for questioning. But it was with a jaunty step that Rogers crossed the room to take the chair Bobby indicated, and there was something almost patronising in the nod of friendly greeting which was now bestowed on Bobby.

"Nothing on me," he announced as he settled himself comfortably in his chair. "You can't break an alibi what's gospel true. If it's faked, same as happens, there's bound to be holes in it. But not when it's gen-u-ine."

"I hope it is," Bobby said, noting with some surprise this new-born confidence in, and reliance upon, truth, on the part of one whose acquaintance with it in the past had been of the most limited and casual character. "Working with your wife in her café, I hear?"

"That's right," agreed Rogers. "No soft job neither, for tough she is, and sleeping in the back kitchen she says is good enough for me. But tough as you like, a woman needs a man to handle them kids as think they know it all. Reckon to come it over her, some of 'em, not paying, or picking on any quiet-looking bloke having a cup of coffee and saying he'd pay, as some do, being scared. But not no more now, when they know that if they ask for a spot of trouble it's there, all ready and waiting." He paused and grinned broadly. "A social worker, guv., that's me."

"Dear me," said Bobby, not quite sure what this meant. "In what way?"

"If I see kids getting larky like, I sit down with 'em," Rogers explained, "and tell 'em about the stretch I've just done. Seven years of it. About as long, I says, as you kids have lived, from the way you act. Seven years, I tell 'em, and they listen. No pictures, I says, no dogs, no girls, no fun—no nothing, in a manner of speaking, only doing what you're told, and food you couldn't eat only for being hungry. In a general way they go off thoughtful like, and if they don't—well, they go off all the same."

"Bravo," Bobby applauded, much intrigued by this picture of ex-convict turned social reformer, but not yet fully persuaded to take it all at face value. "It's that little matter of your alibi, though, I wanted to talk to you about."

"God's own truth, guv.," Rogers assured him again. "You ask them railway blokes what was there."

"First thing we did," Bobby told him. "They agree that someone called for help as the train came in. But they don't know who it was, and none of them remembers seeing anyone in any way resembling you."

"What are you getting at, guv.?" Rogers demanded, beginning now to look a trifle less confident. "Couldn't know all about it, could I? Only for being there, same as I said."

"There was a full report in the papers," Bobby said, watching him closely the while. "Any further detail you could have picked up later from the railway staff."

"Never went near the place again," Rogers insisted. "It was me there, s'elp me. Truth's truth all the world over."

He spoke earnestly, pleadingly almost, but now with much less confidence, and Bobby was silent for a few moments, his steady gaze on Rogers, waiting. Rogers's uneasiness increased. Instead of lolling back in his chair very much at his ease, he was beginning to wriggle, to cast longing glances at the door, as if thinking how much nicer it would be if he were on the other side of it. Bobby said:

"Your wife left you, didn't she? because she didn't like your bringing stolen property home? But you thought that meant she might give information, so you tried to murder her."

"No, guv., not me," Rogers protested. "If I'd meant it, she'd have been a goner all right. I know when to stop and no harm done, not like slashing with a razor, as some do and I don't hold with. Showing her in a friendly sort of way what would be if she squealed. That's all."

"I see," Bobby said. "A Mr Dowie tells me he had rather a similar experience at Twice Over. Three times nearly strangled by someone who also knew when to stop and no harm done. Was that to show him in a friendly sort of way what would happen if he stayed around? The same night, a few hours later, a woman was strangled by someone who may have known when to stop but did not. Not till she was a—goner."

"Mr Owen, sir," Rogers began. "Mr Owen, sir," he repeated, and then looked wildly round and was silent. "Mr Owen, sir," he burst out. "It's God's truth it was me what was there when the bloke was took bad."

"If it was, can you explain why no one saw you?" Bobby asked.

"There wasn't no cause for me to hang around," Rogers muttered. "I didn't know; couldn't, could I? When I saw it in the papers about a skirt being done in, I said; 'Thanks be, no one can't pin that on me.' That's what I said. And now—" He paused and looked entreatingly, desperately indeed, at Bobby, for now it was the drear shadow of the gallows that he seemed to see dark and menacing in that quiet room. "And me as innocent as never was," he wailed. "Mr Owen, sir, won't you believe me?"

"What matters," Bobby told him, "is what judge and jury believe. If it comes to that. But the same method does suggest the same hand. And it is certain you were in Twice Over earlier on that evening. More than one witness to prove it. I think you had better tell me all about it from the start."

"I was nosing round all right," Rogers admitted. "Trying to get a hint where to look for the stuff Charley Cream let on was buried round Twice Over way and told me about. I wasn't going to stand for another bloke on the same lay, so I just gave him a sort of get out notice, meaning no permanent harm, only a friendly warning, same as you said. Lumme, you ought to ha' seen the way he scuttled. Going to squeal to the busies, as like as not, I thought, and no chance of doing more till things quieted down. Just caught the train, I did. That's how it was I was there, and gospel truth, s'elp me."

"No proof yet," Bobby said. "Let's see if we can dig it out, one way or the other," and at this Rogers looked a little more hopeful. "Has your wife still the same dislike to having stolen property in her house?"

"What you getting at, guv.?" Rogers asked doubtfully. "I don't know nothing about stolen property."

"I'm getting at this," Bobby said. "And try to tell the truth for once. If you were in fact there and it was you called for help, why did you go off so quickly, as if you had some very good reason for not being seen? If there was such a reason, what was it?"

"Reckon," Rogers said slowly, sounding both relieved and resigned as he spoke—"reckon as you knew all along—stolen property and all. When the bloke was took ill I went to help, Christian like, same as any decent bloke would. Couldn't help feeling there was a wallet in his pocket, and no sense leaving it for them railway blokes to pinch, like they would, and not think twice about it if they got the chance. So it might as well be me as them, which it was according." He paused and eyed Bobby distrustfully. "What put you on it, guv.?" he asked.

"Most men carry a wallet," Bobby told him. "None was listed among the articles found in the dead man's possession. Missing wallet, you skurrying away in such a hurry no one saw you, your character—it all added up."

"Don't miss much, guv., do you?" grumbled Rogers. "Just my luck, and me thinking it safe as houses. They can't send me down for long on account of a little thing like that, as might happen to anyone, in a manner of speaking."

"Only to someone like you—not only Rogers, but Rogue," Bobby told him sharply. "It took me a long time to get it out of you. I didn't want you to see too soon what I was driving at. Or it might be you would guess and invent a yarn to fit. It could be argued that way still. Have you got the wallet? If you can produce it and it can be identified, I think that would settle it, and your robbery of a dead man prove you innocent of the murder of a dead woman. Which in a way is rather a pity. Well, can you?"

"The old woman settled that on her own," Rogers answered ruefully. "No loving wife about her, no open arms for her man home again after long years of absence he couldn't help. 'No beggars wanted here,' she says the moment she clapped eyes on me. 'Beggars?' says I. 'What do you think you're getting at? Take an eyeful of that,' I says, and I shows her the wallet with eleven pounds ten in it. 'Who did you pinch that from?' she says, nasty like. 'Earned it,' says I. 'By the sweat of me brow,' I says. 'Then why has it got another bloke's name in it?' says she and slammed it in her desk. 'Scoot!' says she. 'Scram. You're not bringing me into it again,' and next thing lets out a yell like a steam whistle gone dotty, because of spotting some kids what had been doing themselves extra proud and now not waiting for the bill. 'Oh, he's paying,' says one of 'em, meaning me, so I up and lammed him one as knocked him cold. Trying to cheat a poor lone widow woman, they was. They paid up then all right, not wanting more of the same their pal had

had—and a bit over for me, as was only right. So when I had kicked the last of 'em out, the old woman says as I could stop there, only sleeping at the back at night and being useful in the day. A nice little business it is, and I don't know but now I'm in I'll ever feel like getting out. Female woman can be tough as hell outside, but still female woman soft inside."

CHAPTER XXVI
THE INQUEST

BOBBY REMAINED silent for a time. He was wondering how far this story would carry conviction to others. For himself he accepted it. But others might think it a little too well invented, too well tailored to fit the circumstance. Rogers was silent, too, but his was an uneasy silence. Badly shaken had been his former instinctive faith in the power of truth to convince—strange as that instinctive faith must seem in one who always had relied upon falsehood to save him when in difficulty. Bobby was the first to speak.

"You said your wife got rid of the wallet. Could you get it back? If you could, that would be good evidence."

"She got rid of it all right," Rogers answered gloomily. "You wouldn't hardly believe it. Slammed it into the post, she did, eleven of the best in it and all, back to them as wouldn't never have missed it, not knowing, and me left without so much as a penny to pay a 'bus fare."

"Do you mean she posted it to the address she found in it?" Bobby asked. "If she did, we can probably get it back again. There might even be your dabs on it still."

Rogers, not noticeably quick in the uptake, set his slow wits to puzzle this out. For him 'dabs' were always the chief enemy to be feared; so treacherous, so dangerous, that even a mere passing touch on some polished surface might bring a man to his doom. Difficult then to assimilate the idea that also they could serve to prove innocence. A novel idea to Bobby, too, for that matter, but now he was busy already issuing instructions to put it to the test. This done, he turned back to the still-bewildered Rogers.

"Is there anything else you got to know from this man Cream? Could you remember the exact words he used?"

Rogers shook his head.

"Popping off, the poor bloke was," he said, "and knew it, and half the time didn't know what he was saying, or too weak to get it out proper; but awful worried about leaving all that stuff behind. 'Could have had a good time with it,' he kept saying. 'Good time,' he says, 'and now it's nix. Don't seem fair, do it?' he says. 'No good time,' says he, and them's the last words he spoke before he croaked."

A grim death-bed scene, Bobby thought in the grim precincts of a gaol, and one that had apparently brought in its train yet another death, and it might be there would be still another. So Bobby thought, wondering a little once again at the way in which things work themselves out. He put these thoughts from him and said abruptly to the still-meditative Rogers:

"Had you known him before you met him in prison? Why did he choose you to talk to?"

"We was kids together—lived in the same street," Rogers explained. "Ran away together when he got hold of his dad's P.O. book. Mr Logan told my dad I was in it too, so I came in for it same as Charley. Then, when we were at Borstal, we did a bunk together, and weren't never caught neither, though your blokes did bring it up years after, along of them dabs being took."

"I see," Bobby said. "Who is Mr Logan?"

"Him? Why, Charley's dad. Changed his name, Charley did, after we bunked from Borstal. Took his mum's instead. Charley said it was safer—safety first, he said. But, lummy, what's the good, when there's always them dabs to trip you up?"

"What indeed?" Bobby agreed. "Did he ever talk to you about the robbery itself or about the murder of one of his pals, a man named Farmer? Farmer was found dead soon afterwards, shot through the head. You remember?"

"That's right," Rogers agreed. "He did use to talk about it sometimes. Charley said most likely it was an outside bloke, trying to push in and get a share he hadn't any right to, not having worked for it. There was a bloke Farmer got sometimes to carry messages and that sort of thing—not one of the regulars, if you see what I mean. Just a sort of odd-job man, and paid according. He might have let on Farmer had the stuff, and someone took advantage according."

"Did he know his name?" Bobby asked. "The runner's, I mean."

"'Fingers' was what Farmer called him," Rogers answered. "Might have been good at lifting things. I don't know. Charley had never seen him, he said. And he hadn't no right to anything more than what he did and was paid for. But he or a pal might have done in Farmer, aiming at Farmer's share, as was plenty. That's what Charley thought. Hard luck on Farmer, as was a good pal, always straight, and planning to retire and live quiet and respectable, same as his wife wanted."

"He was a married man, then?" Bobby asked.

"Well, I don't know about married," Rogers answered doubtfully. "It was a dame he had fallen for—quite took up with her, same as happens easy to the best of us."

"I don't think that was known at the time," Bobby remarked. "Nothing about it in any of the reports I've read. And not much chance of learning any more after all these years, with nothing to go on but a nickname—if 'Fingers' was a nickname and not his own."

He went on to ask a few more questions, without eliciting any further relevant information. Finally he sent Rogers off with instructions that he was to be given a meal in the canteen but was not to be allowed to leave for the present—not till the result of the wallet inquiry came in. When it did arrive—the delay was not long—it was to the effect that the wallet had been duly recovered from the relatives of the dead man, to whom it had been sent through the post, that it had contained the sum mentioned by Rogers, and that it did in fact still show Rogers's finger-prints. So Bobby sent for him.

"You may take it your alibi is accepted," Bobby told him. "Puts you in the clear. You may be called as a witness at the inquest, but nothing need be said about the wallet, as it has been returned and nothing missing. So you can get away back to Mrs Rogers and tell her that, thanks to her, everything's all right."

"Lummy," interposed Rogers, aghast; "if I said a thing like that she would get above herself so there wouldn't be no standing it."

"It might get her to let you stay on," Bobby suggested. "Then you could carry on as a social reformer and sleep quiet at night—and perhaps not always in the back kitchen. Up to you; so good-bye and good luck and—well, may we never meet again."

"Same here, guv.," said Rogers earnestly, accepted the two half-crowns Bobby offered as a solatium for time occupied, and departed, leaving Bobby deep in thought, for it seemed to him that all this contained much that might be of significance, though significant of what he was not sure.

The following day was that on which the inquest on Mrs Field's death was to be held. Bobby knew, of course, that Kimms intended to ask for an adjournment on the ground that 'inquiries were not yet complete'—'at a complete dead end' would, as he had remarked to Bobby, have been a more exact description. All the same, Bobby had made up his mind to be present. There might be unexpected developments. One never knew what might not turn up next in so baffling a case as this; and besides, there was that comparing notes with Kimms which had been tentatively arranged and which both Bobby and Kimms felt to be advisable.

The village hall where the inquest was to be held was already crowded when Bobby arrived, but a place had been reserved for him. He noticed that both Sir Charles and Mr Wynne were present, the former evidently uneasy and restless; the latter imperturbable as ever and showing at times that small, secret smile of his which vanished again almost before it could be seen. Was it by any chance, Bobby wondered, a sign of satisfaction at having pushed Sir Charles into the front while himself remaining in the background, which he apparently so much preferred? Or was there some other, deeper reason?

The brief proceedings over, both of them took opportunity to speak to Bobby, Wynne the first. With his usual quiet, concealed efficiency he managed to be next to Bobby in the general exodus, while Sir Charles, who had made a point of pushing his way out among the first to depart, waited impatiently outside in the obvious intention of waylaying Bobby there and as obviously perturbed when he saw Wynne already at Bobby's side and already chatting to him.

"I was rather relieved to see you here to-day," Wynne was saying amiably. "There's been some talk about your being likely to drop out. With all respect to Mr Kimms—a highly efficient officer in his own way, I'm sure—there is a feeling that he hasn't the experience for handling a case like this. There've been letters in the Press."

"There always are," Bobby said. "The less people know about anything, the more they like to air their opinions about it. Mr Kimms can be trusted to do all that's possible."

"No chance of your taking over, then," Wynne said, with a faint touch of disappointment in his voice, and Bobby was aware of an odd impression that this was what Mr Wynne had wanted to know.

Now with a nod and smile Wynne melted away, and instantly Sir Charles was at Bobby's side.

"I want a word with you," he said truculently. "I'm going to see my lawyers about all this. I take the strongest possible exception to your following me, as I hear you did, to the Hangover."

"Oh, yes; I was hoping for a chat with you," Bobby answered. "But they told me you weren't there and weren't a member."

"Why should you think I was?" demanded Sir Charles, his tone more truculent than ever. "Any business of yours what clubs I belong to? I had never even heard of the place till a friend asked me to lunch there?"

"Mr Veale, was it?" Bobby asked. "The gentleman his friends call 'Fatty' Veale?" and the question shocked Sir Charles completely and instantly out of all his truculence.

"What do you mean?" he demanded. "What's Veale got to do with it?"

"Has he anything?" Bobby asked. "I'm sure I don't know. I met a Mr Dowie there. He was waiting for you, I think?"

"That's another thing," Sir Charles said, struggling to get back some of his former truculence. "I had arranged to meet him about a dodge of his he's invented. He wrote to me, and I wanted him to meet Veale—clever business chap, Veale. My idea was we might float a small private company, if Veale agreed there were possibilities. Gadget to register emanations from gold or silver, perhaps uranium. Might turn out a big thing for prospectors and mining engineers. Others too. Very big thing. And then you interfere and take Dowie off with you. Ought to be actionable. I shall probably lodge a complaint. My whole day ruined. Wasted. Veale was very annoyed. Next time I want to put a business proposition to him very likely he'll turn it down without looking at it. Veale's a busy man."

"Deals in diamonds, doesn't he?" Bobby asked; and once again that question went home through the other's armour of truculence and assurance. "But I really mustn't keep the Superintendent waiting any longer. Lot to do in these cases, you know. Takes time to collect all the facts, and then a lot more time to decide which are relevant. See you again later on, if you don't mind."

CHAPTER XXVII
PHOTOGRAPH

WITHOUT STAYING to hear if Sir Charles did mind or did not, Bobby nodded a farewell and went to join Kimms, waiting for him at a little distance. A good many people were still lingering in the vicinity, exchanging views and opinions and hardly concealing their disappointment at so tame an ending as an adjournment. It was clear from their manner and from a snatch or two of talk that Bobby caught as he passed by that Mr Kimms's prestige was not at the moment at its peak. One such group included Mr Wynne, though he did not seem to be saying much himself, but listening rather to what others had to say.

"Always the bystander, the looker-on," Bobby remarked to Kimms as he joined him. "Wynne, I mean. Never in the centre of things, always watching from outside."

"Knows a lot," Kimms said.

"That's how," Bobby told him, aware of a certain unreasonable irritation against one who seemed to hold himself serenely posed 'above the strife', as once a famous writer had so calmly claimed to be. Not that there was any reason why Wynne should descend from his lofty pedestal of god-like indifference, but—well, irritating, all the same.

Sir Charles had joined another small group a little further away, to whom he was apparently expounding the law and the prophets. One or two of his hearers occasionally glanced in Bobby's direction, and Bobby noticed this and guessed that he himself was probably the target for some of Stuart's more vehement remarks.

"They make an interesting contrast, those two," Bobby observed. "Stuart and Wynne, I mean. One likes to keep his mouth shut, and the other never misses a chance to open it—wide."

"There's talk about them both," Kimms said. "I haven't tried to stop it."

"Good man," Bobby applauded. "The only thing in a case of this sort is to let the pot boil and see what scum comes to the top."

"If there's none?" Kimms said moodily.

"If there wasn't," Bobby retorted, "you and I would soon be out of a job."

"Yes," agreed Kimms. "Not likely," he said on further consideration, and added: "Here's Miss Wynne."

Sylvia was coming towards them down the long village street, and Bobby, well as he remembered the impression she had made on him the first time he saw her, yet was again aware of how vividly she brought with her an aura, as it were of innocence and joy in life. Even Kimms allowed his generally rather glum expression to soften into a smile as he watched her approach.

"Come to pick up her father," he said. "He fair worships her."

One of a little group of chatting women near said aloud: "It don't seem natural like, always happy and smiling. Things aren't so much a laugh as all that."

"Let her while she can," another said, and a third added:

"She'll find out different soon enough; she won't always have her dad to give her all she wants."

Mr Wynne had noticed his daughter's approach. He turned to greet her, and the look he gave as he saw her coming reminded Bobby of the word Kimms had used, 'worship'. It did not seem hyperbole; that look was, indeed, almost reverent in its tenderness.

"I'm not late, am I?" she asked gaily. "Have they finished? I do hope it's all over and done with."

"You must ask those two gentlemen, my dear," Wynne answered, indicating Bobby and Kimms, and at that she gave them one of her lovely smiles, one that seemed to make her not so much pretty as really beautiful.

"Is it?" she asked them. "Oh, do say yes." But Bobby answered:

"I'm afraid not."

"It's making everyone so miserable," she said. "I try not to think of it."

"Yes," Bobby said; and the thought came into his mind that perhaps the joyousness she found in the mere act of living was a little too narrow, too self-centred, with but small understanding of the griefs of others. He watched as she turned away to join her father, and then he heard her say:

"Oh, Daddy, I found that old photo you asked me about, and I put it away somewhere to be safe, and now I can't think where."

"Never mind; it doesn't matter; it'll turn up again," Wynne answered.

His voice sounded for once a little hurried, or at least less calm and equable than usual, and the quick glance he gave over his shoulder to Kimms and Bobby, now beginning to walk away together, did seem to suggest that he was wondering if they had overheard and if they showed any sign that they had done so. There was none, though in fact Bobby had heard clearly enough. Whose photograph? he wondered idly, and then, as he so often did, tucked the trivial incident away in his memory, there to lie dormant for evermore unless the need should arise to call it back to active life.

"Nice girl," Kimms was saying. "Don't know how she does it. Cheers the whole place up. She'll go into the Stores crammed with women grumbling at the cost of everything, and money going before you know it's there, and all trying to get served first, and in half a mo. they're different, smiling and friendly, though she's hardly said a word. Just being there. It's like a miracle."

"A miracle of youth," Bobby suggested lightly. "But, then, youth is a bit of a miracle all by itself," and silently he decided that not the least miracle to be credited to Sylvia was that of having extracted from Kimms so long a speech—the longest speech Bobby had ever heard him make.

They had reached the Over All Arms now, and in the room still serving Kimms as headquarters there lay on the table the copy of the report Bobby had had sent him. Kimms picked it up and said:

"Covers a lot of ground. Dowie out?"

"What he says hangs together," Bobby answered. "It's clear he had no idea that the story he had picked up—it seems to have been all over the London underworld—about the proceeds of a big robbery having been concealed hereabouts meant paper money. Not even the most sanguine inventor could expect a machine designed to detect the precious metals to react to paper, too. Confirmation as well, from Rogers."

"Yes," said Kimms. "What about him?"

"Rogers? Well, we've got to accept his alibi. The story of the wallet is quite clear from the man taken ill in the train to Rogers, from Rogers to his wife in her café, from her to the dead man's relatives, and it couldn't have been like that if at the time Rogers was committing a murder in the Twice Over copse."

"Others still in," said Kimms, after he had again nodded agreement.

"Stuart, who found the body," Bobby said slowly. "Maxton, who has been missing ever since. Wynne, who grows loganberries."

"Eh?" said Kimms, startled by this last word. "What?"

"Loganberries come in somehow," Bobby told him. "A link. They aren't often a feature in crime, but they seem to be this time. Fantastic, of course; but, then, crime so often is. Mrs Field kept a tin of the things on a shelf behind her in full view of everyone who came in for a drink, and she was killed near a loganberry bush. Wynne has a sort of fence or barricade of loganberry bushes arranged under the wall between his garden and the copse—to keep small boys, he said, from raiding his apple trees. The loganberry bush where Mrs Field died didn't plant itself; it must have been put there for some reason. A quite innocent reason possibly, a mere whim it might be. No telling. But also it may be for a purpose, just as Mrs Field may have kept her tin on her shelf behind her for some very definite reason."

"What?" Kimms asked doubtfully, and still more doubtfully added the one word: "Loganberries?"

"Rogers, when I was talking to him," Bobby went on, "happened to mention casually that Charley Cream's real name was Logan, and one of the gang killed in the bombing was called Berry. I imagine that's where they got the idea, and showing the tin was a kind of rallying signal or something of the kind to convey a message to members of the gang. Unfortunately, we have no way of knowing if any of them was likely to hit on such an idea or think it amusing."

"Amusing?" repeated Kimms. "Why amusing? Nothing funny I can see."

"Not 'funny'—amusing," Bobby explained gravely. "'Tickle the fancy'—amusing."

"Oh," said Kimms, trying to fathom this and failing.

"If I'm right so far," Bobby continued, "Mrs Field, at the 'Bell and Boy', which it is said all visit sooner or later, hoped to get in touch with one of them again."

"All accounted for," Kimms said. "Aren't they?"

"The four who actually carried out the raid, yes," Bobby said. "Two killed in the bombing. Charley Cream died in prison recently. Farmer found murdered in a ditch. But there seems to have been a hanger-on, a runner or scout, known as 'Fingers', and a man they called 'the Boss'."

"Farmer himself, most likely," Kimms suggested.

"It might be. The 'Boss' is an illusive character," Bobby answered. "Perhaps non-existent. No telling. But I think we may regard it as certain that the display of the tin was meant as a signal to someone who would know what it meant. Another little item of information that came out casually when I managed to get Rogers talking is that Farmer had recently gone to live with a woman and that he was, according to Rogers, 'dead gone' on her, she being what he called 'an eye-full'."

"Jealous rival?" Kimms said.

"It might be," Bobby agreed once more. "I'm just groping here and there, but it does seem to me there's some sort of pattern beginning to show itself. So much shows signs of fitting. The dead woman had been pretty once; she went by the name of Field—Florrie Field, the same initials as Frank Farmer's. Then she certainly had more money than she earned as barmaid; indeed, apparently had no need to work at all, though we never found out where her money came from or where she kept it. All half hints, I know, but they work in together just as when in a crossword puzzle a letter fits both across and down you feel you are on the right track. For myself, I am adopting as a tenable theory, and one worth trying out—of course, you mayn't agree."

"No," said Kimms thoughtfully. Then he said: "Yes. Go on."

"Well, then," Bobby continued, "my idea is that the dead woman is the one Farmer was living with and, according to what Rogers said, 'dead gone on'. We know Farmer had a big share of the proceeds of the P.O. van robbery. A possibility is that he may have divided it into three parts, given one to his woman to keep for him, and that is what she's been living on; a second part he hid somewhere in Twice Over; a third he kept in his own possession, and it was for that he was murdered. It's the second part, hidden here, that Mrs Field came to recover, or try to. She may have heard the same story Dowie got hold of. You hear many things serving behind the bar at a place like the 'Bell and Boy'."

"Doesn't tell us who killed her or why?—or him either," Kimms said. "Or what brought her there at midnight to her death."

"No," Bobby agreed, "but I think it's a foundation on which to build."

CHAPTER XXVIII
AN EXPLANATION

PRESENTLY, AFTER THE conclusion of his talk or consultation with Kimms, Bobby went on to Overs Abbey; though what it was he hoped for there he was not very sure. All he knew with certainty was that references to dealings in diamonds with the gentleman apparently widely known as 'Fatty' Veale had served markedly to abate Sir Charles's truculence and to lessen his self-confidence. In place thereof uneasiness, even fear, had begun to show themselves, and these are things that, as Bobby well knew from long experience, are as apt to loosen the tongue as ever is strong drink. Few indeed are those with restless consciences who are able to resist the instinct to justify and to excuse—the even stronger instinct to mislead. Indeed, it was in just such a mood of troubled talkativeness that Bobby found Sir Charles when he was shown into the room where Sir Charles was waiting. Drinks were immediately produced, and

Sir Charles's uneasiness was in no way allayed when Bobby declined the proffered hospitality.

"You see," he explained apologetically, "this might be considered an official visit, and it would never do for a senior officer to break the taboo on drinking while on duty. Many thanks, all the same."

"Oh, just as you like," Sir Charles growled, and showed by the strength of the drink he mixed for himself that at any rate to him no such 'taboo' applied. "I thought you told me once Kimms was in sole charge. Are you taking over?"

"Dear me, no," Bobby answered. "But his inquiry and mine interlock at almost every point. There's a lot of unpleasant talk going on—"

"Don't I know it?" interrupted Sir Charles angrily. "And don't I know who I have to thank for it? Wynne. Remember the way he fixed it so it should be me find the body. If you ask me, he's the man you want to watch."

"There seems no motive in Wynne's case," Bobby remarked. "At least, none that we can find even the shadow of."

"I suppose that means," Sir Charles growled, as angrily as before, "you've been hearing that damfool yarn about me being blackmailed by the woman who tried to make a scene on my doorstep. Blackmail." He snorted contemptuously. "Do they think I'm a curate in my first job? Or a married man scared of my wife finding out?" He paused to help himself to another drink, even stiffer than the earlier one. "Thank God, I'm neither," he said. "Mind you, I don't want to see Wynne hanged. Not that he would be any the worse for it, but it would be hard luck on that jolly little girl of his."

"Well, as far as I can see, Mr Wynne is a long way from running any risk like that at present," Bobby remarked, and thought to himself that 'jolly' was the last word he would have thought appropriate for that serene and confident joy in life Sylvia seemed so strangely to spread around her wherever she went.

"Maxton, then," Sir Charles suggested, and let his hand hover for a moment over the whisky bottle and then slowly withdrew it. "He's bunked, hasn't he? Why? Tell me that. Journalist, isn't he? Whole place lousy with them. They wanted to get me talking. When I wouldn't, one of 'em tried to make me drunk. As if I couldn't drink any journalist under the table any day and every day." Clearly fortified by this reflection, he now allowed his again hovering hand to perform as usual with the whisky and the soda-water, though but gently with the latter. "And here's the only one of the whole crew on the spot able to supply local colour gone missing. Good enough for me. Can't the French police find him?"

"No known motive in his case either," Bobby remarked.

"Well, there's Wynne's girl," Sir Charles suggested. "He was keen on her. Anyone could see that; and she ought to come in for a goodish bit if Wynne's been anything like as good in doing other chaps down as he has me. If this woman knew anything to put a stopper on that—motive all right. In the village they are saying there was a woman visited Maxton in that hide-out of his every so often and got money from him. Hire purchase, perhaps. I don't know."

"No doubt Mr Maxton will be able to explain when we get in touch with him again," Bobby said. "We expect to, soon. We are already with his sister."

"His sister isn't him," Sir Charles pointed out, rather as if he thought this was a novel point and one of some importance and Bobby should be reminded of it. Then he rose very firmly to his feet and even more firmly replaced whisky and soda in the cupboard. "Very seldom drink between meals, except for a nightcap," he informed Bobby as he returned, though a little less firmly, to his chair.

"Well, thank you for what you've told me," Bobby said. "You may be sure all the points you've mentioned have been carefully considered—or will be. There's nothing else, is there, you would care to say? The plain fact is we're only groping about in the dark, hoping somehow or another to lay our hands on something useful. If we do run across anything that looks odd, even if it doesn't seem to have much to do with it, we follow it up on the chance that finally it may give us a lead. Of course, if we find a satisfactory explanation or we are given one—well, then we just forget all about it. Nothing else you can think of?"

Sir Charles made no reply. He got to his feet, shook hands in silence and in silence accompanied Bobby to the front door. Apparently it was to prove a fruitless visit, though sometimes it happened that persons who had said little or nothing in response to questions would yet at the last moment show a willingness to talk as great as had been their previous reluctance.

And that something like this was about to happen Bobby began to hope when Sir Charles muttered that he might as well walk down the drive as far as the gate.

"In there," said Sir Charles moodily, with a backward glance over his shoulder, "I catch 'em listening when they think they see a chance." In his turn Bobby was silent, making no comment. They had reached the gate before Sir Charles spoke again. "About those diamonds," he said abruptly. "Veale has been buying some from me now and then. Nothing wrong in that, is there? What put you on it?"

"We get to hear a lot in one way or another during an investigation like this," Bobby explained. "Some of it we forget at once. Our business is with the law, not with private morality. Some of it may seem worth filing, or even worth following up. Some of it is helpful."

"My old aunt bought them in the first place," Sir Charles said. "She was scared out of her life about the Germans coming. There was an awful invasion flap here, you remember. I didn't know at the time. I was in the army, in the thick of it out there." He waved a hand vaguely, presumably to indicate where the 'thick of it' was. "I couldn't make out what she meant when she wrote me a rambling sort of letter about an old suitcase of mine in the attics, and it was for me and it mightn't be in her will; but there it was, and everything in it to go with the title—I had that, of course, since uncle's death; and a fat lot of good it did me, too. The bombing soon got too much for her, though, so she ran off to Ireland, and didn't live very long afterwards. When I got demobbed at last—they hung on to some of us like grim death; found us specially useful, I suppose—the executors had everything cleared up except that they couldn't find out what she had done with her money. Speculating, they thought. Sunk without trace, and there was I left high and dry, no cash to carry on with, and likely to be sold up any day almost. Then I got a letter from Veale to say he had been acting for the old lady and had I any of the diamonds he had been buying for her? If I had, would I like to dispose of any? What would you have done?"

"Well," Bobby answered smilingly, "I expect I should have started to look round—with special reference to any old suitcases I could find."

"Exactly," said Sir Charles, much pleased at what he seemed to take for official approval. "Just what I did. There it was in the attics as before. It had been sent back from Ireland when the old lady died, and, what's more, it was as near as may be sent off again to a jumble sale, only for being full of old junk they thought I might like to look at. Well, the diamonds were there all right. Where do you think?"

"In envelopes under a false bottom," Bobby answered promptly.

"That's right," Sir Charles admitted, though now looking slightly disappointed at receiving so immediate and correct a response. "Unset stones all of them, and all of high quality—not a 'rough' among them. All 'cleans' or 'V.V.S.'s'. So I've been selling through Veale. I must say he gets good prices. Knows the market from tip to tail, and waits his opportunity. What he calls 'grouping'. He says a good stone will often go through half a dozen hands, price up each time, till it gets where it belongs. Veale cuts out all that. Goes direct to the man who wants it most."

"The discovery must have been a pleasant surprise," Bobby remarked.

"You can bet your last potato it was," declared Sir Charles fervently. "Made all the difference. I wake up all in a sweat sometimes thinking how easily it might have gone off to that jumble sale. Wound up in Petticoat Lane, perhaps, or on a dust-heap. It just shows, doesn't it?"

"It does indeed," said Bobby, with almost equal fervour, though without the least idea what it did in fact 'show'. "Anyhow, many thanks for what you've told me."

"Clears everything up, doesn't it?" Sir Charles asked, though now just a little anxiously, as if he had hoped to hear a rather stronger note of reassurance in Bobby's voice. "You'll regard it as highly confidential? Veale is always keen on none of the other dealers getting to know anything about it."

"Everything told a police officer," Bobby answered, repeating a so often given assurance, "is always strictly confidential, unless it is relevant evidence. Then it isn't. As far as I can see at present, your dealings with your aunt's diamonds can hardly have any bearing on either Mrs Field's murder or on the inquiry into the possibility of the proceeds of the P.O. van robbery being still hidden somewhere in Twice Over."

In spite of the deliberately cautious and official tone of this pronouncement—or possibly because of it—Sir Charles seemed now to find his former anxiety much relieved. He went back to the house; and Bobby walked slowly on to the village, pondering as he went over the story he had just heard, and, in the orthodox police phrase, finding himself 'not fully satisfied'.

Extraordinary as the tale was, yet he felt it could not be dismissed as totally incredible. There were, he knew, many stories of people who had concealed money or valuables when invasion seemed imminent and had then forgotten exactly where, or else died or been killed in the bombing without having passed on the secret of the chosen hiding-place.

Fantastic, of course, to think of a battered old suitcase, with a fortune in diamonds hidden in it, going from hand to hand, finally to come to a last resting-place on a heap of rubbish. But, then, these are days when it sometimes seems as if the fantastic had become the commonplace.

All the same, there was one weak point.

"No satisfactory reason," Bobby remarked to Kimms when he had given him a brief account of the interview with Sir Charles, "for all the secrecy. Taken with Rogers's story, it sounds much more like black-market dealing. Why sell through a man of Veale's character at all? You can understand Veale getting hold of an old lady in a state of near panic, but Stuart strikes me as having quite a bit of experience in the shadier walks of life."

"Ah-h," said Kimms when Bobby paused, and managed to make that non-committal exclamation sound like an emphatic agreement.

"There is one obvious explanation, of course," Bobby added thoughtfully. "Guesswork, but holds water."

"Yes," said Kimms. "What?"

"Death duties," Bobby said.

"Oh," said Kimms, considering.

"Dodging 'em," Bobby said. "If the executors had found diamonds, and if they were as valuable as Stuart's story suggests, then a good share would have gone in death duties."

"There's that," Kimms agreed. "No proof. Can't do anything now."

"No," agreed Bobby. "Stuart could say their real value was only a hundred or two, Veale would back him up, and the duty payable would be trifling."

"Fishy," said Kimms. "Very. Clears Stuart, though? More or less."

"More or less," agreed Bobby. "There's another possibility. Pound-notes is what every thief hopes to get hold of."

"No fence to take half," commented Kimms.

"Exactly," said Bobby. "But not quite so easy when it's a sum in tens of thousands. Could Stuart have been mixed up in the original robbery, used his whack to buy diamonds, and then resold them to get clean money?"

"Opens possibilities," said Kimms.

The 'phone rang. He answered, listened, said: "Good, carry on," hung up the receiver and came back to Bobby.

"From Magna Minor," he said, naming the ancient market town a few miles from Twice Over. "Young man answering the description of Martin Maxton reported seen in company of girl believed to be Miss Sylvia Wynne. All our chaps alerted."

CHAPTER XXIX
UNASKED QUESTION

AT THIS announcement Bobby relapsed into one of those 'Bobby Owen trances', in which he seemed somehow to combine two contradictions—complete oblivion to all around with instant apprehension of any relevant word or act. Kimms, equally silent, concentrated his gaze upon the ceiling, as if seeking inspiration there. It was he who spoke first.

"Off again double quick," he said. "Jack-in-the-box business."

"Who? Maxton?" Bobby asked, sitting up in his chair exactly as if he had been suddenly awakened from deep sleep. "Yes. Or he may have made up his mind to come forward."

"Why should he?" demanded Kimms. "What for?"

"Hotels are very sensitive to police observation," Bobby reminded him, "and the one Maxton's sister and her husband manage up North has been watched pretty closely since I was up there. Staff soon notice that sort of thing. They gossip, and then trade is apt to fall off. Maxton may be showing here simply to draw us away from the hotel. His sister may have told him to. Or he may just be wanting to see the girl once more before disappearing for good. No telling."

"Miss Wynne?" Kimms muttered uneasily. "We can't put her through it. Like brawling in church, that would be."

"Well, she'll have to be questioned, all the same," Bobby insisted. "I think there are things she can tell and no one else. It was from her we heard of lights seen in the copse the night before the murder."

"If people get the idea we are bothering her, we'll be lynched," Kimms said, still uneasily. "Or questions in Parliament," and it was clear he thought this last the alternative most to be dreaded.

"It's a risk," Bobby agreed. "And I think Wynne would make himself very nasty indeed if he thought we were trying to bring her in in any way whatever. An ugly customer I fancy he could be if he wanted. But there's a still worse risk."

"What?" Kimms asked, incredulous.

"That she may lose that lovely smile of hers for good," Bobby answered.

"Oh, well," Kimms said. "Even if she is in love with Maxton, she's young enough to get over it."

"Perhaps," Bobby said; "though I don't think she's the kind to get over things easily. Let's hope there'll be no need. But the road must be followed wherever it leads, and she'll have to be asked if she can put us in touch with Maxton. Unless, of course, he does come forward."

"If he is really in love with her," Kimms complained, "why does he want to go committing murders on her doorstep almost?"

"Why indeed?" echoed Bobby; "but, then, we don't know that he did. There are others, and even those who seem cleared we may have to pop back again. How about my trying to get hold of Miss Wynne by myself? It would seem less formal, and no one could object to her being asked to give a message to Maxton. You wouldn't risk local criticism and it wouldn't bother me so much. Besides, you would still be available here if there's any fresh development."

Kimms accepted this suggestion with very evident relief. He even took out his handkerchief to wipe his forehead.

"I had rather tackle a bunch of armed gangsters any day than her," he said.

"I know," Bobby agreed; "but there are things that have to be done, and this is one."

So it was agreed, and Bobby was soon driving to Magna Minor, a detour which did not in fact take him far from the direct road back to London. As he had hoped might be the case, presently he saw another car coming towards him, a car he recognized as Mr Wynne's. Sylvia seemed to be alone in it. As soon as he was sure of her identity he alighted and waved to her to stop. When she did so he went across to her.

"Oh, it's you," she said, opening the car door, and though she smiled as she spoke, it was but a poor watery thing, very different from some he had seen before. The sunshine had gone from it as she asked anxiously: "Is anything the matter?"

"Oh, no," Bobby assured her. "But we would like to get in touch with Mr Maxton if possible. Could you give me his address?"

"It's Hidden Cottage," she answered simply. "Didn't you know?"

"Well, you see," Bobby answered, "he doesn't seem to have been there for some time. You remember the cottage was broken into the same day Mr Wynne found an intruder in his study?"

"Oh, yes," she answered at once; "but he didn't say anything about that, and I didn't either."

"Was that this afternoon?" Bobby asked, and when she nodded, he went on: "Did Mr Maxton say anything about his future movements?"

"Only that he was going away for a long time," she replied. "He didn't say why. I suppose it's his work. He said he didn't know when he would be back," and now there was visible a faint quivering of her upper lip that Bobby noticed and that then was gone.

"That makes it difficult," Bobby said. "We can't do much about the cottage break-in till we know if anything is missing. If there isn't, it's only trespass—and damage to property. Not a police matter. Could you give him a message from us, do you think?"

She shook her head, and when she answered, it was in a very small voice that she almost whispered:

"He said he didn't think it was likely we would ever meet again."

"I see," Bobby said. After a pause, he continued: "I must apologize, then, for troubling you. I thought it was just possible you might be able to help. I'm sorry."

He stepped back then and made as if to return to his own car, but she leaned forward and called to him by name, though in a voice so low he was not even sure he had heard correctly. But he stayed to listen again, and she said:

"It's because of what's happened you want to see him, isn't it? But he doesn't know anything; he told me so," and this was said with a simple faith that Bobby felt he could hardly share.

"The inquiry is going on," he told her, "and must and will, both here and in London, till we get at the truth. You remember the light you saw in the copse the night before the murder. You don't feel you can say anything more about that? It may mean—though of course I don't know—that you will be called as a witness. I think myself you ought to tell Mr Wynne, or it might be better if I called to see him. You said at the time that you didn't know who it was. Could it have been Mr Maxton?"

"I asked him afterwards," she admitted, "and he said it was. But he wasn't there the next night, when it happened. I asked him that, too, and he said No, he wasn't there," and this once again she said with her air of simple faith as though his denial were conclusive, though once again that was hardly how Bobby regarded it.

"It wakened you. You heard something that second night about twelve, didn't you?" Bobby went on. "But you saw there was a light in your father's room—it overlooks the copse, too—so you went to sleep again. Mr Wynne tells us he heard what he thought was a cry. He got out of bed to look—he was lying awake reading—and thinks that was probably what wakened you when he opened the window and then shut it again."

"I expect it was," she agreed when Bobby seemed to expect an answer. "I was awfully sleepy, but so long as Daddy was there I knew it was all right. Sometimes when he's very wakeful he does go out to walk about a little, and it always makes me so nervous, because of course anyone might easily slip in in the dark, couldn't they?"

"I suppose they could, but it wouldn't be likely," Bobby told her. "Not unless Mr Wynne made a habit of it and it was known. Have you any idea what Mr Maxton was doing there so late on the first night?"

"It's his books and things," she explained. "He likes to know about what happens after dark. Ever such a lot goes on, he says—quite as much as in the daytime—only most people don't know, because they're in bed. And that's why, when no one's there, the little frightened people in the fields and the woods haven't so much to be afraid of."

"Isn't that why he took Hidden Cottage?" Bobby asked doubtfully. "That's what I understood. To get material, I mean. Couldn't he have done that just as well where he lived, instead of two or three miles away?"

"It was all awfully silly of him," she explained, her colour slightly heightened. "I never thought he meant it. It was an old story he found, only quite true and awfully sad, and he put it in his book he was writing, about a page ever so long ago, and he was serenading a girl he loved; only her brothers came and killed him. It's most awfully exciting because now he's found out a lot more about it, and he thinks the page was a son of Blondel—you know, the man who went about singing till he found King Richard."

"I expect that will set all the historians talking," Bobby agreed. "But I don't quite see—" He paused, remembering he had heard this tale of an unlucky page before, and that then a vague, fleeting thought had passed through his mind and been at once dismissed as too far-fetched. "Or was Mr Maxton intending to follow the page's example and serenade you?" he asked.

"It was just too silly of him," she repeated. "He said he wished he could, only he hadn't a guitar and wouldn't know how to play it if he had. So I got the giggles and he was offended, and he said he would be there all the same, and he would shine his torch for me to see when I went up to bed if I looked out. I told him I never would, and not to be such an idiot."

"Did you? Look out, I mean."

"Well, not exactly. I did just have a peep, and the light was there, but that's all."

"The next night—the night of the murder—something woke you, didn't it, just about the time it happened?"

"Yes, but Martin wasn't there. I told you. I asked him."

"Well, thank you for what you've told me," Bobby said, and he was thinking to himself that this queer little romantic tale, so simply told, at once touching and absurd, of boy playing troubadour to the girl he loved, would win over at once any jury in the land. No jury would believe, nor would the general public, that a young man seeking to find favour in the eyes of the girl he was courting would turn abruptly to commit what had all the appearance of a premeditated and deliberate murder. Bobby himself was not so sure. Murder and Love. Both born of passion, and sometimes they prove twins in action. "Thank you," he repeated. "It all helps to give a clearer idea of what happened that night. By the way, I hope you found that photograph I heard you say you had mislaid?"

"Oh, yes," she answered, looking both surprised and relieved by this rather abrupt change of subject. "I had it in my bag all the time. Daddy was almost cross at my being so stupid"—and this she said as if she had never till now thought it conceivable that her father could ever be cross with her. "And then he only burnt it when I gave it him," she added.

Bobby spoke no word in answer, but still stood staring at her, and she looked back at him, puzzled by his silence and his expression, and still he stood and stared in silence, till she grew a little frightened.

"Have I said anything I shouldn't?" she asked at last.

"No, no," he muttered, and again was silent.

She said good-bye then and drove away; and long after her car had passed out of sight he was still standing there, a question that had been trembling on the tip of his tongue still unspoken, unasked, unanswered. Then he turned his car and followed her. It was the shortest way back to the direct London road he had left in order to make this detour.

A feeling of guilt, of failure, weighed upon him. It was the first time, he reflected, that he had ever allowed personal or private considerations to interfere with his duty. For he knew it had been his plain duty to ask that question, and yet his tongue had refused to utter it.

Presently he stopped at a telephone booth and rang up Kimms. It was some minutes before he got through. When he did, he gave Kimms an almost verbatim account of his talk with

Sylvia down to the last words they had exchanged. But still he did not mention that last unuttered dreadful question that to him seemed to emerge so clearly from all that had been said before. If that seemed so to Kimms also, and Kimms thought it should be asked, then, Bobby decided, he would at once agree, and indeed offer to return immediately, so as to be present when it was posed. No such suggestion came, though Kimms seemed surprised both at the detailed nature of the report and at its coming from a wayside booth. He even sounded a little impatient at having to listen so long at the 'phone, while at the same time he was being promised a full typed report as soon as it could be prepared.

Back at the Yard, Bobby stayed late to write this out in the fullest possible detail, and next morning he was busy reading the typed copy when a message came to say that a Mr Martin Maxton was below asking if Mr Owen wished to see him, as he had heard was the case.

"Very much so," Bobby answered. "Keep him safe till I send, and then bring him along," and then, with the reflection that life is much easier when those you are searching for turn up of their own accord, continued with his task of reading, correcting and signing the Kimms report.

CHAPTER XXX
TOKEN SERENADE

IT WAS FULLY half an hour before Bobby chose to declare himself ready to receive Martin. No bad thing, he knew by experience, to leave a suspect for a time alone with thoughts that were apt to increase nervousness, suggest pitfalls in his way and how to avoid them, and generally to distract his attention from the confident and plausible story he had presumably prepared. Otherwise he would hardly be willing to submit himself for the close questioning so apt to reveal flaws if concentration wavered for even a moment.

Of course, these considerations did not apply to the witness of truth who came forward with the simple desire to tell all he knew and remembered, and no more. But Bobby did not think this was a category to which Martin Maxton was likely to belong.

When Martin was at last summoned he did in fact show clear signs of being under extreme mental tension, but a tension held in firm control. Unless it broke, and now Bobby was inclined to think that unlikely, equally unlikely that Martin would in any way allow whatever story he meant to tell to collapse or allow himself to walk into any trap of his own preparing. That often happened with the most carefully constructed story; often the more carefully constructed the more easily broken down. But not, Bobby was telling himself, not with Martin Maxton.

Indeed, even from the first, the interview did not take the normal course, as between detective and suspect. For when Bobby sat back in his chair and began to subject Martin to that long, scrutinizing gaze, under which so often a suspect's self-confidence crumbled, it was Martin, settling himself in the chair offered him, who spoke first and with emphasis, saying:

"First of all I want it clearly understood that I am willing to tell you anything you want to know about myself. But I will tell you nothing about anyone else—nothing, at least, that I feel they must tell you themselves if they are willing to."

"Dear me," Bobby remarked, surprised for once. "You know, that sounds much more like a declaration of war, instead of a wish to help."

"I should call it," Martin retorted, "not so much a declaration of war as of armed neutrality, and I have never said I wanted to help."

"If it is not to help us, why have you come to see us?" Bobby asked.

"Because I preferred to come at once rather than wait for you to dig me out. When my sister told me you had been to see her and your men were watching their hotel and how terribly difficult it was and upsetting both her and Tom—her husband, he is—well, it was what I jolly well had to do. Not that I wanted to, but there it was."

"You tried to make us think you had gone to France?"

"Rather a wash-out, that," Martin admitted. "An amateur's trick. At the time I thought it quite a good idea—to choke you off, I mean. I knew that girl would talk if she saw me on board, so I let her see me, and then came straight back on the same boat without even landing."

"Why did you go through such a performance?" Bobby asked. "Was it because a murderer always thinks first of flight?"

"Does he?" Martin asked; and only a slight drawing in of his breath showed that he had noted that dread word Bobby had at last pronounced. Indeed when Martin repeated it, he did so without a tremor in his voice. "I didn't know. But, then, I'm not a murderer, though I suppose I should say so anyhow. Even confessed killers protest they are innocent, don't they? Killers perhaps, but not murderers. I am neither."

"You seem," Bobby said, "to have taken an interest in the psychology of murder."

"Murder," answered Martin, "has become a subject of overwhelming interest to me since I realized I was under suspicion of having committed one myself—and even before, even before," he said, almost to himself, in a tone and with an accent Bobby did not fully understand. "Not," he added with a sudden, rather charming smile, "that I'm in the least afraid that you will ever be able to prove I did something I didn't do. But aren't we rather talking round and round? Or is this an example of your famous technique McKie told me about—an amiable chat about nothing in particular to lull the other fellow to sleep and then pounce."

"I wish McKie would keep his nose out of things that don't concern him," Bobby said crossly.

"He's a journalist; that's their job, pushing their noses in," Martin explained, superfluously, for that was something Bobby knew all about, from which at times he had suffered many things—and gained more. "He offered me a hundred down to write a full confession if I were guilty, with a firm undertaking not to use it until after I had been convicted and hanged, and then another four hundred to anyone I liked to name."

"What did you say?" Bobby asked.

"Oh, I agreed at once; only he had to understand I should name him as the actual murderer and explain I only stood by and looked on—under protest. That rather choked him off."

"I daresay it would," agreed Bobby, a little pleased to hear that the enterprising Mr McKie had been scored off for once, reflecting, too, that a suspect capable of introducing a frivolous note into a talk with an investigating officer was certainly out of the usual. He continued: "Miss Wynne saw a light near the scene of the murder the night before it took place."

"Me," Martin said simply.

"What were you doing there at that time of night?" Bobby asked. "Making yourself familiar with the ground, by any chance?"

"Preparatory to committing a murder?" Martin retorted, ready as ever to dot the 'i' and cross the 't'. "If that had been the idea, I should hardly have told Miss Wynne I would be there, or asked her to look out for my light, should I?"

"Were you in the copse on the night of the murder as well?"

"I was. I told Miss Wynne I wasn't, but I was. But I didn't show a light. I had meant to as soon as she put out her own, just to let her know I was still there."

"Why didn't you?"

"Because there was someone else hanging about. Near that loganberry bush. I imagine it must have been either Mrs Field or her murderer. I don't know. It was a dark night, anyhow, and under the trees it was as black as pitch. I nearly got lost myself though I've trained myself to move in the dark by sound and feel, the way blind people do. On a really dark night, under trees, you are as good as blind. I've rather made a corner for myself in nature-studies by night. I could tell someone was there. There were little noises none of the creatures of the wood would have made. At the time I thought it was probably a boy waiting for his girl. I heard them talking. But definitely not lovers. I couldn't hear what they said and I didn't try. It was getting late, so I gave it up and went home."

"You've said nothing of all this before?"

"No, I haven't, and I wouldn't now," Martin retorted, "if my hand hadn't been forced and my sister on the verge of a breakdown with worry. She's very nervous—has cause to be. I hope now I've told you all this you'll lay off their hotel. Of course, too, I wasn't in any way awfully anxious for it to be known I was there that night. People talk—they'll talk a man to hell if they get half a chance."

"I can believe you didn't want us to know of your presence," Bobby remarked drily. "Did you notice anything else you remember?"

"No," Martin answered. "Unless you mean the light in Wynne's room. I knew he often lay awake reading in bed before going to sleep, but that night it was later than usual. It was one reason why I thought I had better go home. If I showed any light and he saw it and thought it was me, he might suspect there was something on between me and Sylvia, and that might make a bit of trouble."

"What you say is entirely your own story. No supporting evidence?"

"Not a scrap. There isn't any. For you to believe or disbelieve just as you like."

"Your first visit to the copse was simply to impress Miss Wynne with your devotion? Was that it? A sort of serenade, in fact?"

"Rather a token serenade," Martin commented. "But that was more or less the idea. Sounds silly, I know. She never seemed to be aware of me any more than of anyone else. Out of sight, out of mind. Interested in everyone and everything just the same, and how lovely it all was. The world full of a number of things, and everyone as happy as kings. That was how she saw it. A sort of divine content with us all. She loved all the world, and what I wanted was that she should love me. She didn't. No reason why she should. I suppose that has to come of its own accord. The serenade idea was a sort of forlorn hope to get her to feel that I was—well, that I was me. She took it as a kind of joke, only more silly than most. That's all over now. I don't even mind talking about it. A bit of a relief.

It's all as if it were someone else—someone I knew once, but not now."

"You told Miss Wynne, didn't you? that you were going away and would never return. A final good-bye?"

"How do you know? Have you seen her? Yes, that's what I told her. I've always known I ought to. All the same, I hung on, though I knew it was impossible. Wrong." He was silent, and he looked long and thoughtfully at Bobby. He said: "I'm treating you as a sort of father confessor, instead of a detective chap out to get me hanged. Do you know, I don't think I should much care if you did. It would end what ought never to have begun."

"What do you mean by that?" Bobby asked, but this question Martin did not answer. He resumed:

"Perhaps I should, though, if you managed it, though I don't see how you could. I daresay that really, way back at the bottom of my mind, I did rather hope you might believe me. Always the optimist, you see. Sometimes, too, the prospect of getting hanged—well, I do rather panic."

"The risk would be less if you held less back," Bobby said. "You are not telling all."

"I tell my own tale, no one else's," Martin retorted.

"As I understand it," Bobby continued, "you were in love with Miss Wynne and hoped you might win hers. Then suddenly, after the murder, you changed, and now you've told her you are going away and she is not likely ever to see you again. She seems to have found that rather puzzling, and even disturbing."

"I hope you are right," Martin said. "I hope even more that you are wrong."

"That makes it seem something happened—something serious to make you change your mind," Bobby said. "What?"

"Yes, it does, doesn't it?" Martin agreed. "What happened was that I woke up from dreams and faced realities instead. It was all wrong, and I knew I had to go away. That's all."

"What do you mean by 'all wrong'?" Bobby asked, but Martin did not answer. He sat silent, staring straight before him, and his eyes were strange and dark. It was as though they were watching visions from the past, visions that were strange and dark. Bobby said: "Why do you sleep badly?"

CHAPTER XXXI
MARTIN'S STORY

NO ANSWER came. Bobby waited—watchful, patient, as so often before when instinct told him a crisis had come, one that might or might not come to a head but that any spoken word would certainly dispel. For some moments Martin remained silent, motionless, staring straight before him, and when he spoke at last, it was rather as if the words came automatically, without conscious will.

"Yes, I do, don't I?" he was murmuring, and the words were hard to catch. "Sis and I, we sleep badly." Then he passed his hand before his eyes as if to wipe away whatever it was they saw, and said more loudly, "Yes, that's right. How did you know?"

"The first time I saw you," Bobby answered, "I got two impressions. There are things that in police work you get to recognize instinctively. One was that you slept badly. Your eyes, I think. Tired and watchful, they seemed to me—the eyes of a man who often lay awake watching the dark. Also I heard you were much abroad at night and in the small hours of the morning, and that people talked about it."

"'Macbeth hath murdered sleep,' is that the idea?" murmured Martin, and now he seemed more self-possessed, more like his usual self. "If you really want to know, yes, I do have dreams—ugly dreams, nightmares. Is it a crime to have nightmares or to suffer from insomnia?"

"No, but crime might be their cause," Bobby retorted. "You know your cottage was entered while you were away? Have you any idea who it was or why?"

"None," answered Martin. "Have you? I've missed nothing. I did wonder if it had anything to do with all those stories about stuff buried in the copse that were going the rounds. Do you know?"

"We have strong suspicions, but that's all," Bobby answered; "and we suspect, too, that there may be a tie-up with those stories you mentioned. If you've missed nothing, it seems more like a civil action for trespass and damage than a police matter. But there's another thing I thought I noticed that time we first met. I thought you knew me, recognized me. I even had your finger-prints checked. They are not on record."

"How on earth did you manage that?" Martin asked. "To check them, I mean. They've never been taken."

"There were plenty in your cottage," Bobby explained. "When the local police were informed of the break-in they took a number. They were nearly all the same, so presumably made by the occupier—yours, in fact. Most likely the intruder wore gloves. They were sent to Scotland Yard—without result."

"Well, I'm glad I'm cleared on that point, anyhow," Martin commented, more than half mockingly. "Thorough, aren't you? I shall have to be careful, though, in the future. Down on me at once if I misbehave; is that it?"

"As a matter of fact, they've all been destroyed," Bobby assured him. "We are allowed only to keep dabs of convicted persons. It seems I was right in thinking that you slept badly, and I heard you say just now that your sister did, too. Does it run in the family, I wonder? Never mind. Would you care to say if my other idea was correct? That you recognized me and were rather upset by doing so?"

"Was that another guess?" Martin countered. "Good at guessing, aren't you?"

"Everyone calls it guessing," protested Bobby. "I call it deduction from observation. Anyhow, was I right?"

"Well, I was there once when you were shooing off a lot of journalists, trying to get you to tell us something about a case you were handling. Years ago. I was in the back row. I always am. I'm no newshawk, able to smell an exclusive a mile away. I don't expect you even saw me."

"If that was all," Bobby insisted, "why were you so plainly startled, uneasy even, seeing me?"

"Top-rank police officers turning up unexpectedly generally means trouble somewhere," Martin retorted. "And I knew there were some funny rumours going round, though I didn't know exactly what. Or was it just instinct?"

"Our information is that a woman answering the description of Mrs Field was seen earlier in the day of the murder coming from the direction of your cottage."

"I don't know anything about that," Martin said. "So far as I know, I never saw her in my life."

"We have further information that a woman has been paying you regular visits and that you gave her sums of money—rather large sums? Do you care to say anything about that?"

"You are on that, too, are you?" Martin exclaimed. "Is that suspicious? My God! is there anything a man can do that can't be called suspicious? Yes, I do give a woman money at regular intervals. Once I gave her a hundred pounds, and of course that was the time she managed to lose her hand-bag, the hundred pounds and all! Started some of my more amiable neighbours talking about blackmail when they heard."

"A hundred pounds is a lot of money—at least, most of us think so."

"You do when you have to save it up in shillings," Martin retorted. "But that's what television sets cost, if you get a good one. And I don't see why I shouldn't pay for someone else's, if I want to."

"No," Bobby agreed, "but it's unusual, and there are a lot of unusual things in this case, and a good many of them seem to centre round you. However, if that's all you have to tell me, I won't detain you any longer. But I am bound to say that serious consideration will have to be given to the question of charging you."

"I thought that would be next," Martin said. "Pretty flimsy evidence, in my opinion. But no doubt I'm prejudiced. I hoped I might manage to put you off. Sis told me I should only make it worse, but I didn't see what else there was to do. I knew you would go on working. The Yard never stops, does it? All right, I have been keeping things back a lot. Once I swore on the Bible I would never tell. Now I suppose I've got to. I told Sis it might come to that, oath or no oath, and anyhow, getting had up for murder and perhaps hanged wouldn't be much good to anyone—not even to that blessed hotel Tom Toosoon thinks is the beginning and end of all created things."

"Yes?" Bobby said, when Martin paused, as if uncertain how to continue or else unwilling to. "Yes?"

"I saw you once before that other time I told you of," Martin resumed. "But I don't suppose you saw me. Sis and I. We were hiding behind the curtains looking through the window at a woman hammering at the front door with one hand and waving a knife in the other. She wanted to get in to murder me."

"Who was the woman?" Bobby asked.

Martin seemed to have some difficulty in answering. He got up from his chair. He went to the window. For an instant the fear flashed into Bobby's mind that he was going to jump out. But there was no sign of that. Over his shoulder Martin said, and now his voice was loud and clear:

"She was my mother."

He turned from the window then and came back slowly to his chair. There was a long silence. For this at least Bobby had not expected, and he had some difficulty in adjusting his mind to it and to all that it implied. Then at last he said:

"Why did your mother wish to murder you?"

"Because she thought she had," Martin answered; and once more he lapsed into silence, and once more his heavy eyes seemed to be watching strange, dark visions surging up from past years, and it seemed to Bobby that this time he could well guess what those visions were. Martin said abruptly, Bobby's question unanswered: "I don't suppose you remember. Why should you?"

"Do you mean that I was there?" Bobby asked.

"I expect someone rang up the police station, and you came along to see what was happening. It's years ago. It might be yesterday for me. Not for you. I was fifteen. Sis is seven years older. You managed to coax mother to give up the knife and come away. I believe you told her that if she wanted me killed, all right, but it had to be done in the proper way, and it was most unladylike to be making such a disturbance. She must come to the police station so that the necessary steps could be taken and proceedings begun. So she did, and then two nurses arrived, and she went back quietly to the Home she had escaped from. When she remembers, she still asks when the proceedings will begin."

"Had she been long like that?" Bobby asked.

"Since she watched my father die and the baby was born blind," Martin answered. "A car knocked her down crossing the road. Father ran to pick her up. Another car came along and overturned trying to avoid the first. It pinned father down right across mother lying there. By the time they got the car lifted father was dead and mother had watched him die. The baby was born soon afterwards, before its time, and it was blind. Some mischief-making fool started the idea that the baby was blind because mother's unconscious wanted to protect it from ever seeing what mother had seen. She got to know somehow what was being said. I think that was what did it. No one had any idea anything was wrong. Except Sis. She was twelve and she knew, only she didn't know what. One day mother told us she was going to take us all for a nice walk by the river. Sis and me—I was five—and the blind baby. When we got there she sat down, nursing the baby, and I began to play about; but Sis stood a little way away, watching. Mother called to us. I came, but Sis waited. Mother stood up and pushed the baby into the river. I remember saying, 'Oh, mummy, that was baby.' I think I thought it was just a mistake. Mother took my hand. She said: 'Yes, darling; she's going to join father, and we must go, too.' I don't remember any more except being in the water. Sis ran away, crying. Some men heard her. They were in time to get us out, but the baby had disappeared."

When he had finished speaking, Martin sat back and closed his eyes, as if to shut out the vision that so often tormented him. Bobby let some minutes pass before he spoke. Then he said: "Is your mother, then, still suffering from the delusion that you and she must join your father?"

"It's not that exactly," Martin answered. "She believes she did drown me and that I'm dead, and when she sees me she thinks I must be some evil spirit, masquerading as me—a kind of zombie—and it's her duty to kill me again. It's quite logical. She knows she pushed me into the river, and so I must have drowned. If she sees me she goes into such paroxysms that the doctors at the Home where she is now have asked me not to try to see her. The woman who visits me regularly is a nurse from the Home, and she is our only link. She comes to tell me how mother is, and the money I give her is for any little extra comfort and to pay her for her trouble. The hundred pounds you've heard about was for a television set for mother's own use. Very often she won't mix with the other patients. Nurse wants any money I give her to be in cash. She has an idea the Home wouldn't like it if they knew."

CHAPTER XXXII
DOUBTS AND FEARS

ONCE AGAIN THERE was a long silence, but not now because either had become lost in past memories or present thought. Rather it was as though, like two skilled swordsmen, well knowing that in their encounter lay issues of life and death, they had drawn apart for a momentary pause. Yet each still as wary and intent as when keen rapiers had clashed and thrust and parried, flickering to and fro.

In no word that Bobby had uttered had doubt or misgiving found expression, yet a deep awareness was in Martin's mind that in Bobby's such thoughts and feelings had been born. So equally did Bobby know, with equal strong assurance, that everything Martin had told him had been carefully prepared, chosen to conceal some one vital fact, the one that might provide the necessary clue. Yet what that could be he could not conceive. Then Martin stood up, glancing towards the door, as if he felt that now he had told everything he had to tell he was entitled to go.

"That's all," he said. "You can check it all if you want to. It was in all the papers at the time."

"Oh, yes, it will probably be checked," Bobby said. "Matter of routine—red tape, if you like. But no one could suppose that you would invent or suppress"—was there just the faintest emphasis on this last word?—"anything that could be so easily confirmed—or not. No, I accept your story as it stands as factual and complete. There are just one or two minor points. You began by saying you had promised never to tell anyone. Do you mind saying who it was you promised and why your promise—oath, you said—was asked for? Surely it was all well known, and I imagine there was no great risk of your talking about it."

"Well known at the time," Martin agreed. "But people soon forget, and then Sis and I had gone to live with relatives in Canada. I was five when it happened and fifteen when I promised. It was Sis asked me. She was old enough at twelve to feel it all, not old enough to throw it off. For a long time she was half afraid she might go the same way. She told me once she never dared look at a baby. That wore off in time. When we came back to England she met Tom Toosoon. Tom's a good chap, but I always think he puts his hotel before wife and family and everything else. Anyhow, Sis picked him out as her man from the start. I remember finding her one day writing 'Mrs Thomas Toosoon' on a scrap of paper to see how it looked. She got the idea that if Tom knew he might sheer off, and then, if there were children—and she meant there to be because she knew Tom would want them—well, she had it on her mind that they must never hear about their grandmother. So she won't go to visit mother because of the risk of Tom and the children getting to know. I believe myself, though she never says so, that there's still fear at the back of her mind that if she thinks of it too much—and seeing mother would bring it all back again so vividly—then she might go the same way. Perhaps she might."

He paused and said softly: "Nightmares; I have them, too. But she helps with the money when she can wangle some without Tom knowing. It's not that he's mean; it's that an hotel's like a farm—there's always something extra you want and kid yourself it will pay off in the long run, though no guest will ever notice it. Anyhow, that's the whole thing; and now I've told you, I must take my promise back."

"It is an unhappy story," Bobby said. "I am sorry you had to tell it, but I think it was right to do so. Your disappearance immediately after the murder was of course highly suspicious, and other things puzzled us as well."

"I can see all that now," Martin admitted. "I didn't at the time. But when you got going I knew you would dig it all up in time—and probably get it all wrong."

"We shall have to ask you for a written statement," Bobby said.

"No," Martin said. "Written stuff goes on record and stays there. Spoken's different."

"Well, that chiefly concerns Twice Over," Bobby said. "Naturally we are working together, but they are in charge of the murder investigation, while what we are after is recovering stolen property. All one pattern, no doubt; but, for the murder, Mr Kimms is in charge."

"I thought you were," Martin interjected.

"Strictly speaking," continued Bobby, "I ought to have sent you to Twice Over to see Mr Kimms. But we might have lost you again on the way, and it's a sound rule to let a man speak when he's feeling like it. Mr Kimms will want a full report from us, and I'm sure he will want to see you himself—and for you to make that written statement I spoke of."

"He won't get it," said Martin simply.

"We must hope you will change your mind about that," Bobby said, ignoring Martin's shake of the head. "You will be at Hidden Cottage for the next few days, in case we want to get in touch with you?" Martin nodded this time. "Then I don't think there's any need to keep you any longer, except of course that we are greatly obliged to you for coming forward of your own accord."

"I'm beginning to be sorry I did," Martin grumbled as he left, and Bobby made no comment.

Nor had he often felt more doubtful than he did as he pondered over Martin's tale, and wondered what effect such an experience might have had not only on his sister's psychology, but also on Martin's own.

Presently he rang up Kimms and gave him the gist of the story, promising also that he should have a full report as soon as possible. He would send it, Bobby said, by special police dispatch rider, and if Mr Kimms agreed, he would come down himself next morning. It might, he thought, be useful if they talked it over together. Kimms answered that he thought it would be very useful indeed. He added gloomily that it seemed as if they had got to the complete dead end, and Bobby said that on the contrary he felt that now at last things were beginning to move. He went on:

"When you get the full report, as near verbatim as I can manage, you'll see there are various weak points. It doesn't quite ring true. Which may mean nothing—or everything."

He rang off then, made the necessary arrangements, and next morning, with Detective Constable Ford for chauffeur, drove to Twice Over, there to find Kimms looking more excited than was often the case with that normally placid individual.

"All made up," were almost the first words he uttered when Bobby arrived. "That statement. Eh?"

"Well, there are certainly serious inconsistencies," Bobby agreed. "According to Maxton it was so dark that even he, though used to being out at night, wasn't sure of his whereabouts. Yet he knew the other two he talks about met by the loganberry bush where the murder took place. He says he assumed it was a case of boy meeting girl. Not a likely idea to occur to anyone at that time of night—earlier on, perhaps, but not then. He says he was near enough to be sure it was no lover's meeting, but not near enough to hear what they were saying. But can all that be put across to a jury? Defending counsel would pooh, pooh objections like that, call them frivolous and trivial; and it's not easy to make a jury understand that the frivolous and the trivial may be also the serious and the significant. The Public Prosecutor will want a lot more."

But Kimms didn't look as if he were altogether inclined to agree.

"Others all out," he said. "He's still in."

"Well, I don't know," Bobby said doubtfully. "All very much still in the melting-pot, isn't it? I agree they all have their explanations pat—rather too pat, to my mind. I agree, too, we may take it as certain the murderer is one of the five: Stuart and Wynne, Rogers and Dowie, and Maxton himself. It revolves round them, but opposite which one the wheel will stop is still, for me at least, a problem. Rogers seems to have a water-tight alibi, but there is a leak in it, all the same. It might be not Rogers but a pal who was at the railway terminus that night and robbed the dying man of his wallet, passing it on afterwards to Rogers, as arranged, for the very purpose of proving an alibi. Not a shred of evidence, but it might be. Stuart's diamond-dealing may have been no more than a dodge to evade death duties, though it would certainly cost him more to deal through a man like Fatty Veale than paying what was legally due. But some men instinctively prefer the crooked way. Equally it might be an elaborate scheme for getting rid of the compromising pound-notes. In that case he may be the unknown 'Boss'. Again, there may be more to Mr Dowie and his treasure-detector than we've been able to find. And if Stuart was right—and he put up a good show of really believing it—Wynne knew where the murdered woman's body lay. If he did, how and why, and is it an acceptable explanation that he only wanted to avoid fuss and bother and publicity when he fixed it for Stuart to make the discovery?"

By this time Kimms was beginning to feel his head going round. He said presently:

"Back again where we were before we began."

"Or further back still," Bobby said gloomily. "Is it just possible that Maxton has brooded so much and so long on what his mother did that he has become obsessed with murder to such a degree the idea has had at last to be translated into action?"

"Eh?" said Kimms, who had not quite followed this. "That's his sister, isn't it?"

"It might be him as well," Bobby said. "Only more firmly repressed and all the stronger if at last it did break out. I don't know."

"Evidence," said Kimms, abandoning all this that he found merely bewildering, and certainly nothing to do with police work. "Got none."

"None a jury would recognize," Bobby agreed. "I don't think I've ever had a case where we know so much and yet can do so little. What do you say to my going on to try if I can get anything more out of Mr Wynne?"

"Wynne?" repeated Kimms. "I don't see . . ." and there he paused.

"I don't either," Bobby told him. "I just have a feeling I might get something, perhaps even the one necessary clue we need. He has a trick of smiling to himself when he thinks you aren't looking. A worrying little half-hidden smile you can hardly see, as if there were some joke he knew and you didn't, and so it amused him all the more."

"I never noticed it," said Kimms doubtfully.

"Perhaps he only shows it to me," Bobby said, and repeated: "I don't know."

"Want me to come?" Kimms asked.

"Well, I always have the feeling that people talk more freely if there's only one of us. You've seen him once or twice, haven't you?"

"Got a statement. Written. Nothing in it," Kimms replied.

"There was a photograph," Bobby went on, speaking almost as much to himself as to his companion. "I happened to hear Miss Wynne telling her father she had found it and then mislaid it again. I thought it rather disturbed him. My fancy, perhaps. But I did think at the time that he looked at me rather as if wondering if I had heard and hoping I hadn't. Next time I saw her I asked her if she had ever found it. She said she had, and her daddy had been nearly cross with her at first for being careless, though he had only burnt it immediately. It keeps nagging at me."

"What does?" Kimms asked.

"Oh, wondering whose photo it could be Wynne wanted so much he had to burn it immediately he got it," Bobby explained.

"Never know now," said Kimms.

"No, not now it's burnt," agreed Bobby. "Well, I'll push on, shall I? To the Old Dower House. I might pick up something."

"I'll send Jenkins to pick up Maxton," Kimms announced, and obviously thinking that that was a 'picking up' much more likely to be useful, he added, "Second time they often open up more. Once they start, they go on."

"So they do," agreed Bobby. "Especially when they aren't sure they've been quite convincing, try to think up more detail, and start contradicting themselves. Shall you press the loganberry-bush point?"

"No," answered Kimms with decision. "Not till we have it on paper. Or he'll deny he said it."

Bobby nodded approval; and went on to the Old Dower House for an interview to which he did not altogether look forward, though he had the thought in his mind that it might well prove decisive.

CHAPTER XXXIII
BATH AT NOON

IT WAS NO great distance to the Old Dower House. In the mellow sunshine of this fine morning the ancient building, set in its well-kept garden, had a peaceful and a gentle air, as if of grief, strife, and trouble it had known little during the long years of its existence. Or so at least it seemed to Bobby as he walked up the rhododendron-bordered avenue by which it was approached. He knocked, but had to knock again before the door was opened by Mrs Griggs, the village woman who came every day to help Sylvia in her household duties.

"I don't know where the master is, or missy either," she told him, "but if you will wait in the hall I'll try to find them."

Left sitting there, he noticed at once that the fine Atropos statue he remembered so well from his first visit here had now tied round its neck a label marked in large letters: 'Sold'. He got up to look at it, wondering why the label, when he heard Sylvia come running down the stairs; and it seemed to him that she had regained some of that clear, sweet gaiety she had shown before, such as men have imagined there must have been in the primal dawn when innocence prevailed. The thought came to him that this might be because Maxton, for all his declaration that they must never meet again, had now returned to the neighbourhood and she had seen him. It was a thought that did not please him. He said to her:

"I see you've sold the Atropos."

"She's going to a museum, sulky old thing," Sylvia announced happily. "I'm so glad. Daddy didn't want, but I simply made him, and it's ever such a lot more than he paid, and he's giving it all to me, and I'm going to give it to the Vicar for the church, so that will be the absolute end, and we won't have anything more to do with her. I know she would have done something awful and horrid if she had been here any longer."

"And the label?" Bobby asked. "Are there prospective purchasers waiting to make offers?"

"Oh, no," replied Sylvia. "No. I just wanted to remind her now we have nothing more to do with each other and she can be horrid to someone else. Only she can't in a museum, can she?"

"Well, no, I shouldn't think so," Bobby agreed, smiling, and yet somehow impressed against all his common sense. "It's a remarkable piece of work. More suited to a museum, though, than to a private house."

"I only hope the men will come to-day to take her away," Sylvia said. "I shall be ever so glad when she's gone. Was it Daddy you came to see? I'm afraid you can't—not now, at least."

"Is he away?" Bobby asked.

"Oh, no, he's upstairs; but you can't see him." She paused for a moment and looked at him with something of that old lovely smile of hers that had seemed to proclaim so clearly that in her world at least all was well and very well. He had a momentary impression that she was going to give him three guesses. Instead she announced: "He's having a bath."

"A bath?" Bobby repeated; and involuntarily glanced at his wrist watch, for it was now nearly noon—an unusual time for taking a bath.

"He's been moving the coal in the cellar," she explained, "and you just simply can't imagine what a state he got into." Now it was that soft laugh of hers, so gay, so spontaneously happy, that came bubbling forth. "I simply had to chase him upstairs to make himself fit to be seen. He was sure there was a smell of gas all over the house, and it must come from the cellar, so he had to find it."

"Did he?" Bobby asked.

"Oh, yes; it's all right now," she answered. "So we shan't get blown up and I needn't write to the gas people. They do take such a time to do anything."

"Gas leaks are always a little dangerous, especially in cellars," Bobby remarked. "Do you think Mr Wynne will be long?"

"Oh, no," she assured him. "No. Will you wait? I suppose it's all the same thing? Mr Kimms has been here. He made Daddy and me talk and talk, and it was all the same old thing all over again. Are you going to as well?"

"I hope not," Bobby said, "but there are some points that we think perhaps Mr Wynne might be able to clear up. Details—background—that's often so important."

"Nobody can talk of anything else," Sylvia said as she led the way to the room which seemed to be the one more especially used by Mr Wynne. She continued as they entered it, "I do hope something will be found out soon. It's spoiling everything. I asked Vicar if he thought it would be wrong for me to pray that it might be."

"What did he say?" Bobby asked.

"I don't think he wanted me to," Sylvia replied, "but he didn't say it would be wrong, so I did. I don't see it can be wrong to want wicked people to be punished. Do you?"

"I suppose that is what I have to try to get done," Bobby said. "If it isn't, it may spread, like cancer. So it has to be cut out, at any cost."

"Yes," she agreed. "Yes. I'm sure it can't be anyone here. Everyone knows everyone else, so how could it be?"

Bobby did not think the conclusion necessarily followed from the proposition. But neither did he think it necessary to make any reply, nor did she seem to expect one. She pushed forward an armchair for him, said she would knock at the bathroom door and tell her father he was waiting, and so departed.

Left alone, Bobby went to the window and stood there, looking thoughtfully at that kind of hedge or barrier of loganberry bushes running the length of the wall between garden and copse. It was no doubt a very effective check to the depredations of small boys, who could climb walls with the agility of monkeys, but might find a tangle of prickly bushes more difficult to negotiate. Bobby was inclined to suppose it would well protect the rest of Mr Wynne's fruit. And at these bushes he continued to stare as if he thought that from among them might issue the solution to the problem that so tormented him, to find which, indeed, he was risking, as he well knew, his whole future.

The sound of an opening door made him turn. Mr Wynne was there, spruce and smiling from his pre-luncheon bath, all trace of his struggle with the coal in the cellar completely removed.

"Is there any fresh development in this unhappy business?" he asked. "The sooner it's settled, the better for us all. The whole place is full of all kinds of rumours. People are even beginning to look over their shoulders at their neighbours. A most unhealthy situation," and this he said with some severity, as if inclined to lay the blame for it upon the shoulders of the police, individually and collectively.

"Well, not exactly," Bobby said, "though there are one or two small points it's possible you may be able to help us to clear up."

"The police here," Wynne protested, "took very full statements both from me and from my daughter. Unnecessary to bother Sylvia, I thought. I found her in tears afterwards. Almost the first time, I think. I've tried to shield her as much as possible."

"At any rate, I'm sure she has had a very happy life so far," Bobby said. "That will always be something she owes you."

"I've tried," Wynne said, but somehow a little doubtfully, as though he were feeling that might not be enough. "I don't think there was much new either Sylvia or I could say. Or, as far as that goes, much I can add to it now. I'll do my best, naturally."

"Thank you," Bobby said. "I was sure you would say that." He saw that Mr Wynne was looking at him sharply, even questioningly. He went on, "Do you think it possible that the murderer—possibly the victim as well, either separately or together—made use of the door in your garden wall to get into the copse? You keep it locked?"

"Always," declared Wynne with emphasis. "But I daresay it wouldn't be too difficult for anyone who wanted to take an impression of the lock and get a key made. After dark, perhaps, or an evening when Sylvia and I were out. Why? Does that make any difference?"

"The copse was under observation," Bobby explained. "Not of course the close observation planned for the night when we had word the attempt to recover the supposedly buried money was to be made. But there was a man stationed on watch, just in case. He saw nothing, and evidently he wouldn't be likely to if the copse was entered by way of your garden."

"Did he hear anything, as I thought I did?" Mr Wynne asked.

"No, but then it's much further to the edge of the copse where he was stationed than to your house. Besides, the trees would tend to muffle any sound. Miss Wynne woke, but was reassured when she saw the light in your room."

"All this has been gone over very carefully with Superintendent Kimms," Mr Wynne said with more than a touch of impatience in his voice.

"We have information now," Bobby went on, unheeding this sudden show of impatience, which he was not sure might not be rooted in uneasiness, "that Mr Maxton was present in the copse on both these nights. He claims he was there to study wild life at night—a sort of speciality of his apparently—and partly because he intended to signal his presence to Miss Wynne."

"I know, I know," Mr Wynne interrupted. "Sylvia told me all about it. Boy and girl playing together like two ten years old." He was not smiling now, either secretly or openly. He resumed, "I don't like the young man. What it all comes to is that he was doing his best to get Sylvia to give him some sign of encouragement. She will have a fair amount of money presently, and Maxton hasn't a penny in the world except what he makes by his scribbling, and that may die on him at any moment. Of course, if she really wants him and sticks to it, she'll have to have him. Nothing matters except her happiness. It's all I care about. All," he repeated with a certain almost desperate energy, and then he paused and laughed, but not very naturally.

"Do you think there is anything really serious between them?" Bobby asked.

"Oh, no—at any rate I hope not," Wynne answered, and this time more calmly. "There won't be if I can help it. Change. A trip abroad. More opportunities to mingle with other young people. If her mother had lived, all that would be much easier, and I'm afraid I've been selfish in trying to keep her too much to myself. But you didn't come to talk about Sylvia, did you? and I've been letting myself run on. I'm apt to when it's her," he added, an odd little note of shyness in his voice.

"I was hoping," Bobby explained, "you might be able to tell us more about that door between your garden and the copse. It may prove very important. Just possibly we may be able to make an arrest in a day or two, but we must be sure before we act."

"If you mean Maxton," Mr Wynne said, "I'm sure that's all wrong. I don't much like the young man as a son-in-law, but he's no murderer. Absurd to think so for a moment. For one thing, I don't believe he has the guts. A nervous type. You could tell at once if he had anything like that on his mind. Killing, even in self-defence, not murder, does tend to cause bad dreams, doesn't it? I do hope you'll give that idea up. The very thing to get Sylvia all sympathy and turn it into something stronger. She's so sensitive; even a fine morning like this can make her feel all's honey and heaven. And if Maxton were hanged it would be a most terrible shock."

"I feel that, too," Bobby said. "I hope nothing of the sort will happen, but I fear it may."

"There's no possible motive," Mr Wynne insisted, and it was evident that his uneasiness had grown stronger even than before.

"Yes, motive," Bobby agreed; "that's always the crux. There is something, though, we now know about his past that might provide one. A nervous type," he repeated. "I don't know," and then he went away to collect Ford and his car from where they were waiting by the Over All Arms.

Sergeant Jenkins was there too, chatting to Ford.

"The Super's been called away," he said as Bobby came up. "I was to ask if there was anything fresh you got at the Old Dower House?"

"You can tell him," Bobby said slowly, "that Mr Wynne has been in his coal cellar most of the morning, because he said he smelt gas and thought there might be a leak in the pipe there."

"Yes sir," Jenkins said. "I'll tell him, sir."

"Dangerous things, gas leaks in coal-cellars," Bobby remarked, to himself apparently, and Jenkins retreated within the Over All Arms, muttering indignantly the while to himself.

"Trying to be funny," he said to one of the staff he met. "Mr Smarty from Scotland Yard, I call him."

CHAPTER XXXIV
THE CELLAR

UNAWARE HOW FAR he had fallen in the considered opinion of Sergeant Jenkins, Bobby drove back to London, his mind still obsessed by the thought of how extremely dangerous are leaks from gas-pipes in cellars. Why, he had even heard of people searching for them with naked lights—candles or matches.

Later on—Superintendent Kimms and his Chief Constable had to be summoned to attend it—a short conference was held at which Bobby put forth his views, his theories, his doubts, his plans. These were not easily approved. A certain element of risk, it was pointed out. Some details of what was suggested seemed to go beyond the book of rules, which as every police officer knows, must be obeyed to the letter—or else. Why, there might even be questions asked in Parliament—a prospect to make the strongest blanch.

However, in the end it was agreed that Bobby's plan should be carried out exactly as he asked, and so next morning he and Ford were again in Twice Over, where Kimms, looking rather worried, was waiting for them.

"Everything all right so far?" Bobby asked.

"Special duty officer re copse," Kimms said, "reports Maxton present during night. When challenged, stated studying nature. Eh?"

"Well, I should certainly have expected Maxton to have more on his mind just now than nature-study," Bobby admitted.

"Report further states," continued Kimms, "same entered Old Dower House garden towards twelve midnight, but soon returned. Eh?"

"Are you in touch with Maxton now?" Bobby asked.

"Observation evaded," Kimms answered. "Special instructions issued to look out for same and report if seen. Eh?"

"I've no idea what he can have been doing, or why he entered the Dower House garden, or what he wanted there," Bobby said, answering the questions he took it those plaintive 'Eh's' of Kimms had been meant to convey. "Nothing to do, anyhow, but continue as arranged."

"Yes," said Kimms; and with that both lapsed into a brief silence, going over in their minds what lay before them. Then Bobby glanced at his wrist watch and said:

"Well, time I was off. I'm leaving the car here. Constable Ford knows what to do under your orders. But it might be as well, if you think so, to go over it all with him again, just to make sure there's no risk of any misunderstanding."

Kimms nodded; and Bobby took his way once more towards the Old Dower House by the same shady path he had followed before. It was a fine morning, the sunshine warm, caressing; a gentle breeze blew; there was a fresh, sweet scent in the air. Bobby's mind, though, was too full of what grim business lay before him to take much notice of his surroundings. Then he saw coming towards him Sylvia and Maxton, talking earnestly together and apparently on their way to the village. They had seen him, too, and they drew back to the wayside, out of the bright sunshine into the heavy shade cast by the tall beech that stood there. He felt they were watching him with apprehension, and he felt also that they had reason to. He greeted them as he came up, though he knew they had been hoping he would pass by with no more than a lifted hat, and said:

"Do you know if your father is at home, Miss Wynne? I find it will be necessary to see him again."

"Oh, not again. Must you?" she exclaimed. "He was so upset yesterday after you were there. Oh, not again."

"I'm afraid it is necessary," Bobby said. "Neither I nor anyone else can help it, any more than we can help to-morrow coming." To Martin he said: "You were in the copse last night?"

"One of your chaps was there too, wasn't he?" Maxton asked in return. "Well, suppose I was. Why not?"

"It's rather a case of why, isn't it?" Bobby answered slowly and continued: "We know a good deal now. Soon we expect to know a good deal more. Don't try to take any action. You would only make more trouble, both for yourself and others."

"Dilly, dilly, duck, come and be killed. Is that it?" asked Martin bitterly.

Bobby did not answer this. He said farewell and continued on his way. He was aware that they were standing still, watching him as he went. He had a feeling they would follow him, though he hoped they wouldn't. This time when he reached the Dower House he had no need to knock even once, for the door was opened immediately by Mr Wynne.

"I saw you coming," he said. "I was looking out for Sylvia, I get uneasy if she is not there. It was you instead. The constant visitor. Well, what is it this time?"

"What you told me yesterday was very informative and useful," Bobby said. "If you could possibly spare the time . . ."

"Yes, yes, of course," Wynne answered. "As much time as you like. Come this way."

Bobby followed him into the hall and to the passage leading to the room where they had talked before. Bobby noticed that the statue was still there, still with the label 'Sold' in position. He remarked:

"I see you are getting rid of your 'Atropos'."

"The van will be here for it any minute now," Wynne said. "Sylvia says she won't have a minute's peace till it's gone, and she doesn't seem inclined to let me have one either till then."

They had reached the room now. Wynne pushed a chair towards Bobby and seated himself at the desk. He put out his hand to the drawer on his right, and then changed, and opened instead the drawer on his left. From it he took a box of cigarettes and offered it to Bobby. Bobby excused himself politely. Mr Wynne put back the box without helping himself and without comment, though it seemed somehow as though his face grow tighter.

"It's still that communicating door between your garden and the copse that is worrying us," Bobby explained. "As you know, there is strong reason to believe that on the night of the murder both the murderer and his victim entered the copse by it."

"I suppose it's possible," Wynne answered. "In any case, I don't see that I can add anything to what I've said already. The door is always kept locked. But there would be no great difficulty for anyone who wanted to—I can't imagine why they should—to get a key made to fit."

"That is understood," Bobby agreed. "Maxton was in the copse most of last night, and left it at least once to enter your garden."

"You think he has a key?" Wynne said. "I don't know. I think it unlikely. If you mean you are still suspicious of him, I think you ought to come out into the open and say so. I find the idea incredible. If you are trying to hint that the young man was hoping to see Sylvia, I think that is still more absurd. I am sure Sylvia would tell me at once if there was any suggestion of that sort. In any case, I can't imagine what that would have to do with you."

"So many things have so much to do with each other," Bobby said. "May I ask another question? Many people think wall safes give greater security. No back plate to be torn off, and burglars may not be able to find them without losing a lot of time, and that's something burglars are always short of. Do you mind telling me if you have one?"

"As a matter of fact, I have," Wynne replied, "though I can't imagine why that should interest you. Would you like to see it? I suppose as you're a policeman there's no danger of your passing on the information to prospective burglars? Or practising burglary yourself." He rose and took down one of the pictures on the wall to the left of the window. "This is an outside wall," he remarked, "and it's an old house. I imagine the wall here is fully two feet thick, or even more." By now he had deposited the picture against one of the chairs, to the right between him and the desk. He turned back to the wall and showed Bobby a tiny, almost imperceptible hole. "The keyhole," he said. "Unless you know exactly where to look—and I don't think anyone does except me—it would take a long time to find it. You mightn't succeed, for that matter." He drew the signet ring he was wearing from his finger and showed that combined with it was a tiny key. With it he opened the safe. "There you are," he said. "I hope that satisfies you. But I wish you would tell me what it is all about. Sometimes I have fairly large sums in it, but at the moment there's nothing but a few papers."

The door of the room opened—rather, it was thrown violently back. Martin was standing there. He said loudly:

"Police are in the cellars." He came further into the room. He threw out a hand, pointing at Bobby: "One of your men," he said. "I've seen him with you. Ford."

Bobby got up and went to stand nearer the desk, facing the door. He said to Maxton:

"I told you not to meddle."

Wynne was saying slowly, his expression unmoved, his voice so steady as to be almost toneless:

"In the cellars? My cellars? Mr Owen, what does this mean? Have you a search-warrant? If not, I must ask you to leave immediately and take your men with you. You can return when you have your search-warrant—if you get one."

"A search-warrant was not needed," Bobby said, and his voice, too, was quiet and level. "The men were freely admitted. A 'phone message was received at the Gas Show Room to say a leak in the cellar here had been reported, so a fitter was sent, and Constable Ford and a companion—a specialist—came with him."

"Who let them in?" Mr Wynne said. "Was it Sylvia?"

No one answered him. They all knew. But Martin said:

"I asked her if it was all right. She said she knew the fitter; he had been here before."

"Sylvia let them in," Wynne said, and no one contradicted him.

"Where is she?" Maxton said. "She mustn't stay here."

Wynne turned to Bobby.

"It was Sylvia told you about my bath that morning, didn't she? Then you guessed. Was that it? My photograph, too. You heard her?"

Bobby did not answer. He remained watchful and still.

"Where is Sylvia?" Martin said, and said again: "She mustn't stay here. I must find her."

But he did not move, remaining standing in the doorway, a little inside the room.

Wynne said: "This is an outrage. I must ring my lawyer immediately."

He began to move from where he was by the window towards the desk and 'phone. Bobby was standing between them and Wynne and did not move. Wynne did not ask him to do so or try to push by. Instead he turned sharply away to reach the desk from the other side. In doing so, he stumbled over the picture he had placed leaning against a chair and had forgotten was there. That momentary delay, as Wynne kicked away chair and picture lying in his path, gave Bobby time to tear open the right-hand drawer. Just inside it lay a wicked-looking small automatic. Bobby snatched it up and thrust it into his pocket. Wynne recovering the balance he had momentarily lost, leaped at him. Before that frenzied onslaught Bobby went down, Wynne tearing at his throat, tearing at his pocket. They rolled together on the floor. Maxton stood motionless, watching. Wynne was uppermost, then Bobby. Wynne got Bobby's hand between his teeth and bit it severely. Bobby hit him twice on the side of the head with all the force he could command. For a moment Wynne, dazed by the force of the blows, relaxed his grip. In that moment Bobby slipped on the handcuffs with which he had provided himself. He helped Wynne to his feet, and they stood silently, watching each other. Ford came running. The handcuffed Wynne; Bobby, now trying with his handkerchief to bandage his bleeding hand; the broken and displaced furniture; the utter stillness succeeding the sound of violence he had heard; told Ford all. He said:

"We found a wall safe in the cellar—half a ton of coal piled up against it. Mrs Farmer's handbag's there. I heard something going on, so I came at a run—sorry I wasn't quicker." He looked at Wynne. "Guessed it was all up, and tried to cut up rough?"

Bobby, who had got his hand more or less tied up now, took the little automatic from his pocket and handed it to Ford.

"Take charge of that," he said.

Ford whistled softly.

"If he had got a chance to use that . . ." he said and left the sentence unfinished.

"It was not for you; it was for me," Wynne said.

They were all watching him so intently none of them heard a faint sound at the doorway—except Wynne himself, and it was not so much that he heard as that he saw, for he was standing facing the door and they with their backs to it.

Now a strange thing happened. Even as they watched, Wynne seemed to shrink, to grow small and old before their eyes; it was as though the burden of fifty years or more had fallen suddenly upon him and broken him where he stood. Beneath their weight he sighed a little and sat down. Bobby was speaking now. He said:

"I am arresting you on a charge of having murdered a woman known as Mrs Farmer or Mrs Field—"

He got no further, for from behind a low voice said:

"Daddy," and then again, "Daddy."

They all turned quickly. Sylvia was standing there, as she had been for perhaps some sixty seconds, though only her father had heard her approach. A third time she said "Daddy" and came towards him. He was on his feet now, and with his fettered hands he made a gesture to her to keep away.

"It's what I did," he said, in a voice so strained and changed none would have known it was his. "I killed her, for she knew I killed her husband years ago and I had taken the money he hid for her, and I knew what she would do. Take me away," he said to Bobby, "for it is better Sylvia should never see me again." Ford came forward and laid a hand upon his arm. Wynne said, still speaking to Bobby: "God hits hard, doesn't he? A little below the belt, though, I think, hitting through her," and as he spoke he smiled—such a smile as those who saw it hoped they would never see the like of again.

"This way," Ford said, and they were gone.

"I'll come," Sylvia said, as one awakening from a dream into a reality beyond all understanding or comprehension.

"That cannot be," Bobby said, and with one hand held her back. "That cannot be," he repeated when she still tried to follow. To Maxton he said: "A doctor and a nurse will be here immediately. We thought they had better be standing by."

Maxton moved towards Sylvia, speaking her name softly. "Sylvia, Sylvia," he said.

She pushed him away as he came nearer, and said, but still without understanding, knowing only that on her there had fallen some nameless horror:

"Daddy never killed anyone; he never would; he says he did."

"My mother also," Maxton said. "Come to me, for we belong."

Bobby went away then, closing the door behind him, leaving them together, holding each other tightly; for what else had they to cling to?

CHAPTER XXXV
CONCLUSION

ONLY A FEW days later, one afternoon in the following week, Kimms appeared in Bobby's office. He had come from the Public Prosecutor's office, and he still looked very tired after the strain and stress of recent events. Bobby waved him to a chair. Kimms said "Eh?", and Bobby looked up from his paper-strewn desk and nodded agreement.

"They've told you, I suppose?" he said. "Unexpected sort of thing."

This time it was Kimms who nodded agreement.

"Staggerer," he said moodily.

"A perfectly natural development, though," Bobby went on. "Wynne and Sylvia and Maxton being what they are—or rather what circumstances made them."

"Um-m-m," said Kimms, a little as though he felt it was not only circumstances that had moulded them to what they were. "Eh?" he said, and this time his 'Eh?' meant that he gave it up. He went on: "I don't quite see . . . eh?" and now his 'Eh?' of many meanings indicated that he would like to be told exactly how Bobby had arrived at conclusions justifying him in risking so much on finding what was required hidden away in the wall safe in the coal cellar—surely the last place in the world where one would expect to find a wall safe.

"Oh, well," Bobby said, knowing he must explain, much as he hated explanations, much, very much, as he would have preferred to leave it all in a kind of haze of semi-magic, semi-intuition, all very mysterious, and therefore so much the more impressive. "Oh, well," he repeated, "when I knew—and of course we soon did—that there was a lot of renewed talk going on about the first P.O. robbery and what had become of the stolen money, and as soon as we had traced its origin through Rogers to Cream—one of the gang concerned who recently died in gaol—I got out the dossiers of the case. I went over them word by word: some job, often kept me up till three or four in the morning. I got to know every document pretty nearly by heart. I soon felt sure it was the unknown, unnamed 'boss' in the background who had shot Farmer. After the murder in the Twice Over copse there were many small things I noticed that seemed to put Wynne right in the centre of the picture. You may think it fanciful, but that dodge of his of putting a kind of hedge of loganberry bushes almost as a baited trap for small boys, and the way he seemed rather to be pleased and amused when one of them fell into it, did suggest a certain callousness—or worse."

"Small boys stealing fruit deserve all they get," interposed Kimms severely. "Only not to be amused by same."

"Then there was that odd little way Wynne had of smiling all to himself so you could hardly see it. Nervousness, perhaps. But it did suggest to my mind that he knew himself to know things that others didn't know and knew—or thought he knew—that he was secure in that knowledge and the ignorance of others. Again, the first time I saw him he showed he knew there had been four men engaged in carrying out the P.O. robbery, though previously he had said he had only the vaguest memory of the newspaper accounts. It hadn't interested him much, he said. But enough it might be, for the number of the men engaged to stick in his mind. Later on Rogers made a casual reference to a man called 'Fingers'. He described him as a runner to the gang, a sort of scout or side-line helper. I remembered that Wynne had lost a finger from one hand and that the backroom 'boss' had always been very insistent on all his gang wearing gloves. Only to avoid the risk of 'dabs'? Wynne was quick—very quick—to say so, when I mentioned this insistence on gloves. But was there another reason? To keep secret so quick and sure a means of identification? And was it possible the murdered man, Farmer, had found that secret out and was threatening to make use of it? Apparently, too, from what Wynne says now, he wanted to retire and live quietly with his wife and child, and he seems to have felt Farmer didn't intend to let that happen."

"It does begin to add up," Kimms said. "Not watertight."

"No, indeed," agreed Bobby. "If we had taken the case into court at that stage there would probably have been an acquittal, and then Wynne would have been safe for evermore. I had to be careful, too, not to let him have any idea how first one thing and then another was being noticed. If he had got really suspicious he might have vanished abroad, and that would have made everything very much more difficult. And then I had to get the other possibles out of the way on the general principle that if it can't be anyone else—then it must be whoever's left."

"Sound idea," said Kimms, impressed by this maxim, since though he had always acted on it instinctively he had never formulated it clearly to himself or heard it so stated by others.

"Other things you know and we've often talked over," Bobby went on. "There was the very carefully suggested, but never openly claimed alibi. I mean the light in his room on the night of the murder to show he was there, and Stuart's angry declaration that Wynne knew where the dead body lay. It was a possibility. Then there was the odd way in which loganberries began to come more and more into the picture. Even in the Oxton Court flat we found a tin of the things. Clearly all the papers had been taken when the flat was entered in order to remove all traces of past identity. But what had become of them? Well, if Wynne had done the ransacking as I soon suspected, had he still got them? The dead woman's handbag had disappeared, too. If he were the guilty man he might have hidden the papers where he had hidden that. Handbags are not too easy to destroy. Even if you throw them into the Thames they may be fished out again. He had been rather forthcoming about his wall safe. I think now he was growing a little uneasy and he calculated that if there were a search that would be the first thing looked at—and of course found empty. But if I were right he must have a store somewhere of hidden money—the stolen money—as well. What clinched it was when Sylvia, poor child, told me her father had been in the coal cellar looking for a gas leak and had got himself so dirty he had to have a bath. She was laughing a little as she told me so innocently and gaily where to look for the proof of her father's guilt. And I remembered, too, a certain stress had been laid once on Wynne's always bringing up the coal himself. Well, I thought, what about another wall safe there, and had Wynne been busy not looking for gas leaks—the Gas Board's business—but piling up the coal against it to give it better protection? He must have begun to feel by then that we were getting near the truth."

"That photograph she burnt," Kimms said. "His? Eh?"

"I couldn't somehow ask her," Bobby answered. "I knew I ought to but the words wouldn't come—indefensible. I ought to be sacked, I suppose. Then she told me spontaneously what I had to have—the necessary clue to it all. Anyhow, it was all there. Everything. The stolen money, the missing handbag, the papers Wynne took from the Oxton Court flat. They told all. The murdered woman knew her husband belonged to some gang but not who they were. She did know—it was the job they gave her—that if she showed a tin of loganberries where she worked then that was a signal some new coup was being planned and the members of the gang were to meet—somewhere. She thought that if she continued to show such a tin one of the gang would recognize it and get in touch with her again. She hoped to avenge her man's death. She hoped, too, to get to learn where he had hidden the rest of his share. He had given her some to keep for him, kept some himself, and hidden the rest but he had never told her where. Then she heard of Rogers and how he was talking about Twice Over. So she went there herself to try to find the money but found her death instead. It seems probable that she recognized Wynne—by the missing finger, perhaps, her necessary clue—that he talked her over, persuaded her to meet him in the copse at midnight, promising she should have the hidden money, which of course wasn't there, as Wynne himself dug it up after he had disposed of Farmer. It was tucked away in the cellar wall safe. With Mrs Field's papers was the key of a safe deposit where she had stored most of what Farmer had given her—all she hadn't spent. She had used the name Harvest at the safe-deposit place. Well, we've got back a very large share of what was stolen—and I suppose all that will happen to it now is that it will go straight to the furnace. Modern economics take some understanding. Beyond me."

"All over and done with," Kimms said, getting to his feet. "Or soon will be. Eh?"

"Maxton is coming to see me tomorrow," Bobby said. "He rang up to ask if he could. He says he has made up his mind. I don't know what about. He wouldn't say, but I told him to come along if he wanted to. Care to come too?"

But Kimms shook his head. He had too much to do, he said. All sorts of things had had to be neglected while he and all his men had been so busy on the Wynne case, day and night. So Bobby was by himself when Maxton was shown into his room the next afternoon. Bobby thought he looked a little more worn, older, but with a quieter manner, steadier eyes. Nor did he seem to have now that manner of looking suddenly over his shoulder, as though to see if the past were still following him. But he began abruptly enough. He said:

"I want to make it quite clear that if I am called as a witness I shall refuse to speak. Mute of malice they'll call it, won't they? I don't think you'll get anything out of my wife either."

"Why come to tell me?" Bobby countered. "We in the police have nothing to do with the conduct or preparation of the trial. We may be called to give evidence, of course. Your wife, you said? You and Miss Wynne are married, then?"

"Yesterday, by special licence. That's why I rang you up, as soon as we were married and I had the right to stand by her. My sister is with her now; she isn't fit to be left. She has no relatives."

"Yes, I understood that," Bobby said. "When you rang I rather hoped you meant to complete that story of yours. It was so plain you were telling much to hide more. Refusing to answer questions in court is easier said than done, I think. But I can tell you unofficially—even the papers don't know yet—that it won't come to that. Wynne is going to plead guilty, and he's refusing all legal aid. So no witnesses will be called and no evidence will be required."

"To spare Sylvia," Martin said slowly. "I might have expected it. Whatever else he was or did, he cared for Sylvia—cared for her more than for all else. It was for her sake he gave it up."

"For his wife's sake, too," Bobby said. "He told me once it was to please her he retired. He didn't say what from. I think he felt so safe he liked to play on the edge of security."

"Will the plea of guilty be accepted?" Martin asked. "It isn't always, is it?"

"Well, no," Bobby answered. "No, not always, I believe—not in murder cases. But it might be in this case. In view of the circumstances. That is, if it ever comes into court, which I gather may not happen."

"Why not?" asked Maxton, with a sudden gleam of what can only be called hopeless hope.

"It seems doubtful if Wynne will live long enough," Bobby explained. "The trial can't come on for about six weeks. I have seen the medical report. There is nothing wrong with him physically; it's only that he has lost the will to live. You might say he has exchanged the will to live for a stronger urge to die. He sleeps, eats well. He does all he is told, but life is slowly ebbing away, and nothing the doctors do makes any difference. There is nothing left in him, in body or spirit, to hold life, just as there is nothing to hold the wine when the flask it was in is broken. And that means he will die an innocent man as far as the official records go. For the law of England is that every man is innocent till he is proved guilty. Wynne's guilt will never be proved, I think."

"I hope—" Martin said, but only after a long, long pause. His voice was not quite steady when he continued: "I shall have to tell Sylvia—in her father's death is our hope. I have thought she might not be able to bear it . . . the other way. Hope in death," he repeated.

"It will also mean," Bobby continued, "that your wife's claim to all her father's property will be completely valid. If a conviction were obtained it would be forfeit to the Crown."

"She will never touch a penny," Martin exclaimed with vehemence. "I know that for certain. The Crown can have every last farthing."

"That will be for her to say," Bobby told him. "I think you knew all the time, didn't you? that Wynne was guilty. I felt that that was what you were keeping back—that you knew. Your story didn't—didn't gell, as they say. It didn't fit, as the truth always does and must. And I think an investigating officer does develop a kind of sixth sense that warns him when a witness is lying—or suppressing truth, shall we say? Cross examination would probably have shown up more holes still. It laid you open to rather more than suspicion. You made yourself, of course, an accessory after the fact."

"I know," Martin said. "You don't think I was going to give evidence against Sylvia's father, do you? To get him hung? whatever he had done."

"Did you actually see what happened?"

"No," Martin answered. "I heard a woman's cry and I saw a man hurrying away. I didn't see him very clearly, but I knew all right. I made sure she was dead. If she had been alive it would have been different. It took me a few minutes to find her. She was dead all right."

"It was your duty to speak," Bobby said, but softly, for he remembered it had been his duty to put a question to Sylvia that he had never asked.

"I know it was," Martin was saying. "I didn't care. I remember saying out there in the copse: To hell with duty. My first idea was to run for it. No good. You chaps can always run faster. So then I thought up the idea of telling you all about Sis and me, so as to explain why I cleared out. That didn't work either, did it?" He got to his feet quickly. "That's all. I'll go now. Can I?"

"Oh, yes," Bobby said. "Why not? I hope you and Mrs Maxton will be—" but there he paused, not knowing how to finish what he had begun to say.

"Happy," Martin completed his sentence for him. "Happy?" Martin said again. "At any rate, now, when we can't sleep, we can lie awake together."

THE END

MAKING SURE

Originally published in the Evening Standard,
16 February, 1950

BOBBY OWEN watched the woman sitting opposite him. Her face was pallid; there were dark circles beneath her red-rimmed, bloodshot eyes; she was haggard with fear and horror and lack of sleep. At times violent fits of trembling shook her. Then she would recover herself and sit quietly, though still her hands remained pressed tightly together; so tightly that tiny drops of blood could be seen where the finger-nails had bitten deep into the flesh.

All the same, making every allowance for present circumstances, Bobby could not quite understand the enormous attraction she had apparently exercised on almost every man who came near her. Even at her best she could never have been a great beauty. Yet many men had loved her desperately. Her husband indeed had found his love become a tormenting, possessive jealousy. One man had committed suicide when the news of her marriage reached him, though she could not be blamed for this, since she had avoided all contact with him. Now there was young Donald Merton; probably at this moment, Bobby supposed, only kept at a distance by the presence of a uniformed policeman on the doorstep. Even Dr. Long, middle-aged, married, had confessed, more than half seriously, that he too, had felt the strange fascination that she exercised on men.

"It's not that she's so wonderfully beautiful," he had remarked. "Or clever. Or witty. It's just that there's something about her puts a young man's blood aflame. You don't notice it at first, and then you find it's got you; it's her—well, her altogether." He laughed awkwardly. "I'm forty," he said, "so luckily I'm immune. I'm glad I didn't meet her when I was twenty." Bobby had gone away, wondering and thoughtful.

Now, however, on this sunny winter afternoon, the examination Bobby had been conducting was almost over. He said to her:

"You have been warned before that everything in your statement may be given in evidence. You understand that?"

She nodded without speaking. Bobby turned to the only other occupant of the room—a young uniformed policeman who had been taking down in shorthand all that had passed since the interview began.

"How long will it take you to type out your notes?" he asked.

"Well, sir, it's not a long statement," said the constable. "I think I could have it ready between six and seven, not later."

To the woman Bobby said: "Mrs. Rawson, as soon as it is ready you will be asked to read it over. If you are satisfied that it is a fair and accurate report you will be asked to sign it. Till then I should like to suggest that you try to rest."

Her face seemed to break up and for a moment Bobby feared hysteria. She recovered herself. Her voice was perfectly calm and steady as she answered: "Do you think it is easy to rest when you are waiting to be hanged?"

"I don't think we have got that far yet," said Bobby.

"You have made it perfectly plain what you do think," she retorted.

"I hope not," Bobby exclaimed. "Making it plain what you think is just about the worst fault a police officer can commit. Quite inexcusable."

"I'll wait here till the thing is ready, then I'll sign it," she said.

"You must do as you wish."

"When I've signed it, I suppose you will want to take me away?"

"That won't depend on me," Bobby said, "and I wish you wouldn't jump to conclusions. But if you feel equal to it—anyhow, it will be better for you than just sitting and waiting—I would like to go over some of the main points again. You were married about seven years ago when you were only eighteen. There are two children. I think you ran away from home with Mr. Rawson. I think your married life has not been very happy."

"It was at first, the first few months," she answered slowly. "Then John became violently jealous. It amused me at first, I liked to tease him a little. I was so young then. Eighteen. Now I'm twenty-five. It became a sort of mania with him. I don't think anything would have satisfied him except shutting me up away from every other man for always."

"I understand there were some violent scenes?"

She rolled up her sleeve and showed the bruises on her arm. Bobby had seen them before.

"Did he threaten your life?"

"Yes, but he was always sorry afterwards. I don't think he knew how strong he was. If I showed him my arm like this he would begin to kiss it and almost cry and say he would never do it again. It all started all over again, all the same."

"Two days ago," Bobby continued, looking at the notes before him, "Mr. Rawson was found dead in bed. The post-mortem showed that at least two grains of morphia had been taken. It is suggested that the morphia was administered in the cup of hot milk he took at night and that you prepared. It was given to him by the maid as you had gone out, but you left the milk ready for her to warm. You told your husband that you were going to the cinema with a friend. You repeated that statement to the police officer first called in and later to me."

"You soon found out it was a lie, didn't you?" she said wearily. "I went to meet Don Merton. We had a long talk. When I got back John was in bed or dead. I don't know which. I didn't go into his room. I went straight to my own. I didn't feel I could bear seeing John just then."

"Why was that?"

"I knew I had just thrown away my last chance of freedom—of anything like happiness. I know what you think, what everyone else will think—the jury, too. They'll all say I didn't dare look again at my victim. I'm credited with that much decency apparently. That's something."

"Your statement is that you told Mr. Merton you were not prepared to leave your husband?"

"No. I would have left him. It was the children. I had to stay with them. They'll say I planned to keep them and rid myself of John and then I could have Don and the children, too. I can hear the judge saying it and all the jury nodding yes. I didn't. I told Don there were the children and I must go back to John, and so I did—you think to kill him."

"I do wish," Bobby said, "that you wouldn't keep telling me what I think. I don't know that myself yet. At first Mr. Merton confirmed your story but afterwards admitted the cinema tale had been concocted between you."

"I rang him up," she said. "I told him what to say."

"Let us go back a little," Bobby continued. "You visited Dr. Long shortly before your husband's death. He had been sleeping badly and he asked you to get him some sleeping tablets. Dr. Long states that he gave you a small phial containing some. They were quite innocuous and contained no morphia. You have handed this phial over. Two of the tablets are missing."

"I put them in the milk I left ready. I put in nothing else."

"Dr. Long was questioned. He examined his poison cupboard. He found a morphia tablet was missing. He says, and you agree, that he left you alone for a few moments while he went to answer a phone call—a wrong number as it turned out. He had heard the phone ringing, and as he knows his wife is hard of hearing he went to attend to it himself. Your fingerprints are on the small glass container holding the morphia tablets of which one is missing."

"I never touched it," she said again, as she had said before. "I never touched anything all the time that I was there. I didn't even take my gloves off. It's not true." Her voice grew a little wild. "It's not possible," she said. "You're only saying it to trap me. How can they be when I never touched a thing?"

"Nevertheless," Bobby answered, "your prints are there and can be seen plainly. They are very clear prints. That is a fact." She did not answer. He went on: "The poison cupboard is in the dispensary, and that is where Dr. Long saw you. That was because the gas fire in the surgery proper was out of action. The radiants had been accidentally broken. A chair had fallen against them and the new ones ordered had not arrived."

"There was something like that," she agreed, "I didn't notice particularly."

"Dr. Long's house is one of those big, old-fashioned places, isn't it?" Bobby went on. "As you go in, on the left is a large room. It is used as the waiting-room. Opening out of it is a smaller room, the consulting-room or surgery proper where the doctor sees his patients, unless, apparently, it is a cold day and the gas stove is out of order. Finally, built out from the house is a third room, a large room. Dr. Long uses it as a dispensary and also for research work. As he dislikes being disturbed in any way while he is at work there are heavy curtains over the door of this room."

"Why are you going over all this again?" she asked.

"To make sure of details," Bobby answered. "Details are important. Details give the truth, if you can read them aright. I will mention three that interest me. First: two grains of morphia at least were given your husband. Second: the radiants in the gas stove in the consulting-room or surgery were broken. Third: there are heavy curtains over the door of the room where the poison cupboard is."

"What has all that to do with it—or me?" she asked. Bobby continued: "There's one thing more I want to ask about. You and Mr. Rawson were on friendly terms with Dr. and Mrs. Long. You visited each other. Did Dr. Long ever take you into the dispensary to show you what he was working at or specimens of it he thought interesting?"

"Not in the dispensary," Mrs. Rawson told him. "I was never there till this happened. He didn't like people in his room. Mrs. Long said it was because it was so untidy he was ashamed of it. She complained a lot because he wouldn't let her have it cleaned. He always said he wasn't going to have his things disturbed."

"I take it," Bobby said, "you mean he would occasionally fetch things he thought of interest and hand them round to be looked at. What sort of things?"

"I don't know exactly. Why? What does it matter? I didn't like touching them if I could help. They were all horrid. John was interested in them. I wasn't."

"Thank you. That's all at present, I think," Bobby said. "Another detail, you see. Now come with me."

She rose and obeyed mechanically. He led her into the next room where a younger sister of hers, pale, bewildered, anguished, was waiting.

"I have to go now," Bobby said. "Look after Mrs. Rawson till you hear from me. I may be ringing up."

He went out then to where his car was waiting. A young man came running. He called: "I must see her. I must. You've no right—"

"I have given instructions that Mrs. Rawson is to see no one for the present," Bobby answered. "You must wait for a time."

"If you get her hanged," Merton cried, "I'll hang myself as well."

"Mr. Merton." Bobby said, "try to keep your head. It is not certain yet who, if anyone, is going to hang."

"How can I keep my head when I am going mad?" Merton asked.

Bobby got into the car without replying. The constable who was driving started it. At Dr. Long's house they stopped. Bobby knocked and was admitted by Mrs. Long, a small, thin, discontented-looking woman, plainly very hard of hearing. But Bobby made her understand who he was, and he was shown into the waiting-room. In a moment or two Dr. Long entered. He was a middle-aged man, stout in build, almost chubby indeed, though now evidently nervous and suffering from fatigue and loss of sleep.

"A dreadful business this," he explained. "I have felt it all most terribly."

"I can understand that," Bobby said. "I think my case is complete." The doctor did not speak, but his face twitched. Bobby went on: "I would like to see your poison cupboard again."

Still not speaking, Dr. Long led the way to the dispensary. Bobby followed. The doctor held back the heavy curtains to allow Bobby to enter and then let them fall back into place. Bobby looked at the poison cupboard, saw that it was safely locked again, chatted rather aimlessly for a moment or two, looked at his watch, and then asked suddenly: "Do you hear anything?"

"Hear anything? No. Why?" Long said, evidently surprised.

Bobby pulled back the curtains over the door and opened it. He went across the room and opened the door of the next room as well. The phone was ringing and could now be clearly heard.

"A phone call," Bobby said, returning to where Long was waiting, puzzled, faintly troubled. "You needn't answer it. It was for me. I arranged for it and was expecting it, and my driver is there to answer it. Please listen carefully to what I'm going to say. On the day Mrs. Rawson was here you were not expecting any call. Yet you heard it in this inner room, through closed doors and those heavy curtains. You went to answer it. It was a wrong number, so it cannot be traced. But in this way Mrs. Rawson was left alone and thus was given the opportunity to get hold of a morphia tablet. Can you explain how it is you heard the phone ringing that day, though you were not expecting it, while to-day neither you nor I heard it? Yet, anyhow, I was expecting it."

"I really don't know," Long answered. "I suppose I had forgotten to draw the curtains, shut the doors, something like that."

"The curtains seem to fall into position by their own weight." Bobby said. "It would be unusual for you to forget to shut the door when you so much dislike any interruption while at work. Is not that so?"

"Probably I was more on the alert, listening more attentively. As a matter of fact I was expecting a call from one of my patients."

"Will you please give me his name and address?"

"Certainly not. I do not give my patients' names. It would be betraying their confidence."

"Mrs. Rawson." Bobby went on, "was brought into this room because the gas fire in the consulting-room was out of action, its radiants having been accidentally broken. I have ascertained that new radiants were not ordered till the day after Mrs. Rawson was here."

"They must have been forgotten," the doctor said.

"Or was it all part of a plan to get Mrs. Rawson into this room where the poison cupboard is and where she had never been before?"

"How could that account for the fingerprints you found on the morphia tablet container?"

"It seems that occasionally," Bobby said, "you used to show her and her husband specimens of your work. Was one such specimen handed to her in a glass container? Was the contents of that container, with her fingerprints on it, afterwards removed and morphia tablets substituted?"

"Fantastic," the doctor said. "I never remember giving her anything to hold. I might have, of course. But it's not likely. She used to object, said it was horrid."

"You admit, then, that you tried?" Bobby asked, and the doctor did not answer.

Now he had become very pale and Bobby was watching him closely. Bobby went on, speaking slowly:

"The morphia tablet that is missing, and that it is suggested Mrs. Rawson took, contained half a grain. I'm told that is about the biggest dose made up in tablet form. But two grains at least were found at the post-mortem. Does that suggest a specially prepared tablet had been placed at the head of those in the phial of sleeping tablets given Mrs. Rawson?"

"I never thought there would be a post-mortem," Long remarked quietly. "I thought the plain symptoms of morphia poisoning and the fact that one of my tablets was missing would be enough without any post-mortem being held. I had to make sure, hadn't I? Half a grain might not have been enough. So I made up one specially with two grains in it for her to give him."

"Making sure?" Bobby asked.

"Making sure," Long agreed. He said: "She was a woman with a flame in her that ate men up. It had to be stopped."

"And Rawson?" Bobby asked. "Why should you want to destroy him?"

"Could I bear, was it tolerable," Long cried, "that he should live with memories of her in his arms, of kisses, of all no other man had ever had?"

His hand, which he had taken from his pocket, was going to his mouth. Bobby leapt. They struggled for a moment. They were on the floor. Long was struggling desperately to get his hand to his mouth. The policeman-chauffeur came running. In a moment or two Long was handcuffed. He did not speak and a little froth gathered at his mouth. Bobby said:

"Take him to the car. I must ring up Mrs. Rawson and tell her I'm so sorry, but I'm afraid she will have to be a witness at the trial."

Lightning Source UK Ltd.
Milton Keynes UK
UKOW01f1017200617
303734UK00001B/26/P

9 781911 579090